Hauntings and Hoaxes

Witch Haven Cozy Mystery - book 9

K.E. O'Connor

K.E. O'Connor Books

Preface

The Witch Haven series has been created so you spend time with four amazing witches:

Books 1-3 tell Indigo's story: Spells and Spooks, Hexes and Haunts, Curses and Corpses

Books 4-6 tell Luna's story: Muffins and Moonlight, Cupcakes and Cauldrons, Pancakes and Potions

Books 7-9 tell Odessa's story: Hauntings and High Jinx, Hauntings and Havoc, Hauntings and Hoaxes

Books 10-12 tell Storm's story: The Case of the Screaming Skull, The Case of the Poisoned Pumpkin, The Case of the Cursed Candy

And there are two bonus origin stories to enjoy:

Fire Fang and **Silvaria**

Chapter 1

It wasn't every day you saw the ghost of the man you'd given your heart to appear in your bedroom. I blinked once, twice, three times, and he was still there. This wasn't my imagination playing tricks on me.

Brodie Barclay's smile widened as his warm gaze flicked over me. "Are you going to say anything?"

I opened my mouth, but I'd forgotten how to talk. I pointed a finger at him and shook my head.

"Yep. It's me. I'm here. I've been looking for you for such a long time." Brodie's voice had the same deep, warm cadence that always made my toes curl.

I took a step toward him, but my knees buckled, and I hit the floor. Not only had I forgotten how to talk, I'd stopped breathing. Dizziness hit me so hard that I curled into a ball and squeezed my eyes shut. I'd waited so long to see Brodie, and I could do nothing but try to remember how my lungs worked.

"Odessa, what's keeping you so long?" Storm Winter yelled up the stairs. "We're starving, and you promised us dinner. I've already eaten all your pumpkin crackers. And is there anything in this house that isn't pumpkin flavored?"

I raised my head, not sure what I'd see when I did. Brodie was still there. After so many years of longing for him to return, this was too much. My eyes rolled back, and the room went dark.

Someone was tapping my cheek. I opened my eyes to find Storm, Indigo Ash, Luna Brimstone, my favorite scarecrow, Shamrock, and Tuffin surrounding me.

"She's awake." Indigo had her hand on my forehead. "What happened up here?"

I tried to speak, but only a croaking sound came out. I cleared my throat and tried again. "Brodie."

"What about him?" Luna said.

"He was here. You must have seen him." I tried to sit, but Indigo pressed a hand on my shoulder.

"Take your time. Did you hit your head on something?"

"No, my head's fine. But we have to find Brodie." I sat up with my friends' help, although they handled me as if I might break at any second.

Storm pursed her lips. "Brodie's gone. You're moving on. You've got a life with Sol."

"No, I haven't." My gaze flicked to the door, and I saw Sol Vossen standing there. He didn't look happy. "I mean, of course, I do. But not like I had with Brodie. Help me up. I knew he'd come back to me. I never gave up hope."

I didn't miss the worried looks that passed between my friends as they got me on my feet, but I couldn't care about how weird they thought I was being. My gaze shot around my bedroom. Brodie wasn't there.

"So, where's he hiding?" Indigo said.

"Should I check the closet? Or maybe he's under the bed." Storm yanked open a closet door. "No dead lover hiding in here."

"This isn't a joke. He was right here." I jabbed the air. "Brodie spoke to me. I've dreamt about this day so many times, but I wasn't ready. I let him down."

"Are you sure it was Brodie?" Indigo said. "I mean, you've been looking for a long time. And I've lost count of the number of times you were certain you spotted him in a crowd and it turned out to be someone else."

"Or you discovered his ghost in a haunted house," Luna said, a note of sympathy in her voice.

"This is different. It was him. I'm sure of it." I stepped away from my friends and their overwhelming compassion. I didn't need it. Brodie was back, and everything would be fine.

"If he's back, why doesn't he show himself?" Sol said, a quiet anger in his tone. "Or does he have something to hide?"

"No. Nothing! But this must be overwhelming for him, too. He said he'd been looking for me for a long time. I knew he'd gotten lost getting back to me." I pivoted on my heel, desperately seeking Brodie. "Come back. You know where I am now. This is your home, and we can figure everything out."

No one spoke as we looked around the room for Brodie's ghost. Well, I was looking. My friends kept shooting each other worried glances and shrugging.

"Give him a minute," I said. "You know what ghosts are like. If Brodie doesn't have much energy, he won't manifest."

"When you saw him, what did he look like?" Luna said.

"Just like Brodie."

"For real? But he's been a ghost for over three years. I figured he wouldn't be doing so well."

"He looked better than good, actually. Not even a hint of ghost ghoul about him."

"Which is impossible," Storm said.

I didn't like her sharp tone. "It's possible. Ghosts can linger for decades and not transform into something unpleasant. And Brodie has our memories to cling to. They kept him whole." I walked around the bedroom. "Brodie, follow my voice and come back to me."

I kept pacing and calling, but he didn't show. And every time I glanced at my friends, I could see they didn't believe me. "We need to split up. The farm is a big place. Brodie could have ended up in a barn. Maybe he got scared when you all came into the bedroom."

"Brodie knows us. He has no reason to hide," Storm said.

"There'll be a reason. Everyone go look for him. You can all see and sense ghosts, so make yourselves useful."

"I'll search the rest of this floor," Indigo said.

"I'll do downstairs and the basement," Luna said.

"That leaves me to check the barns and not get attacked by the scarecrows," Storm said. "What fun."

I appreciated my friends didn't hang around as they began their search. I stopped in the doorway by Sol. My initial excitement at seeing Brodie faded when I saw the grim expression on Sol's face. "I'm sorry, but I can't abandon Brodie."

He gave a slight shake of his head. "I'd offer to help look for him, but you know I can't see ghosts."

"I wouldn't expect you to, even if you could. And... this must be difficult for you. I never wanted it to be this way, but I was always honest with you. You know I've been looking for Brodie." I walked along the corridor, keeping a lookout for Brodie as I talked.

Sol walked behind me. "He's really here?"

"Yes. I'm certain of it. Tuffin, Shamrock, help me look, too. We need all eyes on this ghost hunt."

"I'm asleep," Tuffin said from the bedroom.

Shamrock lumbered into the corridor. He was holding a squirming Tuffin in his large, straw-filled hands.

"Help Storm search the barns," I said. "Come back and tell me if you find anything."

"Make this scarecrow put me down, before I shred him to pieces." Tuffin hissed in Shamrock's face.

"You go with Shamrock. Make yourself useful, too."

I ignored Tuffin's protests as I kept looking. Sol remained doggedly by my side, and although I was glad of his presence, I felt guilty. I'd been leading him on. I'd imagined a future for us and even contemplated going on a date with Sol. What had I been thinking? I'd almost missed the chance to reunite with Brodie because I'd lost focus. It wouldn't happen again.

We spent the next hour searching the farm and the barns from top to bottom. Brodie still hadn't appeared.

With every minute that passed, my frustration grew. I had seen him. It hadn't been my imagination. I hadn't even been thinking about Brodie when he'd appeared. I looked over to see Sol standing with his hands on the fence, staring out across the fields he tended. I'd been thinking about another man.

I gathered everyone in the kitchen and encountered lots more pitying glances and nods of sympathy. It was too much to bear, and I needed to be on my own. Brodie must want to see me alone. That was the reason he wasn't showing himself.

"What do you want to do next?" Indigo said. "There's no whiff of a ghost around here."

I forced a smile. "You're right. Maybe I imagined him."

My friends exchanged another set of annoying glances.

"You seemed so certain," Luna said. "Why the change of heart?"

"I made a mistake. I'm allowed to do that, aren't I?"

"You said you saw him," Storm said. "You even had me convinced. Well, almost."

I bit my tongue to avoid biting back at her sharpness. "I've had a stressful few days. I need to catch up with my sleep and get into my old routine, then I'll stop hallucinating." I hoped Brodie wasn't listening to this conversation and getting the wrong end of the stick.

"You think Brodie was a hallucination?" Storm shook her head, clearly not believing me.

"He must have been. Because as you said, there's no reason for him to hide. He knows everyone here, and he trusts me. Even if he's confused because he's been a ghost for a long time, it makes no sense." I looked out the window, so I didn't have to make eye contact with my friends as I lied. "This was my mistake. Sorry for wasting your time. You should probably all go."

"What about Brodie?" Luna walked over and wrapped an arm around my shoulders. "We don't mind staying and looking some more. Or we could have that long overdue dinner and see if he shows up. Maybe we did scare him. And if he's not himself—"

"He is himself. Really, it's best you go. And I'm not in the mood for doing dinner tonight. It's late, and I want to be on my own."

"I hate that idea," Storm said. "Someone should stay, especially if you're seeing things that aren't real."

"I can stay a while longer," Sol said. "There's nowhere else I need to be."

I didn't want anyone sticking around, but my friends wouldn't move until I compromised. "Fine. You stay. Everyone else can go, though. I'm embarrassed about what happened."

"Don't be embarrassed," Luna said. "Brodie was your guy. We all know how much you want to see him again. But it's time to move on, don't you think?" Her gaze shifted to Sol.

I nodded. "Thanks for helping. Sorry for wasting everyone's time."

"Don't be an idiot." Indigo walked over and hugged me. "I'm always happy to help you with a little ghost hunting."

Luna also hugged me and Storm gave me a half-hearted fist bump before they left.

I looked around the kitchen, excitement and anxiety bubbling inside me in equal measure. "Sol, I need your help."

"With what?"

"Your ring is still locking the barn with my experiments in it. I need to get inside. If Brodie is back, I have work to do."

"You didn't tell your friends the truth, did you?" Sol made no move from the doorway he stood in. "You're still convinced you saw Brodie's ghost?"

"They never believed he was here. It was pointless for them to stay."

"And you do believe he's back? Brodie is the only person you want?"

I wanted to tell Sol no and reveal I'd planned to ask him on a date just before Brodie had shown up. I cared about Sol and wanted him in my life, but I couldn't have him and Brodie. That was greedy. And I'd given my heart to Brodie so many years ago, I wasn't sure where to find it if I ever wanted it back. Not that I would. Brodie had always looked after it.

"I get it." Sol's sigh was heavy with regret. "You need to complete the magic for Brodie's vessel. And I know you can make it work. Your power is amazing. You dazzle me."

"I appreciate you not judging me," I said. "I know this can't be easy for you."

"Your happiness is what I care about the most. I wanted to make you happy, but I see that'll never work. You've only got space in your heart for one guy."

I reached for his hand but stopped myself and stepped away. "It's how it's always been. It's only ever been Brodie for me."

"I never stood a chance? Even after everything we've been through?"

There had been a moment, just a flicker of uncertainty, that had made me reach for Sol. But that was me being weak and not true to myself.

"It's okay. You don't have to answer those questions. Let's go to the barn. Get you the happy ending you need so badly." Sol's steps were heavy as he went outside.

I waved over Shamrock and Tuffin, and we headed to the barn. My mind was whirring too fast for me to keep up with all the thoughts buzzing through my brain. There was so much I needed to do. I'd yet to perfect a permanent vessel that Brodie could live in. I was also aware the beady eyes of the Magic Council were still on me. I had to be careful not to be arrested again, but if I didn't take this risk, I could lose Brodie for good.

Sol caught hold of the ring that had protected my barn from unwanted Magic Council attention. A silvery glow covered his palm, and the ring slid off the metal chain holding the doors shut. He slid it onto his finger.

I stared at the ring and then my own bare fingers. I was so close to getting everything I wanted. When Brodie was back, we'd be married, we could start a family, expand the farm like he always wanted, and finally, I'd have my happily ever after.

"I should go," Sol said. "You got what you wanted from me."

"Don't be like that. I've loved having you around. I love everything you've done for the farm and the scarecrows."

"But you don't love me. And I accept that. It doesn't make me happy, but this is your choice."

I blinked back tears. "It's the right choice. I always knew one day my true love would return. And it's here. I can't let Brodie go. This is too important."

"You have to follow that," Sol said.

"I... yes, I do. But what about you? What will you do?"

"Figure something else out." Sol caught hold of me by the shoulders and drew me close. "I won't be sticking around for much longer. I've loved you for almost as long as I've known you, so it would be too painful to see you with another guy. When you get Brodie back, I'll be glad, but I can't watch. I need my own life."

I swallowed around the sudden lump in my throat. "I hope we can be friends."

"Maybe. In time." Sol stroked a hand down my cheek then stepped away. "Have a wonderful life. You deserve it." He turned and walked away.

Shamrock shoved into me and growled.

"What? This is the right thing to do. You want to see me happy with Brodie, don't you?"

He caught hold of my arm and made a two-way connection with us, the buzzing filling my head as our thoughts linked so we could communicate.

"Like Sol," he growled.

"So do I. But Brodie is everything to me. He's almost here. He's almost back with us."

"Brodie jerk. Not nice."

"Don't tell lies. Brodie was always good to you."

"Set me on fire once."

"Shamrock! That's not true. Don't be jealous because he's coming back. I'll still have time for you and the other scarecrows. You won't miss out on anything."

"Miss out on Sol. Like him."

I stepped away to break the connection. Shamrock had always had a possessive, jealous streak. He was only worried because Brodie was back and my attention would be elsewhere.

"You stay out here and check the perimeter. Tuffin, stay with Shamrock. I don't want anything to get in the way of Brodie coming back."

"I have no interest in meeting another ghost." Tuffin leaped out of Shamrock's arms and strutted away.

I headed back to the house and walked around, calling for Brodie, but no amount of pleading got him to materialize. I briefly considered a séance or a summoning, but that was extreme. He'd made it back to me on his own, so he could do it again.

I sank into a chair in the kitchen and rubbed my aching forehead. I wanted to cry in frustration. Where was he?

Automatically, I grabbed a pouch of powdered pumpkin on the table and went to take a huge scoop. I hesitated. I'd managed without it when I was helping Arietta Frost solve her murder. She'd constantly drained my power, and though I'd felt awful, I hadn't had any powdered pumpkin, and I'd survived fine. Maybe I was too reliant on my supercharged magical pumpkin dust.

I took a small amount and chewed slowly, welcoming the rush of energy.

There was a shift in the air, and I tensed. I jumped from my seat and looked around, almost too afraid to breathe in case something went wrong. "Brodie?"

Tuffin raced into the kitchen, her fur bristled and her eyes wide. "Something is here."

"I told you to stay outside." I was looking around, frantic for any hint Brodie was back.

"I don't like this," Tuffin said. "It doesn't feel right."

"You never met Brodie, so you don't know what his energy feels like. This must be him."

"He'd better not feel like this, or I'm moving out," Tuffin said.

"You've only just moved in, so that won't be hard to organize." I kept looking around. "Brodie, follow my voice. It's Odessa. I'm right here. Come back to me."

Something shimmered in the corner of the kitchen, and a few seconds later, Brodie appeared.

A startled laugh shot out of me. "It really is you."

Tuffin hissed and backed to the door.

Brodie strode forward and wrapped me in a tight, icy hug. "Hey, babe. It's me. I'm back."

Chapter 2

I clung to Brodie until I was shivering and my bones felt frozen to the marrow, but I didn't let him go. If I did, he may vanish again.

"Come sit with me," he whispered against my hair.

"Standing is perfect. Just don't move." He smelled different. Less like my Brodie, but it was him. Every nerve ending screamed at me he was finally home.

"Babe, you gotta let me go at some point. Although I sure have missed these hugs."

"No, I don't. Not ever." I gripped him tighter. He was surprisingly solid. If it wasn't for the cold, I wouldn't have known he was a ghost.

"Odessa, sweetheart, your teeth are chattering so loudly they're giving me a headache. Come, take a seat. I need your help with something. It's urgent."

Reluctantly, I unwrapped myself from around Brodie and stared up into his striking dark eyes. He was just as I'd remembered, and I was relieved to see there wasn't a hint of ghost ghoul about him. This was my Brodie.

"What do you need?" I said, still drinking in the delicious sight of him.

"I need a boost of energy. Do you mind if I take it from you?"

"Of course not. Take whatever you need. Just promise, you won't vanish on me again."

"I need a lot. You'd better have more powdered pumpkin. I don't want you passing out."

My cheeks flushed. "That was from shock. I've been waiting so long to find you that, when you appeared, I didn't know what to think. My brain short-circuited."

"It's flattering I have that effect on you after all these years." His grin was lopsided as he tugged me over to a seat and settled me on his lap. "Have some powdered pumpkin. We can talk after I'm recharged."

"Whatever you want." I downed an entire bag and chewed on it, swallowing it down with half a cold mug of coffee that had been neglected on the table.

"That's my girl. You always were amazing with your pumpkin magic. Mind if I take some now?" Brodie said.

"It's all yours. Whatever you need to do to stay with me." I tried not to shiver as his icy hands gripped my face. Within seconds, the energy from the powdered pumpkin was fading as Brodie consumed it, and I was racked with chills.

"You taste so good. Better than I remember."

"You used to get bored of my pumpkins. You said I was pumpkin mad."

Brodie chuckled. "That's not how I remember things. And who would ever get bored of you?"

I leaned against him. "I've got so much to ask you."

"What do you need to know?" His image was even more solid as he continued to feed, and his touch slightly less icy.

"Where have you been? How have you been getting on alone? Why did you never come when I looked for you? And why are you back now?" There was more, but I started with the basics.

His familiar, deep laugh spiraled joy around my heart. "I don't have all the answers. Everything was confusing for a time, but one thing I clung to was a memory of you. I knew something terrible had happened to me, but every time I wavered and wondered what to do next, I got an image of you in my thoughts. You were always smiling and so happy. Sometimes only that memory was clear. You were my beacon of hope."

"I knew the memories of us being together would keep you going. I told everyone you wouldn't give up on us."

"And I never did." He was quiet for several seconds. "Who didn't believe I'd come back for you?"

"Just about everyone. It doesn't matter now. You're here, and we can prove them wrong. But... why didn't you show yourself? I looked everywhere. I was worried you might have turned into a ghost ghoul."

"That was never going to happen." He rubbed his stubbled chin. "I'm not sure why it's taken me so long to find you."

"Where have you been, though? I've looked everywhere. I hunted dozens of ghosts in my search to get you back."

"I bet you did. I knew you wouldn't give up on us," Brodie said. "And I wish I could answer that question, but everything is a tangle of weird memories. I'm not even sure how I died."

"Oh! You didn't look into it?" I was shivering so hard, I almost bit my tongue, but I wasn't going to tell Brodie to stop taking my energy. He needed it, and I needed him right here.

"I remember being at work and people panicking. I also remember a sensation of feeling crushed. Was that what killed me?"

"It must have been." I stroked a hand down his back. "We never found your body. The trolls attacked the mine when you were working late one night. They set off explosions, and you got trapped. The mine was too dangerous to go back in, so you were left behind."

"Wow! I'm still in there? You didn't get my body out?"

"I couldn't. It would have caused more of the mine to collapse. But people searched for weeks. When you weren't found, you were declared dead. We had a ceremony, but I didn't take part because I knew you'd come back. You wouldn't give up."

"Of course not. You've always been the best part of me. I was never giving that up."

The sigh that slid out of me was a mixture of relief and exhaustion. "I'm so glad you're back, but how did you figure out where to find me after such a long time?"

Brodie turned his head and looked over his shoulder. "I don't know. I just suddenly knew. It's not been that long, though."

I rested my hands over the top of his so we could be more connected. "You have been looking for me, haven't you?"

His expression darkened, and he looked away. "Not always. But not because I didn't want to. Sometimes, I forgot your name. I knew you were important but couldn't figure out why." Brodie kept looking over his shoulder. "I'm sensing something. It's calling to me. Do you feel it?"

Tuffin, who was curled at the edge of the table, narrowed her eyes at him. "I'm sensing something, too. This ghost isn't telling the truth. Did Brodie lie to you when he was alive?"

"Shush. Of course he's telling the truth."

Brodie flicked a glance at Tuffin. "Who's this?"

"Tuffin recently joined the household. She was the familiar to a guy who was killed. He left her to me just before he crossed over. We're still figuring things out, but we're making it work."

"I'm not so sure about that," Tuffin said. "Especially if you're keeping this ghost around."

I swayed in my seat, overcome with lightheadedness as Brodie continued taking my energy. "Of course, I'm keeping him. And you'll get used to each other. This is my Brodie, and you're my familiar."

"I hate your choice in men," Tuffin said. "I preferred the other one."

"The other one?" Brodie said. "You got another guy? I mean, of course, you should. I guess I have been gone a while. Maybe a year."

"Oh, no. You really don't know how long you've been dead?" I said.

"It seems like I don't. You'd better fill me in."

I sat up so I could look him in the eye. "It's been over three years."

Brodie's mouth dropped open, and he broke our connection, making me almost pass out again. I grabbed another bag of powdered pumpkin and chewed on it, feeling instantly restored.

Brodie shook his head, his form shimmering with my orange magic. "That's impossible. I've left you alone all this time?"

"You didn't know what you were doing. And it doesn't matter. I knew we'd eventually be together."

"What about this other guy, though? You've got someone important in your life? Someone's been looking out for you?"

"In a way. He's not here anymore. And..." I was going to say Sol didn't matter, but that was a lie. He'd become more than a friend. We hadn't crossed any lines in our relationship, but I'd thought about it. More than once.

Brodie brushed a hand down my face. "I'm not angry with you. I died and left you alone. You're a stunning, clever witch with so much power that it takes my breath away. Of course, you'd catch someone's eye. But where does that leave us?"

"Here. As we should be. We're together. And I've been working on a plan to bring you back properly."

"Properly? What do you mean?"

"You won't just be a ghost."

"You've lost me."

"My reanimation magic can bring back the dead, but I only use my ability to create scarecrows. I've adapted my spells to make a vessel for you to use. You can live inside it."

His brow furrowed. "You want to turn me into a scarecrow?"

"No. Well, a supercharged, humanlike scarecrow. I need to make a few tweaks to the final spells, but I'm so close, and having you here is a huge missing piece of the puzzle." I kissed his cheek. "Brodie, I'm getting you back. We can be together for the rest of our lives."

He nodded but kept looking over his shoulder, not seeming as thrilled as I hoped he would. "I don't know. And I see a light. That's new."

I jumped up and caught hold of his hand, my heart beating out a frantic rhythm of panic. "No! Don't look at the light. Stay with me."

"It's inviting. I've never seen it before. I've just been wandering about, trying to figure out what I'm supposed to do. It feels like I should go there. Should I?"

"No, your place is here with me. You must not go into the light. If you do, you won't come back. Please, stay with me."

"But it feels like it would be warm." His voice sounded faint, as if I was losing him. "Being a ghost is strange. I don't always feel whole. I don't know what I'd have done if I didn't have that memory of you."

"Think about that now. Look at me and see I'm right here. Think about the rest of our lives together. There's so much I want to show you, and we can start with your new vessel. We can change it so you can look however you like. I've been testing the magic so I can change the form." My heart almost shattered as Brodie stepped away and shook his head.

"I want to go. I think it's my time. Maybe this was what I was meant to do before I was ready to leave. I had to find you and say a proper goodbye."

"It isn't. You're wrong." Tears ran down my cheeks. "Brodie, stay with me. This is our chance to have a happily ever after. We're meant to be together. I can't have found you, only for you to leave me. That's not how it ends for us. Please, don't go." His form was fading, but I wasn't giving up. I threw reanimation magic at Brodie, not sure if it would have any effect, but I had to keep him tethered to me. I lashed him with a restraining spell, but it passed through him.

"Babe, don't fight this. It's just my time," he whispered.

"Think about our future. You had all those ideas for the farm. I'll expand if you want me to. Or we could start something different. We can have a business together. But you have to stay."

"With scarecrows?" He glanced at me, but his gaze was drawn back to that evil, enticing light that threatened to take away everything I cared about.

"I love my scarecrows, but we could try something new. I'll keep the scarecrows, and you start something different. Something you'd enjoy, too. And we can travel the world and start a family. You've always wanted children."

"This vessel you've created can do that? I could be a dad?"

"Yes! You'll be better than you were. Stronger, faster, and have more power. And we'll be linked. My energy will channel through you."

"I... I don't want to leave. I'm remembering more now I'm here. You always loved this old farm. You didn't even mind the drafts creeping under the door, or the way the boiler creaked and groaned, as if it was on its last legs. You were so happy when you were covered in straw and pumpkins, weaving your magic into those scarecrows."

I laughed and swiped at my eyes. "That's always been me. It's what I've always loved to do. But you make me happy, too."

"That's great to hear. I'm glad we had a good life together."

Brodie was talking like he'd made up his mind, but I wasn't letting him go. "Stay a while longer. I'll show you around, and all the memories will return. You'll remember how amazing we were together. Nothing can beat that. You might even remember to finally marry me."

He tilted his head. "Marriage?"

"That's what we wanted, wasn't it?"

Brodie shook his head. "I'm so confused. And I've been alone for a long time. I want to rest."

"Rest with me. Take more of my energy. I need to make more powdered pumpkin, but I can do that by the morning. Keep feeding off me, and everything will be back to how it was. You'll go into your vessel, we start living our lives together, and you'll be happy. We can both be blissfully happy."

"Odessa, you're sweet, but I'm done here. I've been too long in the shadows, and I'm worn out. Even taking that energy from you has barely changed me."

"It has. I can see it. You're already stronger. You're more you."

"Not enough. I need so much more. Take care of yourself. But it's time I went."

Shock slammed into me like a fire blast from a dragon, and I staggered back. "Brodie Barclay, no! I'll do anything, but you can't leave me. I won't allow it."

A shadowy figure emerged from behind Brodie, looped an arm around him, and he vanished.

Chapter 3

I screamed and threw magic at the shadow. "Stay away from Brodie. You can't have him. He's staying with me. Go back to the light. Close that door and never open it again. Brodie stays here."

Tuffin leaped to her feet and growled. "More enemy?"

The shadowy figure solidified, and Brodie reappeared. Although his form wavered, he didn't move away as he was pinned in place by this new arrival.

I primed more magic, ready to attack the male shadow figure, my breath heaving out of me and my palms sweaty.

The shadowy form came into sharper focus and revealed a man of around forty, with slicked back dark hair and a single line of brilliant white running through it. He had a nervous smile on his face. "Relax, witch. I'm not here to cause any harm. I heard your call for help, and I had to come. I was drawn to you."

"I don't need you here. Who are you? What are you doing with Brodie?" I directed my magic at this new ghost, holding it primed on my fingertips.

"Giving him a time out." The ghost whispered in Brodie's ear, and he faded away.

"Bring him back!" I slammed a spell at the ghost's feet.

"He's not gone far. Please, I couldn't ignore your distress. Let me help you keep your guy. And I promise, I won't hurt either of you, but I could never ignore a damsel in distress when I was alive. I guess some things never change."

"Who are you?" I wasn't trusting this ghost. He was getting in the way of me seeing Brodie.

"I promise you, I'm here as a friend. And you have powerful magic. I couldn't resist finding out more about you."

"You still haven't told me what you're doing to Brodie." I flared my magic. "And yes, I am powerful. You'll find out just how powerful if you keep messing with me."

The ghost raised his hands in a gesture of supplication. "Brodie is fine. But as soon as I arrived, I sensed his turmoil. He wants to stay with you, but he's also drawn to the light."

"He hasn't gone, has he? Did you send him into it?" My heart raced, and I held a hand against my stomach. "I've only just found him again. Why would he leave?"

"He's still here. He's sitting in what I call the in-between. I expect it has an official name, but I'm new to being a ghost, so I'm figuring out how everything works. It's a sort of nice waiting room. We can use it while we adjust to our new situation."

"Tell Brodie to come back," I said. "There's so much I need to tell him. I have to convince him to stay."

"He'll be back. I'm certain of it. But he needs a time out."

"You know a lot about being a ghost, considering you told me you haven't been one for long." Was this ghost lying to me? What would he have to gain from doing that?

"You have to learn quickly, especially when your death is unexpected. Maybe if I'd died when I was older, I'd have been more prepared, but I was thrust into this existence, or is it an anti-existence? I'm not sure how to define what being a ghost is. Anyway, I had to think on my feet. My now floating feet." The ghost looked at the floor. "It's still so weird not to need to walk anymore."

"I don't trust this guy," Tuffin muttered.

"Promise me, you haven't hurt Brodie," I said.

"He's safe. But he was serious about going into the light. I had to shove him into the waiting room so he didn't cross over."

My heart dropped to my boots. "You really stopped him from leaving?"

"I think he'd have gone if I hadn't been around. He felt ready. But there was some conflict. I could tell he was struggling with something."

I carefully studied the ghost as the edges smoothed off my panic. He looked familiar. "Did you live in Witch Haven when you were alive?"

"Yes. On the eastern edge. I lived there with my wife." The ghost frowned. "You seem a lot nicer than her. I'd really like to help you, if you let me."

"How can you help me?"

"I just did. With Brodie. That's his name, right?"

I nodded.

"He'd have gone by now if it weren't for me."

"What do you want in return?" Tuffin said.

"Your cat is wise," the ghost said. "And I do need some help."

I shook my head. "I have none to give. I don't have time to help another ghost."

"Oh! You've helped ghosts before?" A hopeful look entered his eyes.

"Yes, but Brodie is the only ghost I need in my life. Please, get him to come back so I can talk sense into him."

"That's a bad idea. He can't cross over from the waiting room. He's safe for now. He can take time to get his head together and figure out what he wants to do."

I hated that idea. I wanted to see Brodie and get answers out of him. None of this made any sense.

"You're Odessa, aren't you?" the ghost said.

"That's right. Odessa Grimsbane. This is my farm. Brodie used to live here with me."

"You were a couple?"

"For a long time. He died in a mining accident. I've been looking for his ghost ever since then."

"Well, you've almost got him back, so a little longer won't hurt."

I pressed a hand against my heart. It was hurting.

"Odessa, please, be patient. Brodie's energy was all over the place. Let me talk to him. I can get him calm, so he'll stay with you. I can tell you're a kind lady. You just want to do the right thing."

I let out a sigh. "I do. You definitely won't hurt him?"

"No. But I do need your help."

"Don't do it," Tuffin said. "These ghosts are always more trouble than they're worth."

"I won't be any trouble. But I'm so new to being a ghost, and I'm confused. I thought, when I died, I'd have a clear path of where to go next. But I'm not being shown anywhere. It feels like I can't move on because there's something I need to do here."

"What do you think that is?" Now I took the time to look over this ghost, I definitely knew him from somewhere, but I still couldn't place him.

"I need to know what happened to me. I was a young guy. Well, early middle age. I don't know how I died."

"No one remembers their death," I said. "Maybe that's all you're confused about. The last few minutes of your life get blocked. I imagine it's to help those who had a traumatic death."

"Makes sense. But I wasn't sick, and I don't think I was in an accident. Maybe that's why I'm here. I need to find out what happened to me. I was planning my future, and then... I don't know. It was all gone."

"What's your name?" I said.

"This is a mistake," Tuffin said. "You're getting involved."

"I'm not. I'm just finding out the basics. I can look at the details, tell this ghost how he died, and he can move on. It doesn't need to be complicated."

"Yet, it always is." Tuffin turned in a circle and presented her back to me as she settled on the edge of the table.

"I'm Zohar Delarosa. I moved to Witch Haven three years ago."

"Delarosa? I do know you." I grabbed a bottle of water from the fridge and sat at the table. "Didn't you and your wife win the crystal jackpot?"

He grinned. "That's me. I can still remember how shocked I was when the crystals aligned. It was life changing. I left my job, my wife resigned from hers, and after travelling for a bit, we built a place on the edge of the village. That was my wife's idea."

"I remember that happening. Well, since you're local, your death must have been reported in the paper or online. Although, I haven't read about it. I've been distracted recently. Let me see what I can find out."

"Big mistake," Tuffin grumbled.

I fired up my laptop before typing in a search for Zohar Delarosa.

He moved closer and hovered behind me. "Anything showing up?"

"There are plenty of articles about you and Elsbeth hitting the crystal jackpot. Have you been married long?"

"Ages. We met in school, and I married Elsbeth when she turned twenty-one. I'm a few years older than her."

"Any kids?" I scrolled through the news articles, expecting to find some mention of his death, but so far, there was nothing.

"No. It never happened for us." Zohar floated away.

"Having a family isn't for everyone," I said. "I had big plans with Brodie, but things changed in a heartbeat when he died so suddenly."

"Is that why he's still here?"

"I think so. That and he'd never leave me. Maybe that's why you're still here. You need to see your wife and say goodbye."

"If it was a sudden death, I could be in shock." He shook his head. "But something feels wrong. I need to know what happened to me."

After checking through several pages of search results, I couldn't find any information on Zohar's death. "Do you remember how long ago you died?"

"Two days at the most. Time moves a little differently on this side, but it hasn't been long."

"You don't look like you're changing." His form was fuzzy, but there was no hint of ghost ghoul about him.

"Changing?"

"You know, into a ghost ghoul."

He shuddered. "I don't want that."

I spent a few more minutes checking the search results but drew a blank.

"Your family must be keeping quiet about your death. From the look of these results, you got a ton of media attention with your crystal jackpot win. It's possible people may take advantage of your family when they're vulnerable. The Magic Council could have banned releasing information about your death to keep them safe."

"What if something bad happened to me?" Zohar said. "The Magic Council is keeping quiet because they're investigating my death."

"Do you have any reason to think someone hurt you?"

He was quiet for a long time before drifting to the window and looking out across my fields. "We all make a few enemies, but I can't think of anyone who'd want me dead."

"I'm sure it's not that. Did you have any medical conditions?"

"I'm as healthy as a unicorn. I used to run three times a week and lift weights. I've even got a gym at the house, so there was no excuse for me not to keep fit. My wife had us on this whole food plant-based diet for a couple of months. I lost weight and even got a six-pack. There was nothing wrong with me."

I sat back in my seat. "I don't know what to say. I can't find anything about your death online. Have you been to visit your home since you became a ghost?"

"No. I was wandering about feeling aimless and not sure what to do, when your magic drew me to the farm." Zohar moved closer. "Odessa, will you help me solve this, so I can cross over?"

Tuffin made a snorting sound.

"I wish I could, but I have to focus on Brodie. And this farm won't run itself. My scarecrows need careful handling."

"I'll help with Brodie. I'll keep him stable and make sure he doesn't cross over."

I jumped from my seat. "Will you, really? No matter what I said, it seemed like Brodie wanted to leave."

Tuffin lifted her head from her paws. "How will you do that? You know nothing about being a ghost."

Zohar tilted his head. "Maybe not, but I've always been good with people, and I got Brodie in the waiting room. That's a positive start."

"And you must keep him there," I said.

"Idiot," Tuffin muttered.

I shot her a glare. "Can I see Brodie?"

Zohar hummed under his breath for a second. "That's not a great idea. He seems stressed. I'll talk to him and set things right then get him back here as soon as I can."

"Oh, are you sure? I want to make sure he's doing okay."

"He was wavering about going into the light. You don't want to add any stress, or you might push him over the edge."

"No! I don't want to do that." My heart gave an unhappy thud. I really wanted to see my guy again.

"I'll focus on Brodie, and you focus on finding out how I died. Deal?" Zohar said.

"Don't do the deal," Tuffin said. "We've got enough going on. Selma Black, Sol, the scarecrows, making sure my fish order arrives on time."

I had plenty on my plate, but Brodie needed to take precedence. "It's a deal. I'll help you."

Chapter 4

I kept checking the time and pacing the kitchen, waiting until it was late enough so I could visit Olympus Duke and find out about Zohar's death. Olympus must know what was going on, since he oversaw all the important cases in Witch Haven.

I'd managed about two hours' sleep in the chair in the kitchen last night, barely able to settle because I had so much on my mind. After my conversation with Zohar, he'd left to talk to Brodie, and I hadn't seen either of them again.

And that left me on edge and anxious. I had to know what was going on with Brodie. Why had he reacted the way he did? He must want to stay. He was just confused. He'd been a ghost for a long time and hadn't been able to find me. It had been stressful for me too, searching for Brodie and coming up empty-handed.

I forced myself not to look at the time again as I brewed another coffee and ate powdered pumpkin coated candy. It wasn't the breakfast of champions, but I needed comfort and instant energy.

"It's not even dawn, and you're on your third strong coffee." Tuffin's head appeared over the edge of the table, where she'd been snoozing on a chair.

"I didn't realize you kept count of my coffee consumption." I added cream and stirred.

"It makes you jittery. Add in that powdered pumpkin, and you're a shaky, anxious nightmare to be around."

"I need all the help I can get to make sure I don't miss Brodie when he comes back."

Tuffin rested her chin on the table. "Why do you want him back so badly? You've got a great setup here. The farm's working, the scarecrows are being unusually placid, and you've got Sol to help. And me. Your life is perfect."

"It'll only be perfect once Brodie is here. And I'm not giving up on him." I turned to the window and sipped my coffee as I stared at the expanse of farmland. I did have a great life. I was lucky to have so much, but it didn't seem to matter without Brodie by my side.

"I still don't think you should help this other ghost," Tuffin said. "He's bad news. Shifty. So is Brodie. They were giving out a weird vibe."

"I didn't pick it up. Brodie was just distracted, since he was being pulled in two directions. But I can't lose him. And Zohar said he'd help, so I'm trusting him. He needs me to find out how he died, so I have leverage."

"You're too trusting for your own good."

"And you're too cynical for yours." I finished my coffee, tidied the kitchen, then forced myself to have a slow shower and get dressed. I deliberately took my time, because I knew Olympus wouldn't be at his office much before nine in the morning.

After tidying the kitchen for a second time and wiping down the counters, it was still only seven-thirty. "Let's go see the scarecrows."

"No, thanks. They'll be in a foul mood because you're so stressed. I'm staying here. And I'll be expecting a fresh fish breakfast soon. Buttered kippers and a side order of smoked salmon sounds good."

"You'll get something fishy from a tin." I headed outside. Normally, Sol would turn up for work soon, but I didn't expect to see him.

I tugged on my lower lip as I walked around the barns. There was a deep pang of regret low in my stomach about what I'd said to Sol. I loved Brodie, and I had gotten by without him, but it always felt like a struggle. When Sol arrived, things changed. He hadn't been a replacement, but he'd been a new path I'd been tempted to walk along. He'd made me see there was still happiness to be had, and always looking back at the past wasn't a great thing to do.

But I had so many happy memories of being with Brodie that I couldn't let them go. And now he was back, I wouldn't have to. My small flirtation with Sol was over.

I unlocked the far end barn and went inside. Everything was laid out as it should be, including my scarecrow vessel. I still had a few kinks to iron out, but now Brodie's ghost was here, I had every reason to get it right. And I was close. I'd soon have the perfect vessel.

When I emerged from the barn, Shamrock was lurking outside, his hands clenched and his red eyes glowing. "Is something wrong?"

He lunged and grabbed my arm. I didn't flinch. Most of my scarecrows tended to lunge and grab. Buzzing filled my head as we made a two-way connection.

"Not happy. No one is," Shamrock said.

"What's the problem?"

"Where's Sol?"

"Oh, he's leaving. Or already left. I'm not sure. We're going to need a new Sol. Or when Brodie gets back to full strength, he can help. He might be more interested in the farm this time around."

"No. Hate him."

"Let's not go over that again. He's coming back."

"Don't want him. Want Sol. So do you."

"Well, we can't have everything we want. Don't you have work to get on with?"

"Sol hasn't given orders. No orders, no work."

"Shamrock, don't be difficult. We'll all have to adjust when Brodie gets back. You could start today."

"No adjusting. Make him leave."

I was usually patient with my scarecrows. But I was exhausted, frustrated about not seeing Brodie, and annoyed I hadn't yet figured out Zohar's problem. "Enough! Work in the lower field. Those thistles need to come out."

Shamrock growled at me. No one enjoyed dealing with the thistles. They were almost waist high and had wicked sharp thorns.

"That's an order. And take the others with you."

Shamrock jerked away, scowled at me, and ran off, making the ground shake as he stamped out his unhappiness.

I didn't have time for my demanding scarecrows today. After another check around the farm buildings, I locked up and walked into Witch Haven. I paced outside Olympus's office for twenty minutes before he showed up, Indigo with him.

"Hey, what are you doing here?" she said.

"I need to find out about a case you're working on, Olympus," I said.

He passed his takeout coffee mug to Indigo and unlocked the door. "A case? Which one?"

I followed him inside with Indigo. "Zohar Delarosa."

His gaze shot to me as he opened the blinds. "I don't know who you're talking about. Do you want a coffee?"

"No coffee. Just information."

"How are you doing?" Indigo said. "I was worried about you last night. I didn't want to leave you on your own."

I waved away her concern. "I was fine. Sol stayed for a while."

"You sent him away, too?"

"Of course. Olympus, tell me about Zohar Delarosa."

He took his mug from Indigo, walked around his desk, and settled in his seat. "There's nothing to tell."

"And Brodie?" Indigo wasn't getting the hint I didn't want to talk about my private life.

I shook my head. She'd only think I was weird if I told her about him. My friends didn't understand. I was on my own in getting Brodie back. "Olympus, this is important."

He shuffled through some folders on his desk. "I can't help."

"Look him up on the system. Find out what you can about this guy."

Olympus shook his head. "Why? Do you know something about him?"

Indigo caught hold of my elbow. "What's going on? You're jittery, and you've got powdered pumpkin down your front." She brushed a hand across my cleavage.

I shrugged and stepped away. "It's nothing. I just had an early start and one too many coffees."

"You're sure that's all?" Indigo said.

"Yes! Olympus, what's going on with Zohar? I can tell you're hiding something. What happened to him?"

Olympus studied me with a level gaze. "There's nothing you need to know."

Indigo turned her attention to Olympus, and her eyes narrowed. "I've heard you say that phrase before. It means you know something, but don't want to share. What gives with this guy?"

"Thanks for nothing," Olympus muttered. "Give away my secrets, why don't you?"

"We're all friends here, and you can trust Odessa not to gossip."

"It's not that."

"I recognize the name. It's the guy who won the crystal jackpot, isn't it? He lives in that enormous glass mansion. Has someone burgled his home?" Indigo slid around the desk and rubbed Olympus's shoulders.

"That's the guy I'm interested in," I said.

"Come on, you know something about Zohar. Share with us." Indigo kissed Olympus's cheek.

"This is emotional blackmail," he said.

"Do you want me to stop rubbing your shoulders?" Indigo winked at me.

"No! Yes. I should."

"This Zohar guy seems important to Odessa. Tell us the gossip."

Olympus groaned and tipped back his head. "I'm not getting any peace until I tell you, am I?"

"No. And I think Zohar's in trouble," I said.

Olympus sat back in his seat and placed down his coffee mug. "The case is odd, which is why we're keeping quiet about it."

"What's odd about it?" Indigo said. "Does it involve unicorns? Or invisible trolls?"

"Neither. A friend visiting him found Zohar dead."

"That's unfortunate but not odd," Indigo said.

"The odd part is that Zohar's body is missing."

"Ooooh! Okay, this is more interesting. Did the friend make a mistake about Zohar being dead?"

"No. Ballard Quinn, Zohar's friend, came back to the house to find the place turned over. He looked out an upper floor window and saw Zohar on the ground. He ran to check on him and couldn't find a pulse. He was on the phone, getting help, when he was attacked by the burglar and knocked out. His wife found him and called us for assistance. Ballard told us what he'd seen, but when we looked, Zohar was gone."

"Zohar was definitely dead?" Indigo said. "Maybe Ballard made a mistake and couldn't find the pulse point. Or it could have been really faint and hard to detect if Zohar was injured."

"He's dead," I said. "Zohar showed up as a ghost at my house last night."

"That explains your interest," Indigo said.

"This is good news, in a way," Olympus said. "Although we still need to find his body, or this investigation is going nowhere. Without a body, there's little we can do. We don't even know if his death was accidental."

"Zohar is worried something bad happened to him," I said. "He's asked me to look into it."

"You're getting a reputation for ghost whispering," Olympus said.

"Not by choice. But Zohar showed up, and I agreed to help." I kept the deal we'd made as my little secret, since it wasn't relevant to the investigation.

"What was taken in the burglary?" Indigo was studying me closely as she asked the question. "There must be plenty of rich pickings in a house like that."

"There were a few things taken and maybe some jewelry," Olympus said, "but they left plenty behind, including a stash of money. We assumed the burglar panicked when Ballard came in and ran."

"You don't think the burglar took Zohar's body, too?" I said.

Indigo shuddered. "You're thinking dark magic? They want to use the body parts in rituals?"

"No, I wasn't thinking that. But the dead don't get up and walk away."

"They do when you're around." Indigo grinned at me, but I struggled to muster a smile. I needed more information than this, or Zohar wouldn't be happy, and if he was unhappy, he may not stick to his side of the deal.

"There could be evidence on the body the killer needed to hide." Olympus checked the wall clock. "I wanted to take the scent bears to see if we could follow any trails leading from the house. Unfortunately, they're on a job three-hundred miles away. So..." His gaze went to the enormous empty panther bed in the corner of the office. "Monty is having some quick training to see if he can follow a scent trail. Storm has also agreed to loan us Fire Fang. Apparently, he can sniff out anything."

"Use Tuffin, too," I said. "She's got an amazing sense of smell."

"Three noses are better than two," Olympus said. "And I'm really not sure how Monty will get on. He's easily distracted."

"We need to try," I said. "Zohar's stuck and can't move on until he knows how he died."

"He may be stuck for a while," Olympus said. "We've got no clues as to who murdered him or even how. We need to find his body."

"I'll go grab Tuffin. Meet you back here in half an hour." I could see Indigo had more questions for me, but I didn't have time for her prying about Brodie or my involvement in solving Zohar's death, so I dashed away without a backward glance.

It took plenty of pleading with Tuffin and the promise of even more fresh fish before she agreed to be a part of the scent team.

A translocation spell zoomed us back to the office, and while we were sorting out Monty, Fire Fang, and Tuffin, Olympus contacted the family to let them know what was going on.

"Take a break," Indigo said quietly after I'd run through scent drills with Tuffin for the tenth time. "There's still half an hour before we can go to the house. And you keep yawning. It's making me tired just watching you."

"Maybe just five minutes."

"And you need something to eat."

"I'm good." My growling stomach revealed my lie.

"Sure you are. Rest and food. And are you still worrying about Brodie?"

I glanced at Olympus, who was still on the phone. "No. I mean, not really. I'm working on a solution."

A determined look entered Indigo's eyes. "You're coming with me. Olympus, we're getting food. I'll bring you back something."

He raised a hand in acknowledgement, and we left his office and walked to a nearby café.

I needed to get a grip on myself. I couldn't let on how worried I was about Brodie, but I was desperate to talk about it. If I did, I didn't want Indigo judging me.

"Let's get the cherry and almond croissants. They're always good from here," Indigo said as we browsed the menu.

"Fine. Whatever you want. But let's eat outside. I could do with some air." My stomach churned. What would she think if I told her what I had planned for Brodie?

"You got it. You go grab that empty bench, and I'll be right out."

I hurried to the bench outside the café and perched on the edge.

"Here you go." Indigo arrived a moment later and passed me a warm croissant in a paper bag as she settled next to me.

I took it and had a bite, barely tasting the sweet almonds and tart cherries as I swallowed. "Thanks."

We ate in silence, people watching as they headed to the stores or their day jobs.

Indigo nudged me with her elbow. "So, what's going on?"

"Just had a busy night," I said.

"You look like you haven't slept."

"I slept some. But I had a lot to think about."

"Did you see Brodie again?"

I slid her a sharp look. "If I tell you, I don't want any judgment."

"Hey, I won't judge. I want what's best for you. If you think that's Brodie's ghost, I want that. I'll support you in keeping him around."

"Yeah, you really sound like you will."

Indigo lowered her croissant. "I will. I promise. I just don't want you being stressed when you don't have to be. Maybe the ghost you saw only looked like Brodie."

"It was him." I finished my croissant in four bites, regretting eating so quickly as it sat unhappily in my stomach like a lump of moldy unicorn dung.

"Okay, so he's back. That's great news. You've wanted this for a long time. What happens next?"

I stared into the distance, not looking at anything. "Brodie's not sure he wants to stay with me."

"That's crazy. Of course, he'll stay."

"He saw the light." Now I was opening up, I didn't want to stop. "Brodie came back after everyone left, and we talked. Suddenly, he said he had to go. The light was encouraging him to leave. He said he only needed to find me to say goodbye." I swallowed to unblock my throat. "I panicked. I worried I was about to lose him again."

"What did you do?"

"Made a deal when Zohar appeared. He said he'd help Brodie and keep him stable. In return, I need to find out how he died."

"That doesn't sound such a bad deal. And it now makes sense why you were hassling Olympus," Indigo said. "How will Zohar help Brodie?"

"He's convincing him to stay. I didn't seem to have any luck in doing that." I stared at my feet. I was wearing mismatching shoes. "I can't lose Brodie. Not again."

"You won't. If he's meant to be here with you, then he'll stay."

"Of course he's meant to be here. Where else is he supposed to be?"

Indigo reached over and squeezed my knee. "You've been apart for a long time. People change, and they move on. I think ghosts do too."

"Yes, they change into ghost ghouls. But Brodie hasn't changed. It was him."

"I'm not saying any of this to be unkind, but I don't want you to get your hopes up. You were moving on with Sol and planning a different future. One without Brodie. Maybe you can keep doing that if Brodie feels he needs to go."

I slid her a glare as I shuffled along the bench. "You'd like that."

"I'd like you to be happy. And maybe that happiness won't come from living in the past."

"Brodie isn't in my past. He's right here." I jabbed a finger at the ground.

"But not for long if what he's said is true. Why come back just to leave you again? It's twisted."

"It's not! He's confused. So am I." I scowled at her. "I'm right about this. Don't spoil things."

"I'm not spoiling things. I'm just trying to get you to see—"

"No! This is how it's supposed to be. Don't put doubts in my head about Brodie. He's back, and I'm getting him back for good."

Indigo stared at me, not speaking for several seconds. "How are you going to do that?"

"I'll figure it out." I scrunched up the paper bag and tossed it in the trash. "Come on. Let's go scent hunting. We have a body to find."

Chapter 5

I headed to Zohar's house with just Tuffin, leaving everyone else at the office. My chat with Indigo had gone in the wrong direction, but it proved to me I was right about not including my friends. They still didn't understand how important Brodie was to me.

"Why do I have to be involved?" Tuffin yawned loudly as she sauntered behind me.

"You're always saying what an incredible sense of smell you have. Now's your chance to put it to good use."

"I only had a small amount of breakfast. And it's nearly noon. I don't work on an empty stomach."

"Try." I let out a sigh. "Sorry. I just can't mess this up. This ghost is the only thing keeping Brodie grounded enough, so he doesn't cross over."

Tuffin caught up with me and head-butted my calf. "Maybe he should move on. What's the guy been doing all these years, anyway?"

"You heard him. He's been confused. He sometimes couldn't even remember who I was."

"I'm not buying that. He wants something. Brodie must have known where you were. If your relationship was as amazing as you always claimed it was—"

"It is. It was. And it will be again. Tuffin, I don't ask much of you—"

"You do. Since I've been here, the Magic Council has almost arrested me, I've had several near misses with your crazy scarecrows, and had to deal with serious issues regarding overcooked fish. Now, I'm having to sniff out a corpse. You ask a lot. Most familiars would run a mile rather than get messed up in your witchy drama."

"I... Maybe I do ask a lot of you. My life isn't normally like this, but these are extreme circumstances." My eyes were full of tears, and I blinked to chase them away. It was only stress making me feel weepy. "You don't have to be involved, but I really need your help."

"I'm here, aren't I?"

More tears appeared. "You are. And thanks. The quicker we solve what happened to Zohar, the quicker I'll get Brodie back. And then you'll see what a great guy he is. He may even be better at cooking fish than me."

"Doubtful. Although you are terrible with anything savory." Tuffin mooched along for a few steps. "My first impressions of people are always right. I don't like him. And he looked at me funny."

"Brodie loves animals. And he'll adore you once he gets to know you." I rounded a bend, and my eyes widened as I took in the huge mansion standing in the late morning sunshine. It was dazzling white, had four stories, and dozens of enormous windows.

There was a balcony at the top of the house with a wraparound glass veranda.

"How many people live here?" Tuffin said.

"As far as I know, it was only Zohar and his wife."

"They must have been planning on a huge family. You could get lost in there. Not me, of course. My sense of direction is faultless."

A menacing growl rumbled behind us, and I turned to see Fire Fang loping toward us, Storm not far behind him.

She raised a hand in acknowledgement. "I heard you were getting involved in this missing body search."

"Deliberately. Zohar's ghost came to find me." I risked a pet of Fire Fang's head. Tuffin had wisely jumped on my shoulders and was clinging on with her claws as she hissed at Fire Fang.

He growled, and acrid smoke bellowed from his huge nostrils.

Storm rolled her eyes. "We should just let them duke it out, or this could go on for hours as they vie for the top spot."

"Um... Tuffin is tiny next to Fire Fang. He could eat her in a single bite."

Tuffin hissed again. "I could eat this hound. It would take a few goes, but I could do it, especially if I marinate him in fish sauce."

"You can all be friends," I said. "You're here for the same thing."

"Look out! Monty is incoming."

I recognized Olympus's voice, even though I couldn't see him, and had just enough time to brace for impact as Monty raced around the bend and leaped at me. His sandpaper-like tongue rasped up my cheek, and then he tried to lick Tuffin, who hissed and slashed out with sharp claws.

He whimpered and dropped onto his huge leopard paws. "I'm the best body hunter. I'll sniff out this rotting corpse. We should have a competition. Whoever finds the body first gets a prize. Would you like that, tiny furball?" He looked up at Tuffin, who was still growling right by my ear.

"Tuffin, Monty's friendly. So is Fire Fang, sometimes. You need to work together on this."

"We can team up," Monty said. "Do you like steak? I love it. I eat several in one sitting, but I always share with friends. Would you like to be my friend, mini fluffy?"

Tuffin stopped growling and regarded Monty with suspicion in her eyes. "I prefer fresh salmon. Lightly poached in cream. Do you eat that?"

"That sounds delicious. We should get some of that, too. We should invite Fire Fang, too. He eats anything. I once saw him chew up a pair of shoes left by a dumpster. He didn't even get gas afterward."

Fire Fang growled and shook out his fur, looking proud of his gross shoe eating exploits. Tuffin hopped down, and after a bit of nose and butt sniffing, the three of them began a game of crazy chasing.

Olympus jogged up to join me and Storm. "Sorry. I told him no jumping. He knocked someone over in the street the other day because he went to say hello and they weren't expecting him. Monty is a menace."

"He's an adorable menace," I said. "So, how are we going to do this?"

"I called ahead and told Zohar's wife, Elsbeth, and their friends, Ballard and Hester, what we plan to do. They're expecting us. Shall we?" Olympus gestured toward the driveway.

I nodded, and we walked toward the house.

"They had no problems with us doing this?" Storm said.

"No, they're all concerned about what's going on."

"I bet. Especially if one of them killed Zohar," Storm said.

"Have you got your suspicions about any of them?" I said to Olympus.

"No, nothing obvious. But it's early days. Without Zohar's body, we're stuck. Let's hope our familiars don't let us down." He rang the bell at the front door, and a moment later, a stunning brunette with pale skin and big dark eyes opened the door. She wore a long floaty dress down to her ankles, with a high waist that sat under her ample bust. Diamonds sparkled in her earlobes, and she had several large rocks on her fingers, too.

"Elsbeth Delarosa, these are the colleagues I spoke to you about, Storm Winter and Odessa Grimsbane." Olympus made the introductions.

She nodded and shook hands with both of us. "Please, come in. Where are your familiars?"

"They're scouting the area." Olympus went in first, and we followed.

The inside of the house was as impressive and flashy as the outside. There was modern art on the walls, all of which looked original, a mirror that took up almost an entire wall, and white tiled flooring.

"Come through. Hester and Ballard are in the living room. We're all anxious to find Zohar."

Storm nudged me with her elbow and leaned in close. "I could fit about thirty of my apartments in this place. Who needs so much room?"

I shrugged and had to admit it seemed over the top. But then they'd won the crystal jackpot, so they didn't have to worry about money ever again.

We went into another white room. Waiting for us was a round-faced, nervous-looking blonde woman, standing close to a guy of about forty who wore a Hawaiian shirt and had a neat, dark goatee.

"These are two of my oldest friends, Hester and Ballard Quinn. We've known each other for years," Elsbeth said. "We invited them to vacation in Witch Haven and catch up on old times."

We all introduced ourselves, and then everyone looked at Olympus.

He stepped forward. "We've brought over skilled operatives to follow any scent trail to help us locate Zohar."

"May I ask a few questions before we start the search?" I said.

Olympus nodded. "Of course."

"Where were you all when you learned about what happened to Zohar?"

"I found him," Ballard said. "I went into the village with Hester to have a look around. We'd been there an hour, but I had to get back. I was going out with Zohar for the day for a round of golf. I came back, let myself in, but couldn't find him. I thought he was messing with me, so I checked every room. Then I looked out the window, and I saw him."

"Where was his body?" I said.

"At the back of the house." Ballard scrubbed at the back of his neck, and Hester caught hold of his hand and nodded at him. "I wondered if he'd fallen from the veranda. The door was open when I went up. Again, just for a second, I thought he was messing around. Zohar was a huge joker and loved to play pranks. I yelled at him to stop being an idiot, but he didn't move. I raced down the stairs, checked his pulse, and there was nothing."

Elsbeth looked away and covered her mouth with a hand.

"What about you, Mrs. Delarosa?" I said to Elsbeth.

Her eyes were cloudy with tears as she looked at me. "I was at the smoothie bar. I often go there."

I looked at Olympus, and he nodded to show she was telling the truth.

"Was anything odd or out of place when you got back here?" I said to Ballard.

"A couple of the rooms had been messed up. It looked like a burglary gone wrong, although I wasn't paying attention when I first got here. It was only when I saw Zohar that everything else hit. I don't know, maybe someone was watching the house and saw me and Hester leave and thought it was empty. Things were taken, weren't they, Elsbeth?"

She nodded. "Mainly cash and a few small electrical items. Ballard must have disturbed the burglar when he came back, so they left everything else."

"Mind if I look around?" Storm said.

"Of course not. Right this way. Not all the rooms were searched, though." Elsbeth led us into two more rooms.

"You can look around without disturbing evidence," Olympus said. "We checked for prints but came up blank."

"This is where I got hit on the back of the head." Ballard pointed to the door. "I was calling Hester to tell her what I'd seen."

"You didn't think to call the Magic Council first?" I said.

He ran a hand down his face. "I should have, but I was so panicked. I was on the phone when I was whacked. When I woke, Zohar was gone, and Hester was by my side."

"How long were you unconscious?"

"It wasn't more than ten minutes," Hester said. "I knew something terrible had happened when the line went dead. I ran all the way from the village and found him on the floor. He was just coming to when I arrived."

"I don't understand how anyone could move Zohar's body without being seen," Elsbeth said. "And why do that?"

Storm turned from the window she was looking out of. "You're isolated here. You don't have any neighbors?"

"We have some. There are small cottages close by. You can't see them because the trees provide a natural shield, but they're often at home. They're all retirees."

"Did any of them see anything suspicious?" I said.

Olympus shook his head. "No. And it would have been impossible to be discreet when moving Zohar. He was a big guy."

"Please, help us find him," Elsbeth said. "I haven't been able to sleep since this happened. I don't feel safe in my home."

"We're here for you." Hester hugged Elsbeth. "You're not alone."

"Let's round up our operatives," Olympus said. "We'll take a look around and see what they find."

We headed outside, and I was pleased to see Monty, Fire Fang, and Tuffin waiting patiently like the good little operatives they were supposed to be.

"Have you got something that smells of Zohar?" Olympus said to Elsbeth. "It will help with the search."

"I'll check the laundry hamper." Elsbeth left and returned a moment later with several shirts.

"Perfect. Hold them to the operatives' noses. Give them a few seconds to have a smell." Olympus was being so serious that I couldn't help but smile. Storm was looking anywhere but me, most likely also stifling laughter.

I gave Tuffin a warning look to behave.

Her tail swished from side-to-side, but she made no comment and even accepted the soiled shirt under her nose with all the good grace she could muster.

"We'll start at the site where you saw Zohar's body," Olympus said. "We'll work our way out from there."

We headed to the back yard.

"This is it," Ballard said. "I feel sick remembering it. I've known the guy for years, and he's suddenly gone."

"How did you know each other?" I said.

"We were neighbors," Hester said. "That was before they hit the jackpot and built their own place out here. We all got along really well. I was sad when they moved, but I understand why. This place is beautiful."

"Operatives, focus up," Olympus said in his most authoritative voice. "You know the scent. Work your way around and see if you can pick up anything."

Tuffin muttered something rude under her breath, but no one else seemed to have heard her, so I let her off.

We stood back and watched the familiars work. Monty was his usual enthusiastic self, sniffing the ground in rapid, short bursts, his tail wagging wildly. Tuffin sloped away, sniffing things now and again, but not dedicated to the cause. Fire Fang was growling so loudly, I was at risk of getting a headache. But his nose was on the ground, and he seemed to have picked up something.

"Fire Fang's got a scent," Storm said. "Let's follow him."

I glanced at Tuffin, who was heading in the other direction, then hurried along with the others.

"What have you got, boy?" Storm said.

Fire Fang's head shot up, and he raced away, snarling.

"There's something over here," Monty said from inside a dense patch of bushes. "It's a body part."

Elsbeth gasped, and Hester caught hold of her.

"I'll bring it over," Monty yelled.

"No! Leave it where it is," Olympus said.

Monty ignored him. He raced over, something black and covered in green slime hanging out of his mouth.

"Put that down," Olympus growled.

Monty spat it out and poked his tongue out several times. "It's rotten. It's part of a corpse, I'm sure of it. Did I do good?"

Olympus inspected the mess. "It looks like rancid pond weed and maybe part of a dead beaver. A long dead beaver."

"That's a corpse. I scored. Do I win a prize?" Monty bounded around.

There was a yelp and cries of protest, and we all looked around to see Fire Fang dragging an elderly woman toward us.

"Mrs. Langton." Elsbeth rushed over to the woman but kept a safe distance from Fire Fang.

"This creature won't let me go. He wants to eat me." Mrs. Langton's eyes were huge as Fire Fang continued to drag her toward us.

"Put the woman down." Storm marched over, grabbed Fire Fang around the neck, and hauled him away.

Reluctantly, he let go of the little old lady.

"Why did he attack Mrs. Langton?" Elsbeth placed a comforting arm around the other woman's shoulders.

"He wouldn't have dragged her here if she wasn't involved in what happened to Zohar." Storm petted Fire Fang.

"What am I involved in?" Mrs. Langton was shaking from head to toe.

"I'm so sorry," I said. "These are... operatives from the Magic Council. They're here to find out what happened to Zohar."

"Oh! I... I heard he was missing." Mrs. Langton backed away. "Why would this creature think I'm involved?"

"You haven't been hurt, have you?" Olympus rushed over and caught hold of the old lady's arm.

"No, I'm more shaken than anything else. I was attending to the lavender in my garden when this creature lunged at me. He rolled me several times before dragging me here. I thought I was a goner."

"Fire Fang's just enthusiastic about his work," Storm said. "Are you sure you didn't murder Zohar Delarosa?"

"Oh, my! No. He's been killed?"

"You may go." Olympus walked the old lady away from the rest of us. "Sorry for the inconvenience."

Mrs. Langton looked at Fire Fang one final time then turned and raced away. She was sprightly for such an elderly lady. But then, being mauled by a huge hellhound would make anyone want to flee as fast as they could.

Olympus marched over to Storm. "We aren't talking murder just yet."

"We should. And she looked suspicious to me. There was something about her face I didn't like."

"She's a retiree from the white witch community in Sweet Valley Meadow. Mrs. Langton wouldn't even have dark thoughts, let alone cast dark spells. And she wouldn't kill anyone."

Storm shrugged. "Fire Fang rarely gets things wrong."

"Are you sure these operatives know what they're doing?" Ballard said.

Fire Fang growled. He struggled free from Storm and raced to a large set of double gates at the side of the back yard. He pawed at them, and when Olympus opened them, he hurried out. Fire Fang sniffed around a partial tire tread on the ground.

Storm knelt and inspected it. She looked up at Elsbeth. "Do you keep a vehicle out here?"

"No. This is a dirt track. It leads to the main road eventually, but you wouldn't know about it unless you lived here."

"Then we've found a clue," Storm said. "This could be where the killer brought Zohar's body. They had a vehicle here, stashed him in the back, and drove off."

Elsbeth staggered back and tears filled her eyes. "But why? Why take him?"

"That's what we're here to find out," I said.

Elsbeth looked at me, recognition dawning in her sad eyes. "I know you. You have that farm with the scarecrows. Do you also freelance for the Magic Council?"

"Not exactly."

"Odessa is working freelance for us, at the moment." Olympus shot me a warning look.

"Actually, I'm here to help Zohar. I've met him."

"Now's not the right time," Olympus cautioned me.

I shook my head at him. Elsbeth needed to know the truth. "I'm here because your husband's ghost contacted me. He thinks he was killed, and he's not able to cross over until he finds the truth and we capture his killer."

Elsbeth's face drained of color. She swayed from side to side and fainted.

Chapter 6

"That wasn't the best idea in the world," Olympus muttered as we stood around Elsbeth, while Hester and Ballard kneeled and tried to rouse her.

"She needed to know the truth," I said. "Zohar's in trouble, and he needs help. And I'm determined to get it for him as quickly as possible."

"Why?" Storm said.

"A man was killed. Doesn't he deserve justice?"

"Sure. But what else is going on?"

"Nothing. You're always so suspicious of everyone."

"I'm suspicious when you act weirdly. And you're more wired than usual. What's going on with you?"

I focused on Elsbeth as she roused. "Let's concentrate on the case, shall we? Fire Fang found a tire track. That could be the clue we need to locate Zohar's body."

"I didn't want to believe it," Elsbeth mumbled as she remained on the ground. "Zohar is never coming back."

"You stay where you are," Hester said. "You've had a shock. We all have."

"I want to get up." Elsbeth struggled to her feet with Hester's help. She focused on me. "He's definitely gone? I thought, since there wasn't a body, maybe this was a mistake."

"He wasn't alive when I found him," Ballard said. "I'm no doctor, but even I know how to find a pulse. He was gone. His eyes were open, and he was seeing nothing. He wasn't breathing."

Elsbeth shook her head and wiped her damp eyes. "Even so, I still had hope, which was foolish. Since you've seen his ghost, he's definitely left me."

"We should go inside," Olympus said.

Ballard and Olympus stepped up to their knights in shining armor roles and stood on either side of Elsbeth as they escorted her into the house. Storm raced off to collect Fire Fang, who'd shot off on a mission to take down a group of squirrels yelling squeaky insults from a nearby tree. Monty and Tuffin were nowhere to be seen.

Hester walked along beside me, not saying anything until the others were some way ahead. "I didn't want to say this in front of Elsbeth, but Zohar was bad news."

"Why do you say that?"

"Their marriage wasn't happy. Elsbeth didn't want to be with him anymore."

"She told you that?"

"Not in so many words. Elsbeth put on a great act when we got here, but it was easy to see something was wrong. Zohar was being over the top and showing off, too. And I noticed they didn't look at each other. They'd speak to each other, but it was as if they were playing a role, acting like the happy couple, when it couldn't be further from the truth."

"While Elsbeth's getting settled in the house, would you mind showing me the veranda?" I said. "Your husband seemed to think Zohar could have fallen from there."

"Of course. If you think it'll help. I want this mystery solved. Elsbeth's all on her own, and I'm worried about her."

Once we were inside, I whispered to Olympus what I was doing then headed to the top of the house with Hester.

Hester stood back as I looked around the large tiled veranda with stunning views of Witch Haven.

"Maybe he did simply fall, and this was a horrible accident." I peered over the edge of the high glass wall. "Although he'd have needed to jump to make it over here. Or been standing on something." I looked around, but there were no boxes or a ladder he could have used.

"Maybe he was pushed."

"By anyone in particular?" I glanced at Hester.

"Oh, no. I mean, not that I can think of. Zohar was an okay guy."

"Just okay?"

She shrugged. "Maybe he's changed. He could be a bit pushy."

"Until we locate his body and see the extent of his injuries, it'll be hard to know what happened. Did Ballard mention any head injuries or anything like that? Any marks on the body that could have been caused by a fall from this height?"

"Ballard didn't spend much time with Zohar when he found him. And he was so panicked when he called. My heart stopped for several seconds when I heard the news. Then I freaked out when Ballard stopped talking. I thought he'd been killed, too."

"Did you hear another voice or any clue as to who hit Ballard?"

"No. Ballard made a gurgling noise, and then there was a thud. I did hear footsteps. Someone running away."

"Heavy footsteps or soft footsteps?"

"I'm not sure. I was yelling Ballard's name and trying to get him to talk. They were moving fast, whoever they were. Ballard must have startled them."

I walked around the veranda, trying to slot the pieces together. "The killer could have snuck into the house and Zohar confronted them. They fought, which could have ended up here, and the killer threw Zohar over the edge. How strong would you say Zohar was?"

"He was a fit guy. There's a gym in the house, and he was always working out. He liked to flaunt his two-pack."

"Which means, the killer was stronger than him or got lucky if they pushed him off here," I said.

Hester shuddered. "I guess so. What a gruesome thought."

"Unless he didn't fall from here, and there's more to this mystery."

"I'm not the expert. I'll leave that to you and the Magic Council. I just want this over with. I feel so sorry for Elsbeth. Their marriage wasn't happy, but she wouldn't have wanted it to end like this."

"How serious were their problems?" After doing another circuit of the veranda and not finding anything useful, I followed Hester back down the stairs.

"I reckon it was pretty bad. Several times, I asked them if there was a problem, but Zohar brushed me off. I even got Ballard to keep Zohar up late one night to get him to talk man to man. My husband is such a night owl, always preferring to stay up until the early hours. He tried, but Zohar made the excuse of being tired and left."

"You don't think the marriage could be saved?"

"I'm really not sure. The evening before Zohar died, Elsbeth seemed anxious. She said she needed to make big changes but wasn't sure how to go about it. I asked if she was talking about her marriage, but she wouldn't say. I pressed her on it, but she changed the subject and told me not to keep asking questions."

"What else could it have been if not marriage problems?"

"I don't know, but I was worried about her. Neither of them knew anyone local when they moved to Witch Haven, so it was a big change for them. I was concerned Elsbeth had no one to confide in if she was struggling. And..."

"There's something else?"

"It's probably nothing, but after Ballard found Zohar's body and called me, we couldn't find Elsbeth. She went missing."

"She said she went to the smoothie bar."

"Yes, but that's not far from here. And she didn't tell any of us about her plan. It seemed odd she'd go out and not invite me. And when Elsbeth got back, she didn't have a drink with her."

"Maybe she drank it there or on her way home."

"Sure. But why not get something for all of us?" Hester shrugged. "I don't know."

"Do you think Elsbeth was making a run for it? Maybe she argued with Zohar and something bad happened. She panicked, left the house, but then changed her mind and came back?"

"Possibly. But why did the place look like it had been burgled?"

"That is a mystery," I said. "Are there any surveillance cameras or trackers we can look at?"

Hester shook her head. "I kept telling them they should get some installed. There are all kinds of weird people out there, and I didn't want them being preyed upon because they came into a lot of money."

"Have they had problems with that?"

"Nothing serious, but Elsbeth mentioned they got begging letters from all over the country. People would find out about their crystal jackpot win and send these heartbreaking stories of illness and problems and expect a handout."

"That must have been hard to deal with."

"Which is why I told them they needed to have better security, just in case one of those weirdos visited and demanded money." Hester shook her head. "This new world of wealth overtook them. We're all from modest means, and I certainly wouldn't know what to do with all that money and the public interest. I wouldn't want it, personally. I like my life simple and quiet."

"Yes, sometimes, a simple life is best," I said.

Hester stopped me before we headed in to join the others. "You said you've seen Zohar's ghost?"

"That's right. He appeared at my farmhouse. I'm kind of a ghost whisperer. They seem to like me."

She glanced around. "Is Zohar here now? Does he know what's going on?"

"He's not. He's helping me with something at the farm. Why do you ask?"

Hester chewed on her bottom lip for a few seconds. "I didn't want to say this in front of Elsbeth, in case it upset her, but I've always been afraid of Zohar. When I first met him, he was full of jokes, and everything was light-hearted, but he could be mean. And when he had a few drinks, he had a temper. I even checked in with Elsbeth after they'd had a fight at their old house to see if she was okay. I heard shouting and things being thrown, and I was worried he might have hurt her."

"Did he ever hurt her?"

"If he did, Elsbeth never told me. It's so sad, but you never really know what goes on behind closed doors. People are amazing at putting on a front and making out everything is fine, when the opposite is true. Someone could be spiraling, and you don't know until it's too late."

I knew all about spiraling. My life felt like I was on a huge helter skelter, and I seriously needed a break. And some pumpkin and sugar candy floss. Maybe that was what happened here. The fighting got out of control, they fought, and Elsbeth had to defend herself.

"Has Elsbeth been questioned about the problems in their marriage?" I said.

"I don't know if she said anything to the Magic Council, but if Elsbeth's hiding things from me, she's probably doing the same with them."

Elsbeth appeared in the corridor, her arms crossed over her chest and an angry expression on her face. "Hester, are you gossiping about me?"

Chapter 7

"I... No! I mean, I wasn't gossiping." Hester rushed over and caught hold of Elsbeth's arm. "But I am worried about you. I know things haven't been easy with you and Zohar."

"You know nothing about my marriage. Stop telling lies." Elsbeth stepped away from Hester.

"But you used to fight. I'd hear you through the walls. You remember how thin they were in our old houses?"

"That was a long time ago. And every marriage goes through rocky patches." Elsbeth glared at me. "This has nothing to do with what happened to Zohar. Don't report this to the Magic Council."

"Do you admit you had problems, though?" I said.

"Who doesn't? Are you married?"

"Yes. I mean, almost. It's complicated."

"There you go. Every relationship has complications. What I had with Zohar was no different. But I loved him, and I didn't kill him because he dropped his socks on the floor and didn't stack the dishwasher right."

"Why don't we go into the main room and talk about it some more?" I wanted Olympus to be involved in this conversation.

"I don't want anyone hearing Hester spreading lies." Her eyes narrowed as she glared at Hester. "We used to be friends."

"We still are. It's been a while since we've seen each other, but I still consider you a good friend. And I don't want anything bad to happen to you," Hester said. "I'm looking out for you."

"How about we step out the front door?" I said. "We can talk outside, and no one will hear us."

Elsbeth huffed out a breath. "Fine. I'm only doing this because I don't like the thought of Zohar's ghost trapped and unable to move on. But I assure you, our bickering had nothing to do with his death."

"I'm sure he'll appreciate the help." After we'd moved outside, I eased the front door closed. "Let's start with the basics. Tell me your alibi again."

"I went to get a smoothie."

"That was it?" I said.

Elsbeth spent a few seconds adjusting the waistband of her floaty dress. "Yes. I like smoothies."

"You were gone a while," Hester said. "The smoothie bar is ten minutes from here."

"I walk slowly."

"I know the place," I said. "Even if you crawled on your hands and knees, you'd make it there and back in forty minutes."

"Maybe I got distracted. It doesn't mean I killed Zohar."

Maybe not, but it meant Elsbeth's alibi was shaky. "Would you describe your marriage to Zohar as generally happy?"

"I've already said yes. Other than a few small bumps along the way, we were fine." She stared at Hester as if daring her to say anything.

"You did used to fight, though," Hester almost whispered.

"And then we stopped fighting. You and Ballard argue."

"You had no big issues you were struggling to work through?" I said. "Most relationships would find it a challenge to come into so much money so quickly."

Elsbeth's gaze lowered. "Maybe we argued now and again. The money was causing a few problems."

"What kind of problems?"

Her shoulders lifted up and down as she sighed. "You always think, when you have all the money you could ever want, the troubles will disappear. You can afford what you like, luxury vacations and amazing clothes, but we ended up fighting over different things."

"I'm sorry to hear that," I said. "Had you been arguing a lot recently?"

Elsbeth closed her eyes for a second. "Zohar wasn't happy about our move to Witch Haven. We'd been here for day trips, and I've always loved the place. I remember spotting this piece of land and saying to Zohar, if money was no object, we'd buy it and build our dream home. It was a joke we often went back to, imagining the layout and furnishings. Then the crystal jackpot happened."

"It didn't turn out to be the dream you hoped it would be?"

She shook her head. "It was great for a while. The fighting stopped, and we were getting along fine. But Zohar missed his friends, and he kept reminiscing about our old life. It was one of the reasons we reached out to Ballard and Hester. We'd been neighbors for years and always gotten along. I thought Zohar might appreciate seeing some old faces. Not that you're old, Hester, but you know what I mean."

"I do. We were glad to hear from you," Hester said. "We lost touch so quickly after you moved. I reached out a few times, but..."

"That was my fault," Elsbeth said. "I let the money go to my head. I even joined some exclusive clubs to find friends, but they were full of snobs and people who bragged about the things they had. And they looked down on me because we'd won our money, rather than worked for it."

"That must have been tough, being in a new place and not finding people you can connect with," I said.

"I thought I had made a few new friends, but after a couple of months, they started asking for things and expecting me to pay for everything when we went out. I didn't mind, but it was just the assumption I'd do it that grated."

"It's hard to know who to trust when you come into a lot of money."

"Tell me about it. The crystal jackpot was supposed to make our lives easier. Now, everything has fallen apart. And Zohar is gone." Elsbeth pressed a hand against her mouth. "I still can't believe you've seen his ghost. How was he?"

"Confused. And he wants answers. Let's go back to the morning he died. Walk me through everything you did."

"There's not much to tell," Elsbeth said. "I got up, had a swim, and got dressed. We all ate breakfast together, then Ballard and Hester went off to browse the stores."

Hester nodded. "We weren't going for long because Zohar and Ballard were having a boy's day on the golf course. But I wanted to have a look around, so Ballard came with me."

"That left you alone with Zohar?" I said to Elsbeth. "There was no one else here?"

"That's right. Then I went to get my smoothie, and by the time I came back, well, it was too late. The Magic Council had arrived, and Zohar... was gone."

"The only thing you did was walk to the smoothie shop and back?"

Elsbeth tilted her head. "Oh! Well, I took a detour."

"You're just remembering that now?" I said.

"Yes, sorry. I've been forgetful lately. I don't know what's happening to me. My brain's turned to mush."

I glanced at Hester to see she looked as puzzled as I felt. How did you forget something that important? Elsbeth was a suspect in Zohar's murder, and she'd forgotten part of her alibi.

"Where did this detour take you?" I asked.

"Nowhere special. I wandered around for a bit. I wanted some air and was in no hurry to get back."

"Why would that be?"

"It's not important. I just didn't want to be here."

"Elsbeth, it is important," Hester said. "Someone might have seen you."

"It doesn't matter if anyone saw me or not, because I didn't kill my husband," Elsbeth said. "Ballard will back me on this. He was attacked by the same person who killed Zohar. It was a burglary gone wrong. I'd never hurt Ballard, just like I'd never hurt Zohar."

"You must be able to remember the route you took," I said.

"I don't. You'll have to blame my hormones. Just last week, I lost my keys for a day. It was only when I opened the freezer to make dinner that I discovered them. I wonder if I'm having an early menopause. Something is making me so forgetful."

I doubted that. Elsbeth was glowing with youth and energy. There was no way her thoughts were muddled because of aging hormones.

"This is serious," Hester said. "You don't want to be under suspicion."

"Of course not. But that's what happened. I went for a walk, I didn't pay attention to where I was going, and my route took me to the smoothie bar. If you have doubts about that, go check there. There weren't many other people in the place, but I'm a regular. Finn served me. He'll confirm the time I arrived. I couldn't have been at the smoothie bar and killing Zohar at the same time."

True, but maybe Elsbeth had shoved Zohar off the veranda then got a refreshing smoothie to reward herself for removing a nagging problem from her life. She'd have had the time.

There was a swirl of cold air around me, and Zohar appeared. He didn't look happy.

Hester looked around, and her forehead furrowed. "I can sense something. Is Zohar here?"

Elsbeth gasped. "Talk to him. He'll tell you I'm innocent."

I gestured Zohar to back off as Hester went pale. She must be sensitive to ghost energy. "It doesn't work like that. I wish it was that simple, but no ghost remembers the moment of their death. That's why Zohar is confused. He knows something bad happened but doesn't know how, why, or who did it. He's stuck here and won't move on until this is resolved."

"I don't want Zohar unhappy," Elsbeth said. "We had our struggles, but he was a good man."

Hester swayed on her feet, her skin an unhealthy shade of gray.

"Give me a minute to talk to Zohar." I gestured him to move away so Hester wouldn't faint and strode to the side of the house. "Why are you here?"

"I came to see what you've been doing. It sounds like you haven't gotten far."

"Give me a chance! I haven't been here long. And shouldn't you be with Brodie? How is he?"

"Everything is under control," Zohar said.

"Tell me more. Is he staying?"

"It's looking good. Brodie asked for a few minutes on his own, so I came here."

"You mustn't leave him. He could have crossed over while you were gone. I need to get back to the farm. I have to stop him from doing anything stupid."

Zohar blocked my path. "Relax. Your guy isn't going anywhere. We talked, and he's calmed down. Brodie even told me the light had faded."

"You're sure? The light could come back."

"It won't. Brodie is chilled. And he wants to stay with you."

"He said that?"

"Yes, he did."

"You still shouldn't have left him. We had a deal."

"And I'm upholding my end. But what about my death? What have you found out?"

I glanced over to see Hester and Elsbeth talking quietly and occasionally shooting me nervous looks. "I've got everyone's alibi, and I was talking to Elsbeth to confirm where she was when you died."

"You think it was my wife?"

"She said you've been having problems, although it was in the past. Have you been fighting recently?"

Zohar grimaced. "It's not been great between us for a while. We tried different things to make it better, couples days and fun experiences, but it wasn't working. I only agreed to move to Witch Haven in an attempt to get things back to how they used to be. Our marriage was perfect when we first got hitched."

"I didn't know things were that bad," I said. "Although Hester mentioned you fought a lot."

"And I expect Elsbeth told her everything that happened between us. That was another reason to move. The neighbors were too nosy. Hester was always snooping into our business."

"Maybe she had a right to do so. It sounds like things got intense between you and Elsbeth. Hester must have wanted to keep her friend safe."

"Elsbeth was safe with me. Sure, we had a fiery relationship, but it wasn't terrible. Well, not all the time."

"You weren't happy here, though? The move didn't solve anything?"

Zohar looked at Elsbeth, and a deep sadness entered his eyes. "Neither of us were happy. It's true what they say. Money can't buy happiness."

"Odessa, is everything okay with Zohar?" Hester called out.

"It will be. He's just concerned. I'm making sure he's okay."

"Can I talk to him?" Elsbeth said.

"Sure. He can hear you," I said.

Elsbeth kept her gaze on the ground as she inched closer. "I'm sorry about what happened. I wish I'd been here. I could have helped."

"Maybe she'd have helped by not killing me," Zohar muttered. "No! I didn't mean that. At least, I think I don't. This is so confusing."

Elsbeth shuddered. "He's not happy with me, is he? I'm not a ghost whisperer, but even I feel the chill in the air."

"Not really. Zohar is struggling with this situation," I said.

"Ask her if she did it." Zohar nudged me forward. "I need to know my wife is innocent."

I shooed him away, but he wouldn't budge, so I focused on Elsbeth. It was time for some truth seeking. "Elsbeth, you have to admit, you have a great motive for wanting Zohar dead. With him gone, you get the money from your crystal jackpot win."

Her cheeks flushed scarlet. "I didn't kill Zohar for the money. Besides, I actually had the winning numbers and agreed to share with him. Maybe I should have taken it and walked away, then we wouldn't be in this mess, and I wouldn't be a suspect in his death."

"It sounds like you thought about leaving with all the money," I said.

"Maybe for five minutes. But we talked it over and decided to use the money to repair our relationship. We agreed on a fresh start in a new place. We were reinventing ourselves."

"The reinvention didn't go to plan?"

"Clearly not, since my husband is dead." Elsbeth rested a hand on the wall of the house. "I don't feel good. I think I might faint again."

"Let me take you inside." Hester caught hold of Elsbeth's elbow. "This stress isn't doing us any good."

Elsbeth nodded and didn't resist as Hester led her away.

I waited until the front door closed and then turned to Zohar. "So, which one of them killed you?"

He shrugged as his gaze flickered over the house. "I have no idea. But that's what you need to find out. Was I murdered, or was this an accident? Are you up to the challenge?"

"Of course." I'd do what I had to do in order to help this ghost and make sure Brodie stayed with me forever.

77

Chapter 8

After making my excuses to Olympus and collecting Tuffin, I headed back to the farm. Zohar had come with me, but drifted off after I'd begged him to check on Brodie.

That had been over an hour ago, and he hadn't returned. I wasn't sure if that meant bad news. But in my heart, I knew Brodie was still with me.

With a mysterious death to mull over, I figured some support was needed. I called Hettie Crane, my friendly local former coroner, but her phone went to voicemail.

I'm on vacation with the dead. A week's exploration of the catacombs of lesser demons on Mount Pleasant. If you need a rental for a horse, I'm fully booked. If you want to talk to me about a corpse, try again in a week.

With the click of a button, I disconnected the call, not leaving a message. Hopefully, this would all be solved soon, so I wouldn't have to disturb Hettie's macabre vacation treat. I was on my own with this mystery.

I headed outside and hunted through the barns for a blank whiteboard. I could use it as a suspect board and lay out the information I had so far on Zohar. After swiping cobwebs off an old board tucked behind some rags, I heaved it out of the barn and walked back into the farmhouse. I set it on the kitchen table and leaned it against the wall. It slid down and fell to the floor.

I picked it up and set it back in place. I didn't have any marker pens. I also didn't have any pictures of my suspects. But there were only three of them, so I'd draw cartoon stick figures to represent them.

There was the possibility of an unknown assailant who attacked Zohar to avoid being caught during a burglary, but that made little sense to me. The house had been rammed with expensive items, and most of them were still there when I'd looked around.

I found some sticky notes and wrote the names of the three suspects on them, along with a cartoon image. I stuck them to the board. They fell off.

This wasn't going so well. I needed Sol's help. He was great with the suspect boards. Guilt hit me in the stomach like an unwelcome headbutt from a goblin. I'd let Sol walk away at the first sighting of Brodie. He'd been helping me for half a year. and I'd thanked him by ignoring him and sending him away.

I should make it up to him, but I didn't know how or even if I should. I had my guy back, and there was no room for distractions, no matter what an amazing distraction Sol was. He'd stuck by me even when he'd been trapped by that awful ghost, Arietta Frost, and forced to help solve her murder. He hadn't flinched. And how had I repaid him? I hadn't. I'd have to figure out how to live with that guilt.

But it didn't feel possible, so I picked up my phone and scrolled through my contacts until I found his name. I could call Sol and make sure he was okay. I hated the thought of him leaving, but maybe he needed to.

I was about to hit the call button when Brodie blinked into sight. I dropped the phone and ran to him, but rather than touching him, I blasted through his ghost and almost hit the wall.

I staggered and landed on my knees as a ghostly chill shook through me. "What's wrong with you?" I turned and examined Brodie's form. He was so faint I could see through him, and his expression looked strained. "Brodie, what's the matter?"

He lifted a hand. "Sorry, I'm struggling. I can't always keep a solid form. It takes a lot of energy."

"Of course, I understand." I scrambled to my feet. "I'm so glad you're here. You are staying, aren't you?"

"I'm staying. Zohar's been having long conversations with me. That guy sure doesn't know how to be quiet."

"I'm glad. He's helping me, and I'm helping to figure out how he died. We made a deal because I really don't want you to go."

"Neither do I. And I'm sorry for scaring you. But when I got here, suddenly, everything made sense. I saw you, and I was happy, and then a light appeared. I felt more than ready to go."

"Is the light still around? You don't feel tempted by it, do you?" I stepped closer to Brodie, and instantly, his form grew brighter.

"I see something faint, but it's not tempting me half as much as you are." His smile had a familiar wickedness to it that always made my knees shake. "I didn't mean to mess up and stress you out. My head's still not right. Being dead for so long is a shocker."

"You don't feel you're changing, though? You know, into a ghost ghoul?"

"Do I look like one?"

"You look just as I remember. Still as handsome as ever."

He chuckled. "I don't feel out of control, and I'm not having dark thoughts. You're safe with me."

"I know. I trust you." I reached for his hand but then stopped, since he was still a little wispy around the edges. "There's so much I have to tell you."

Brodie lifted a hand. "Let's take this slowly, shall we? I just want to spend time with you. I've missed a lot."

"You have. And we have over three years to catch up on."

His gaze flicked around the room. "The farm still looks good. And you look amazing."

"The farm is great. And thanks for the compliment. I've been busy with orders. The scarecrow business is booming." It felt good to talk about normal things, but an overwhelming wave of pent up emotion whacked through me. "Oh, Brodie, I hated not having you around. When you died, I

81

didn't want anyone else here. I just wanted to be on my own."

"It looks like you're doing okay now. Better than okay. You're a super witch. You always bounce back."

"I didn't want to do anything other than hibernate, but my friends dragged me out of my misery. They made me see I had to keep going, even though it felt like everything was over. So, after a miserable few months of hiding under the duvet, I started living again. Kind of living, anyway." I dabbed at my eyes.

"Angel, don't cry."

"I was faking being happy a lot of the time. It felt wrong without you here."

"It makes me miserable to think of you being unhappy and alone in this big place."

I sniffed back my sadness. Brodie was here now, so the lingering misery that had lodged in my heart could take a long walk off a short pier. "Now I've got you back, the farm and business will only get better."

Brodie's nose wrinkled. "Babe, I love you, but scarecrows were never my thing."

"I know you never loved my scarecrows, but I hope you'll change your mind about that."

"Why? What are you thinking?"

"There's something I need to show you."

"What's that?"

I jigged on the spot. "I've been working on a plan to get you back for good."

"Get me back how?"

"Come with me." Nerves jumbled in with my excitement as I led Brodie out of the farmhouse and to the end barn, where I kept my experiments. I unlocked the barn doors and pulled them back.

Brodie drifted inside and looked around. "These are different. Are you working on a new model of scarecrow? This one looks almost human if you squint your eyes."

"In a way." It was time for the big reveal. "I've been working on perfecting a vessel for you to live in. It's a modified version of a ghost jar."

His mouth twisted to the side. "Don't you use ghost jars to trap misbehaving spirits?"

"That's right. The magic in the jars holds the ghosts in place. It stops them from getting out. But what I've created is so much more. It's like a containment unit, but one you'd be able to operate as if it was your body."

"Huh. Interesting." He drifted over to the humanlike scarecrow laid out on a table. "This guy kind of looks like me."

I stood beside him, thrilled to be in Brodie's company again. Being so close to him always made me giddy. "That's the point. I wanted to create a vessel that looked like you, so you could use it when you came back."

"You want me to live inside this scarecrow?"

"Yes! But it's a super scarecrow."

Brodie studied the scarecrow some more. "How long have you been working on this?"

"Ever since I dragged myself out of bed and realized we'd never gotten our happily ever after.

We always talked about being together forever. I still want that."

"Odessa, this is incredible. But it must take a ton of magic to keep this vessel together. You can handle that?"

"It's not been easy, and I've burned through a lot of magic to make it work. I don't think there's a library I haven't searched, looking for something that ties this all together. The vessel is almost stable enough to use." I gestured at the table. "And now you're back, you can try the different models and see which one fits the best. Or you can tell me how you want to look. I can design anything."

"I know you can. You've always been an amazing witch." Brodie ran a hand down his face. "This is unbelievable."

"I'd do anything for you," I said. "My heart shattered when you died. I never thought I'd feel anything ever again. And for a long time, I was so numb, it felt like I'd died, too. Every second I was awake, I missed you. Every breath I took, it felt wrong, because you weren't here to share it with me."

"Angel, I never wanted you to go through that. If I could have stayed with you, I would." Brodie drifted closer, his eyes full of sadness.

"I know. Which is why I got to work on finding a way to reunite us."

His grin was soft and playful. "And you never lost hope? Didn't you worry I might have crossed over?"

"No. Because I know you, and I knew you'd never do that to us. We both want the same things."

"Yeah, we do. And I want this more than anything. I want to be back with you again, but..."

"What? You don't like the plan?"

"I love it. But are you sure you're strong enough to hold me in this thing? This is serious power we're talking about. It's like all the energy you use to keep your scarecrows going. Maybe more."

I let out a long sigh. "That's something I'm stuck on. It's complicated magic. It is similar to what I use with my scarecrows, though, so it's nothing alien to me. And if I form a connection with the vessel, it holds steady. I can channel my magic into it. But it's keeping that high level of magic steady that I'm struggling with. It takes all my focus."

"Does your powdered pumpkin help?" Brodie said. "You use a lot of that stuff when working on the scarecrows."

"It does, but it's not enough. And I'm trying to ease back on the powdered pumpkin power. It messes with my natural magic."

"Nah! You're the queen of pumpkins. This whole place is alive because of the power of that pumpkin magic. And it's all natural. How can it mess with you?"

"Maybe you're right. I don't know. I don't want to rely on it too much."

Brodie drifted around the barn, not speaking for several minutes as he examined several of the failed vessels I'd disassembled. He returned to me and looked steadily into my eyes. "I've got an idea. It's way out there, so hear me out before dismissing it."

"I'm open to anything if it'll help bring you back."

"You use Grimsbane magic to keep the scarecrows animated, right?"

"Sure. That's how it works."

"And can you form a link with this vessel and keep all the links with your scarecrows open, too? Or is that too much to handle?"

"That's my stumbling block. My scarecrows need a certain amount of magic, but once they're infused with it, I just tug on the connections now and again to make sure things are working. The older models, like Shamrock, adapt and become independent. It's as if I know what they're doing without having to think about them. We're so connected."

"Okay. So, here's the out there bit. What if you sever the connections with the scarecrows and just focus on me?"

My heart fluttered in my chest. "They'd be lost. They'd have no guide. I created them, so it would be like cutting off communication with my children."

"Babe, they're only scarecrows. I mean, sure, I get you have this link and care about each one, but it sounds like you can't have them and me."

I swallowed as I processed what Brodie was saying. This concern had been playing on my mind for a while, but I'd refused to acknowledge it.

His chilled fingers brushed my cheek. "If you focus your energy only on my vessel, wouldn't that be enough?"

I looked over my shoulder to see Shamrock peeking around the side of the open barn door. He ducked out of sight the second I spotted him, but I was certain he'd heard what Brodie said. My scarecrows were part of my huge, messy, extended family. But I'd always said I'd do anything to be with Brodie. Did that include abandoning my legacy and letting go of all the scarecrows?

"I know I'm asking a lot, but I'm thinking through all the alternatives," Brodie said. "And it's killing me that I'm here and I can't be the man you need me to be. All I want to do is hold you and kiss you and never let you go again."

"And I'm so glad you're here," I said. "But if I break my link with the scarecrows, one of two things will happen. They might simply fade away. They won't have new magic being fed into them, so they'd slowly die."

"That doesn't sound so bad. It wouldn't hurt them. I know they don't feel pain."

"True. But the option I don't want to think about is that they go rogue. They're powerful magical creatures with a lot of energy, and I've been feeding it to some of them for over a decade. If I break the link, I could let loose hundreds of dangerous, out-of-control super scarecrows. Lots of people will get hurt."

Brodie's form flickered, but he nodded. "No, you're right. It was a dumb idea. I'm just desperate to be back with you. I can see how hard you've worked to make this happen, though. I can also see how much magic you'll need to get me in that vessel and keep me there."

"We just need more time to figure it out. I've almost cracked it. There'll be a way to make this work."

"We may not have time, though. What if the light comes back?"

"We're so close to success," I said. "And with me and Zohar keeping you grounded, you just have to hold on a bit longer."

"I want to believe that. I really want to be here with you and make you happy." Brodie looked over his shoulder.

"You can be. We'll find a workaround. We'll do this. Now you're back, I just need to tweak the spells."

"Your magic and the link you create with this vessel are the key," Brodie said. "There must be a way we can connect to that power without messing with your scarecrows."

"I don't know how. The previous links I've formed with a vessel have broken down in less than twenty-four hours. I might get you back, but you'd only work for one day a week, and I wouldn't be able to control my scarecrows during that time. The farm would become chaotic."

"That won't do. And I want to be working full time so I can be with you," Brodie said.

I wanted that so badly I almost wept. Success was just out of my reach, and it was driving me insane.

"You have your ancestors buried around here, don't you? I remember you taking me to the cemetery on an anniversary," Brodie said.

"Sure. The largest Grimsbane family crypt is in the cemetery in Witch Haven. Grimsbanes have been living in this village for centuries. And they've owned this farmland for almost as long. Why do you ask?"

"If you've got ancestors here, you'll have access to their ancient power. Magical energy lingers for a long time. How many people have you got in the crypt?"

I closed my eyes and conjured an image of the inside of the crypt. It had been at least a year since I'd been there. "There are twenty ancestors. And you're right, there is power there. But to access it, I'd have to use their remains. And..." It felt like a desecration of everything my family held dear. Scarecrows were our lives. Could I use that power for something else? Should I?

"You don't have to say it. I know, it's your ancestors. And this isn't a simple spell we're discussing. I'm just a guy. I'm not that important."

"You are to me. But I need to think about this." Once I opened a link to my ancestors' magic, I wasn't sure how easy it would be to control.

"Don't think for too long. I want us back together as soon as possible."

"So do I, but my ancestors were powerful magic users, and some of them leaned toward the darker side. What if I open something I can't keep stable?"

"Odessa, you're a powerful witch. You control an army of magically enchanted scarecrows who'd do anything for you. Don't underestimate yourself. You can figure a way to get this link open. And when you do, I think it could work." His icy fingers skimmed my arm. "We'd finally get our forever."

I leaned against the table, lost in thought. This could work, but it carried a huge risk. I looked at Brodie. The reward would be worth it.

"Hello, is anyone out here?"

I hurried to the entrance of the barn and looked outside. "Hester. What are you doing here?"

She bustled toward me with a man beside her. "Hey! I hope you don't mind me looking you up, but I've brought someone with me. He knows something about what happened to Zohar."

Chapter 9

My attention turned to the short, rotund man standing just behind Hester. He was shifting from foot to foot and occasionally dabbing at his top lip.

"Are you busy?" Hester said. "I figured this was important, so I thought I'd better come here straightaway. I contacted the Magic Council to let them know but kept getting stuck in the phone system."

"Sure. Give me a second." I eased the barn door closed and walked over to her, my attention on the man. "If there's anything you know about what happened to Zohar, I'd be interested in hearing it."

Brodie floated out of the barn and drifted around Hester.

She shivered and clasped her arms with her hands. "This is Kasper. I met him just after lunch today. He was asking how things were going with the investigation and said something that could be useful. Something I wanted you to hear."

"What's that?" I said to Kasper.

He dabbed his top lip again. "I don't like to gossip about my neighbors, but ever since Zohar and Elsbeth moved in, they've been disturbing my peace. I chose to live on the edge of Witch Haven because it's such a quiet place. Barely anyone comes out that way unless they're visiting someone who lives there. But after they arrived, there's been nothing but trouble."

"What kind of trouble?"

"Mainly fights and lots of shouting. To begin with, it was once a week. They always argued with the windows open or when they were in the back yard. I didn't deliberately listen in, but more recently, it was happening almost daily, so it became hard to ignore."

"Were you able to hear what they argued about?"

"It usually had something to do with money. And I've heard Elsbeth, she's such a sweet lady, more than once yell that she wished she'd kept the money and left Zohar. Things got ugly several times, and I've even heard things being broken." Kasper glanced at Hester.

"You can trust Odessa. She's helping the Magic Council figure out what happened to Zohar."

"I don't consider myself a hero, but I went to the house a few times because I was worried things were getting out of hand," Kasper said.

"What happened when you did that?" I asked.

"Nothing. Elsbeth was always the one who came to the door, and she'd tell me not to worry. But I was concerned about her safety. Zohar was a big guy, and he liked to drink. I got an invitation over there a few times when they first moved in, and he was always generous with the alcohol. Zohar could put it away."

"When you went over there, did you notice any bruising on Elsbeth or think Zohar had hit her?"

His hand quivered as he dabbed his face. "No! Nothing like that, but I was still worried. Elsbeth was always sociable, but Zohar not so much. He became more hermit-like the longer they lived here. The invitations to go for dinner and drinks stopped, and I wondered if that was because of Zohar."

"He didn't want company coming over because of the fighting?"

"I have to assume so. And he seemed to struggle to find friends. The neighborhood is mainly made up of older people, and we like the quiet, so I was surprised when a younger couple built a house there. We're not exactly having raves every weekend." He chuckled at his small joke.

This was interesting. Elsbeth hadn't mentioned all the fighting. Maybe she was concealing it because she knew it would make her look guilty.

"I heard it could have been a burglary," Kasper said. "It's never happened around here before, but maybe it was because of their lack of security. When I visited, I noticed they had no alarm system."

"A burglary gone wrong is a theory being looked into," I said.

"This is terrible news. I often sit on my porch when the weather is nice, but I didn't see anyone approaching the house that day. I have a good view because I'm up the hill, so I'm sure I'd have noticed anyone creeping to the house. I even saw your husband out walking late one night." His jaw quivered as he looked at Hester.

"I'm not surprised. Ballard is a terrible sleeper. When he can't sleep, he takes a walk. It's typical Ballard. He'd rather go out in the chilly night air than disturb me by tossing and turning. He's such a sweetheart."

"If there is a burglar in the area, we must set up a neighborhood watch scheme," Kasper said. "We could patrol and watch out for trouble. Make sure whoever did it doesn't come back. We don't want anyone else to be hurt."

"If that would bring you comfort, look into it," I said. "But I'm hoping this was an isolated incident."

Kasper nodded. "May I ask what happened to Zohar? I mean, I know he died, but when the Magic Council spoke to me, their investigator was tight-lipped."

"There's nothing more I can tell you," I said.

"I wondered if his magic had failed him if he fought someone," Kasper said. "Elsbeth is the stronger magic user, and I got the impression Zohar didn't like that. I'm all for equal rights, though. Go feminism!"

Brodie moved closer to Hester. "Is this what you've been doing while I've been gone? Helping other ghosts?"

I nodded but kept my focus on Hester and Kasper. "Once the Magic Council has finished its investigation, they'll release the details of what happened. Try not to worry, Kasper. Witch Haven is a safe place. And it sounds like you've been protecting yourself against trouble."

"I do my best. You could always post one of your scarecrows nearby," Kasper said. "They terrify me. They'd chase away a burglar, though."

Hester edged away from Brodie, seeming to sense he was hovering by her side. "Is Zohar here? I feel as if I'm being watched."

"No, it's not Zohar."

Her gaze moved to the barn. "What are you keeping in there? It's giving out an unusual vibe. I'm picking up all kinds of strange magic."

"It's my reanimation magic," I said. "When I'm working on a new scarecrow, I keep them in the barns until they're stable and have passed all the tests."

"Maybe that's what I'm feeling. Although it feels troubling." Hester glanced around and rubbed her arms.

"It's something new I'm working on, but it's nothing to fear," I said. "Thanks for the information, Kasper. It's been useful."

"Anything to help. And just between us, although I'm sorry Zohar is dead, I'll be glad to get back to the peaceful environment."

Hester edged closer to the barn, but I blocked her path before she got too close. "There's nothing exciting in there. Just half-finished scarecrows and a lot of mess. It's best you don't look inside."

"Are you sure? I'm feeling really uneasy about something."

I discreetly gestured Brodie to back off, and he moved into the barn, an amused look on his face, as if it entertained him to unsettle Hester.

"I'm positive. My scarecrow energy can just be unnerving if you're not used to being around it."

"Oh! I forgot to say," Kasper said, "the day Zohar was found, I saw Elsbeth race off in a car. She was going so fast, I was worried she'd lose control and hurt herself or someone else."

"What time was that?" I kept half an eye on Hester to make sure she didn't investigate my barn.

"It was just after nine o'clock in the morning. They'd been arguing as usual, and then I heard a car door slam and saw Elsbeth behind the wheel."

"She was definitely driving?" So much for her alibi about taking a long walk to the smoothie bar.

"Yes. It was her." His jowls wobbled again as he jutted out his chin. "I try not to think badly of anyone, but I was worried the argument had gotten heated and Elsbeth had hurt Zohar. I didn't hear a peep from him after she left." Kasper shook his head. "But she wouldn't do that. She's such a nice lady when I speak to her. She sometimes brings me leftovers for my dinner. I live alone, so I don't cook much."

"Did you tell the Magic Council about seeing Elsbeth in a car?"

"Of course. But Hester said you're helping with the investigation, too, and you can actually see Zohar's ghost. That must be exciting."

"It has its moments. And I'm sure, between us, we'll have everything figured out soon." Including puzzling out why Elsbeth hadn't mentioned driving to the smoothie bar. That would have given her even more time to kill Zohar, hide his body, and give herself an alibi.

Kasper stepped closer. "I heard a rumor Zohar's body is missing. You don't think a dark magic user took it, do you?"

"Let's get you home, Kasper." Hester caught hold of his elbow and gently steered him away. "Wait for me at the end of the lane. I just want to have a quick word with Odessa before we leave."

"Oh, of course. And I must get home soon. My favorite game show will be on, and I never miss an episode. Even the repeats." He tottered away.

Hester turned to me. "Kasper's a lonely old gossip, but I got worried when I heard what he said about the fight and then Elsbeth driving off, especially after your operatives found that tire track. I wondered if the two things were connected."

"Elsbeth said few people know about that entrance. What was she doing using it just after she'd had a fight with Zohar?"

"I don't know. I love Elsbeth, but I'm worried she did something stupid. And Kasper's correct that she's much more powerful than Zohar. It caused problems between them. I think he got jealous of her magic. He could only do basic spells, but Elsbeth is amazing with manipulating fire."

"Hester, do you think Elsbeth killed Zohar?"

She shook her head. "I don't want to, and I've known Elsbeth for a long time, but I'm not sure I trust her anymore. She's keeping secrets, and that's not like her. She seems different."

"Be careful around Elsbeth, just in case she learns you're digging into her secrets."

"We're friends. She'd never hurt me."

"I expect Zohar thought the same thing."

"Oh! Yes, I suppose so." Hester looked over her shoulder. "I'd better get Kasper back home. I'll see you soon." She hurried away and caught up with Kasper.

I looked around for Brodie, but he'd vanished, so I headed into the barn. "Brodie, are you in here?"

He didn't answer.

I looked around some more and even called for Zohar, but neither ghost seemed interested in communicating. I checked my watch. The smoothie bar Elsbeth was supposed to have gone to would be open. It was time to check her alibi.

Chapter 10

When I got to the smoothie bar, I was pleased to see they were running a twenty percent off everything deal if you ordered a deluxe tropical fruit smoothie and any brownie. I mean, how could I resist such a deal?

I walked inside and found half the tables occupied and several people waiting for their takeout orders by the counter. I headed over and spent a couple of minutes studying the delicious sounding smoothies on the chalkboard behind the counter.

"Take your time having a look," a cute guy with blond dreadlocks and a winning smile said to me from behind the counter. "You'll be spoiled for choice."

I nodded my thanks and finally settled on a tropical paradise smoothie with a mango and coconut white chocolate brownie. When it was my turn, I placed my order and moved to the end of the counter to wait for it.

A middle-aged woman with short dark hair hurried out from the kitchen at the back. She dashed to a table to clear it of empty plates and glasses. When she returned, I caught her eye.

"Hi. I wonder if you can help me."

"I'm not taking orders. Finn will look after you." She nodded at the guy with the dreadlocks.

"He is. I've got my order in. But I'm looking for information about someone who came in recently." I leaned closer to the woman as she stacked glasses into the sink.

"Who's that?"

"Elsbeth Delarosa."

The woman glanced at me. "I don't know her. I mean, she comes in here, but I've never really spoken to her."

"I know Elsbeth," Finn said. "Let me finish your order, and I'll see if I can help you."

"Thanks."

The woman hurried away, and I waited for Finn to bring me my enormous takeout smoothie and one of the biggest, most delicious brownies I'd seen in a while.

He placed down my order with a flourish and smiled. "So, what do you need to know about Elsbeth?"

"I don't know if you've heard, but her husband died recently."

Finn sucked in a breath and winced. "I did. I was sorry to hear that. I didn't know him, though. Apparently, smoothies didn't interest him. But Elsbeth is a regular. She comes in several times a week."

"Do you remember seeing her here four days ago, first thing in the morning? It would have been between nine and ten o'clock."

"I do. She was here. I always remember the cute customers." He winked at me. "And I'll definitely remember you. I've not seen you in here before."

I blushed as I collected my order. "I'm usually working when you're open."

"Does that mean you work for the Magic Council?" Finn wiped down the counter.

"Not really."

"I'm no Sherlock Holmes, but since you're talking about Zohar's death, I figured you were an investigator. Do they send in the pretty ones if they're not getting far on a case?"

"Not that I know of. I am helping with this investigation in a sort of freelance role. What do you know about Elsbeth?"

"She's good looking and an amazing tipper. And I always put in extra effort with those who tip well." He grinned at me and tilted his head at the almost full tip jar by the cash register.

I rifled through my purse and slid money into the jar. "Do you know how Elsbeth got here that morning?"

"Err... I don't. It was busy. We had a business meeting in and orders for a fancy breakfast. There were thirty orders to process and only two of us. I was doing the cleanup when Elsbeth came in."

"And how did she seem to you that morning?"

"The same as always."

"Was she happy, sad, or frustrated about something? Did anything seem odd about her?"

"Not that I noticed. She was just Elsbeth. I mean, we had a chat, and she had her usual order. I didn't think there was anything wrong."

"Elsbeth always came here alone?"

"She did. She brought her husband once, but he left most of his smoothie. He said it was too sweet. After that, she always turned up alone. She said she liked the peace. We'd often chat, and then she'd take her order to a small table out the back. Or if the weather was nice, she'd sit out the front where we have a few tables."

"What impression did you get of Elsbeth and Zohar when you saw them together?"

"Not much. I mean, I only saw them together once." He grinned. "I'm not being helpful, am I? Maybe you should take back that tip."

"No, it's fine. You said Elsbeth came here to get peace. What was she getting away from?"

Finn scooped ice into a large blender. "I know what you're getting at. You want to know if she had a happy marriage."

"I do."

"She never said anything about Zohar or the state of her marriage, but I wondered why such a nice lady was always on her own. If I had a woman like that, I'd never leave her side."

"Maybe Zohar didn't want to leave her side, but she wasn't happy with him."

"It could be that. I didn't pry much. I'm always friendly with customers and happy to chat, but I never push. If someone wants to share, then they will. Elsbeth didn't share much information about her husband." He swirled the ice in the blender. "You know, I told all this to the Magic Council. Are you sure you work for them? You're not some reporter trying to get a scoop, are you?"

I nodded. "I'm legit. We have an understanding."

"It must be great to have friends in high places."

"I wouldn't go that far." I leaned against the counter. "Did Elsbeth say anything about going for a walk before she came here?"

"Nope. I'm really sorry. I've no clue how she got here. She could have walked. She doesn't live far away. Does that matter?"

"It could be important to the investigation." From what I was learning, Elsbeth hadn't told the whole truth about what happened with Zohar that morning. She said she'd gone to the smoothie bar but then remembered she'd taken a detour. Then Kasper heard a car race off and was convinced Elsbeth was driving. Things weren't looking great for Elsbeth if I kept turning up these inconsistencies.

"I don't want to get Elsbeth in trouble," Finn said. "And from what other customers have said, Zohar got messed up in a burglary that went wrong. I know they were loaded, so maybe someone took advantage."

"How do you know about their money?"

"It was easy to see from the clothes Elsbeth wore and her jewelry. And even though she didn't brag, everyone knew about their crystal jackpot win. I was just glad Elsbeth spent some of her money here. This is only a small place, so we need all the customers we can get." Finn opened a smoothie recipe book. "I don't see her as a killer. And why kill the guy? If she wasn't happy with Zohar, get a divorce."

I'd wondered about that. Maybe Elsbeth had decided she wanted all the money. A divorce would have meant giving half to Zohar.

"Thanks for the information and the smoothie and brownie. It all looks delicious."

"The best in the village." He chuckled. "Especially since we're the only smoothie place. Enjoy."

"I will. And if you think of anything else relating to Elsbeth and Zohar, let me know."

"Sure. How can I get in touch with you?"

"I run the pumpkin farm."

His eyes widened. "You're the scarecrow lady! I thought you looked familiar. Scarecrows to murder. That's a leap, isn't it? How did you get mixed up in this?"

"It's a long story. Thanks again." I headed outside and settled on a bench. As I sipped my delicious smoothie and munched on my tasty brownie, I considered everything I'd learned about Elsbeth. Her marriage to Zohar was unhappy, and there was a huge amount of money at stake if a divorce happened. Then there were the frequent arguments, Zohar's temper, and Elsbeth being more powerful than him. And there was also Elsbeth's increasingly dubious alibi.

Finn had confirmed she'd been here the morning of the murder, but she'd somehow forgotten she'd gone for a walk. There was also the mystery about the car. Had she hidden that, too, or had Kasper made a mistake about seeing her?

After finishing my giant smoothie and gooey brownie and feeling deliciously stuffed, I took a detour to the cemetery. Since I couldn't figure out Zohar's mystery yet, I'd focus on my own.

Gravel crunched under my feet as I headed to the Grimsbane crypt. Tia Grimsbane had erected it in the fifteenth century. She'd been an immensely powerful witch and had established the family as the premier creators of magically enchanted scarecrows. It was a niche but popular market.

Grimsbane magic was intense and life giving, as well as life taking. It could be channeled into all kinds of things to bring them to life. We'd always focused on scarecrows, but there'd been a few ancestors who practised the dark art of necromancy.

Using this power to get Brodie back was more than possible. And I wouldn't give up on him. I was so close to getting him back. But I didn't want to give up my farm and my scarecrows. Basically, I wanted it all. And that meant finding a compromise that worked for all of us.

My fingers brushed the outside of the cool stone crypt as I reached the entrance. There were generations of powerful witches' remains inside. I pressed my hand against the stone, and a familiar swell of power radiated out.

The sensation always made me smile. My ancestors recognized and accepted me. I always meant to visit more regularly, but since losing Brodie, I rarely came to the cemetery. A headstone had been erected for him, but I never looked at it because it confirmed my worst fears. Now, I could get the headstone taken down, since there was no need to have a memorial for Brodie. Although it was a gray area. Was a ghost living inside a vessel actually alive?

As far as I was concerned, it was.

"Sorry it's been a while since my last visit." I moved to the door and waved my hand across it. The large stone door slowly grated open, and I slid into the darkened interior. I shot out some magic to light the white candles that sat in stone recesses in the wall, and the place was soon awash with a welcome glow.

"Hey, everyone. What have you all been up to? I hope no one has gotten in any trouble."

The stones vibrated around me as if they were chuckling to themselves.

"Witch Haven has been as hectic as ever. But you'll be pleased to know, the scarecrow business is booming. I'm not letting you down. And I've got far too many orders." I decided not to mention the small hiccup with Selma Black. She seemed to be leaving me alone, and I was grateful for that.

Don't lose focus. The words scratched into the wall of the crypt.

"I know. I'm sorry. I have been." And that was my fault due to my never-ending quest to find Brodie.

Need help?

"I had some. He's gone, so I'm on my own again." I missed Sol's natural affinity with the scarecrows. Brodie was never interested in getting hands-on with them. It had never bothered me, but then I'd never known how much fun it could be working with a partner. Or, if I was being honest, working with Sol.

Brodie had always had his mining interests, so we'd worked separately, although I'd always wished he'd taken more interest in the scarecrows. They were important to me. They were a part of me.

The stones rumbled around me, as if encouraging me to continue.

"With your help, I may not be on my own for much longer." I paced slowly around the crypt. "You all know about Brodie. Well, I never gave up on him. And I was right to keep looking for him. His ghost is back. Brodie never left me."

The candles flickered wildly, elongating the shadows.

"I know. It's a head spin for me, too. And I didn't mean to keep this from you, but when I told my friends about wanting Brodie back, they thought I was being odd and told me it wasn't possible. But I couldn't let Brodie go. We promised each other we'd be together forever. Now, we can be."

The place was as quiet as... well, as quiet as a grave, which was fitting, but I could tell my ancestors were listening.

"I've found a way to bring Brodie back. He wouldn't be human, but he wouldn't be a ghost, either. I've been adapting the magic we use to create the scarecrows, and I can manipulate it to make a vessel stable enough to house Brodie. His ghost would inhabit this vessel, so he'll be able to walk around and experience life as if he was alive."

The silence remained, but the atmosphere shifted, and not in a positive way.

"I know this is a huge thing, and it's not without its complications. I also know some people won't accept a vessel containing Brodie's ghost is him. They'll think it's unnatural. But if they do, I just won't talk to them."

The candles flickered again, and I wasn't sure if it meant my ancestors agreed with me or not.

"You all know how much I love Brodie. When we met, everything felt so right." I brushed my fingers against the stone. "I've always felt a bit out of place. My scarecrows freak people out, and my pumpkin magic isn't to everyone's taste. Brodie never saw me as strange. He accepted me."

A scratching came on the wall and the word *young* appeared.

I shook my head. It didn't matter how old we were when we met. You know when you find the right one. I'd always believed in finding that one true love, and it had hit me between the eyes when I met Brodie. And he felt the same about me.

The scratching came again, and the word *change* revealed itself.

I frowned. I'd expected support from my ancestors. Maybe some concerns about using their magic but nothing else. Not the suggestion I was making a mistake.

"I've thought about this. I know people change. I know I've changed, but not so much that I won't still be blissfully happy with Brodie for the rest of my life. That's all I want. It's the most important thing."

There was silence, followed by a soft growl, and the word *scarecrow* appeared on the wall.

I let out a sigh. "I love the scarecrows, too. And what I plan to do with Brodie will complicate things. I've been trying to get the balance of magic right, but it's going to take immense power to keep Brodie stable and make sure the vessel works. It's the kind of power I use to sustain all the scarecrows."

What looked like a giant tear slid down the wall and hit the floor.

"It's not for definite I'll have to give them up. But if I'm going to keep them and Brodie, I need your help. I may be able to channel our joined energy and keep Brodie forever and the scarecrows, too."

A long silence followed my words.

"I won't force you to do this, but I would like your support. At least to try to forge a stable connection."

There was an unnerving scratching from several of the stone crypt coffins. I half expected the lids to pop off and my ancestors' bones to slide out and scold me, but it didn't happen. The noise died down and then the word *Sol* appeared on the wall.

"You know about him?"

The word intensified and glowed.

"He's another complication, but I have my forever with Brodie to focus on. My relationship with Sol is new, and I can't give up something that's always meant so much to me. I've had to let Sol go."

The word change and *scarecrows* appeared again.

I stepped back and raised my hands. "If you need time to think about this, I understand. But I would like to test the magic. This may not even work if the power in the crypt isn't strong enough. Do I have your permission to do that?"

The word *yes* appeared on the wall after a short pause.

"Thank you. I just need a bone to hold to channel our magic."

This time, one of the stone lids did creep open. I shoved my hand inside and lifted out a small finger bone. I clasped it between my hands and closed my eyes. I got an instant jolt of power so strong it made the hairs on the back of my neck stand up and a hot shiver run through me. This would do it. With a few bones and the right spells, this magic would sustain Brodie.

"That was amazing. You're all incredible witches, and I'm so grateful to be a part of this family." I carefully set the bone back in the right place, and the lid slid shut.

I walked slowly around the inside of the crypt again. I could use this power, but it was so strong that it would need constant monitoring, and I wouldn't be able to divide my time fairly between Brodie and the farm. And then there were my scarecrows. If I was channeling all this energy to make sure Brodie was stable, I might still have to let them go.

My heart gave an unhappy thud at the thought of there being no more Shamrock, intimidating anyone who got too close and being his usual overprotective self. What if my control slipped and the scarecrows became dangerous? That would be just what Selma Black would want. She didn't trust my scarecrows, and if I lost control of them, it would give her the ammunition she needed to shut me down for good.

But I'd wanted this happiness for so long that I couldn't back away from it. Maybe I would lose some scarecrows and face questions from my friends, but they'd understand. They knew how much I'd struggled when I lost Brodie. I had to test this and see if it would work. And it would be so worth it if I got this right.

The crypt door slammed open and Silvaria Digby burst in, bristling with magic as she slammed her crooked stick to the floor. "What are you doing?"

"Err... hi, Silvaria. I'm just visiting my ancestors. Am I here at the wrong time?"

She strode over. "You're messing with the cemetery magic."

"I'm not. I'm testing a theory. What's the problem?"

"Get outside and see for yourself." She caught hold of my arm and dragged me outside.

The second I stepped into the chilly air, my jaw dropped and my eyes widened. There were a dozen corpses walking around the cemetery. "Were you expecting the dead to rise?"

"No! You did it. I felt the power of your magic zap me in the head. You've awoken the dead. You know how I feel about corpses wandering around in my cemetery. Whatever you're doing, you have to stop."

I blinked rapidly as another corpse struggled from its grave, ragged clothing hanging off its bones and the bottom half of its jaw missing. "Silvaria, I'm sorry. I didn't mean to do this."

"Don't be so daft. You use reanimation magic to get those scarecrows going. What did you think would happen when you wandered into your ancestors' crypt and opened their magic?"

"Not this. I wasn't even thinking about re-animating corpses. I wanted to see how strong my ancestors' power is."

"As you can see, the magic is too powerful. Put an end to this before the corpses cause problems."

"I will. Give me a minute." I dashed back inside, shoved open the coffin lid, and took the finger bone again. "I only need this for a minute. We've had a snafu with the magic." I hurried outside, clasping the finger bone, and imagined the dead back in their coffins where they belonged.

It took five minutes before the cemetery was cleared of wandering corpses. The air still smelled faintly of decay, but there were no more shamblers to deal with. I turned to Silvaria and grinned. "Problem solved."

She grunted. "Do not do that again. I'm tempted to ban you for disturbing the dead."

"I promise, this was an isolated incident. Don't stop me from visiting my family."

"You're lucky I'm in a good mood. You need to watch yourself."

"I will. Just let me put back the finger bone." I returned to the crypt and settled the bone back in place. "I think our link needs finessing, but thanks for helping."

The stones vibrated, and the door slid shut as I hurried out.

When I got outside, Silvaria was striding away, muttering to herself about silly witches not knowing how to use their ability.

I looked around the now quiet cemetery. I needed to watch this power. I had to make sure I had control of it, and not the other way around, or I'd be in trouble and not just with the cemetery guardian.

As I stepped through the cemetery gates, a figure moved out of the shadows. My instinct was to duck and run the second I realized it was Selma Black.

Her shark-like grin suggested trouble as she approached me. "I knew you were using magic for misdeeds. You're under arrest."

Chapter 11

"Again!" I stared at Selma. "Under arrest for what?"

"I saw the corpses walking around the cemetery. And what a coincidence, you come out a few minutes later. Don't tell me that wasn't your doing." Selma's palm glittered with a swirl of gray magic.

"That was a misunderstanding."

"It was also illegal. You're coming with me."

I was backing away, but Selma slammed me with a strong restraining spell before I got more than a few steps.

"No, you don't. I always knew there was something strange about your magic, and I just witnessed it. You can't be trusted to use your power responsibly."

"I can. I'm the most trustworthy witch you'll ever meet." I twisted in her magic, but it held tight like an iron fist.

"I need to find out what plans you have for raising the dead."

"I have no plans to do that." Well, I had one plan but only to help Brodie.

"Once I've spoken to Silvaria, I'll know more. I saw her sending you away. She hates it when anyone messes with her cemetery. She won't protect you if she believes you want to harm her corpses."

"I don't have time for your mistakes." I fought against Selma's magic.

"Make time, witch."

"But I'm helping with a murder investigation. You can't arrest me."

"Helping! A likely story. We don't need your help to solve crime. You're coming with me."

No matter how much I negotiated as Selma dragged me to the cells in Olympus's office, I couldn't get her to change her mind that I was up to no good.

She filled out the paperwork, processed my information, shoved me into a cell, and locked it.

"I'll be back soon to question you," Selma said. "And don't even think about getting your friends to bust you out this time. Other people may believe you're innocent, but I know better."

"Ask Olympus Duke! He'll tell you I'm helping with Zohar Delarosa's murder. I'm crucial to the investigation."

Selma jabbed a finger at me. "Stop telling lies. I won't tolerate the dead being manipulated."

"I wasn't manipulating them. It was a... hiccup."

"A costly hiccup. And one I'll make sure you regret." Selma slammed the door behind her, leaving me alone.

I leaned against the wall and let out a sigh. I hadn't meant to disturb the corpses. That shouldn't have happened, and I couldn't figure out why it had. Would the corpses rise every time I linked in with that power, or was it a one-off? Maybe I needed to refine the link so it only connected to Brodie.

I had to test the theory more. But while I was inside this cell, I couldn't do anything other than wish gentle curses on Selma and hope she'd leave me alone and chase down the real bad guys.

An hour passed before I heard footsteps. Selma appeared, but she wasn't alone. Olympus was with her, and he wasn't looking happy.

"Am I being released?" I hurried over and peered through the cell door.

Selma glowered as she fished a key out of her pocket. "You are."

Olympus smiled at me from behind Selma's back. "Sorry, Odessa, I only just heard about you being arrested. I got in touch with Selma and informed her we're utilizing your ghost whispering skills to help with a murder investigation."

I bit my tongue, desperate to tell Selma I told her so.

Selma reluctantly unlocked the cell door. "I still have questions. And you can't go around raising the dead whenever you feel like it."

"And I'll answer them when I have the time. And it wasn't my intention to create an undead army. Raising them was a mistake."

"You don't need an undead army. You already have those scarecrows doing your bidding."

"About that. You still have some of my guys. When am I getting them back? You must have finished with them by now. Are they okay? You didn't hurt them during your experiments, did you?"

Olympus gestured for me to stop talking, but now I had Selma here, I needed answers.

"Your scarecrows are difficult creatures. I blame the magic in them," Selma said. "And they're uncooperative when tested."

"All your scarecrows will be at the farm by the time you get home," Olympus said. "Selma found nothing to concern her, so there's no need for us to hold your property any longer than necessary."

"I didn't agree to that." Selma turned and glared at Olympus. "I may have further tests to run. The magic maintaining those scarecrows is complicated."

"I can explain it to you if you're struggling." I grinned as sweetly as I could, loving how Olympus was pulling rank over Selma.

She spun back toward me. "I will figure it out. But I need them for longer."

"You've had enough time with Odessa's scarecrows," Olympus said. "We can't have her distracted while she's working on an important case. She's also kindly donating her time for free, so it won't cost the Magic Council anything to have an expert on board."

"Expert troublemaker. This isn't over," Selma said. "I know you're using unnatural magic, and I will find out what it is."

"Selma, I promise you, I'm not doing anything that'll hurt people. I know you're not a fan of reanimation magic after everything that happened, but—"

"What do you mean? I treat all magic users fairly."

"I, um, well, I heard what happened to your aunt. The whole being eaten by a doll thing. Which I'm sorry about, by the way. But my scarecrows don't eat people." There had been a few occasions when I'd found bones in a barn, but I was almost certain they came from cattle.

Selma stepped back, a furious look in her eyes. "That has nothing to do with this situation. I'm a professional, and I keep my personal life separate from work."

"I expect you want to, but nobody would be unaffected by what happened to your aunt. You must miss her."

Selma turned and strode away. "I'll be in touch soon." The door slammed behind her.

"You touched a nerve by bringing that up. How did you find out about Selma's aunt?" Olympus said. "She never talks about it. I only found out from her file."

"Hettie Crane told me." I stepped out of the cell. "And I get why Selma hates my magic, but I wish she'd stop picking on me."

"I'm trying to keep her off your back," Olympus said. "I keep suggesting other cases she could follow up, but she's intent on finding something wrong with your scarecrows."

"I'm just grateful you've been helping me. Otherwise, I may have to start calling this cell home."

"Always happy to help. Besides, Indigo yells at me if I don't intervene when her friends get arrested." Olympus grinned as he led me into his office. There was no sign of Selma. Monty was snoozing on his huge bed in the corner.

"I keep meaning to catch up with Indigo and the others. I've just been so busy."

"I told her what's going on with the case. She said to bring you over for something to eat once you're a free witch."

"That sounds great," I said.

"I've got some paperwork to finish up here, and we need to process your release before you can go."

"How long will that take?"

"An hour. Maybe two."

"To set me free?"

"Sorry. You know how much the Magic Council loves paperwork. Do you want to message Indigo, let her know what's going on?" He handed me my phone, which had been taken by Selma, and the rest of my personal effects.

"Thanks." I opened a group chat message to Indigo, Storm, and Luna. I needed help to deal with my scarecrow problem, and I couldn't do it alone, especially not with Selma watching my every move.

Hey. I need a favor. Could you go to the farm and empty a barn for me?

I only had to wait a few seconds before I got a reply from Indigo. *Sure. I take it you're no longer locked up?*

Olympus got me out. But I need some things moved. It's the far end barn. There's magic around it, but I'll deactivate it remotely once you're there.

I wish I could help, but I'm not in Witch Haven. That was Luna. *Cole's mom insisted I stay with her and meet more of the pack.*

Have fun with the werewolves, I said.

There was no reply from Storm, so I assumed she was working a case.

I'll head over now, Indigo said. *Make sure your scarecrows are expecting me. I don't want to be mauled.*

I'll let them know you're on your way. Thanks. I owe you.

Any time.

It was a risk asking Indigo to move the vessel I had stashed for Brodie, but the truth would come out soon enough, and I needed it gone before Selma went sneaking about.

Olympus's desk phone rang as I finished messaging the girls, and he answered it. After listening for a few seconds, he glanced over and gestured me closer. "I understand. Thanks. I'll be there soon." He put down the phone.

"What is it? Not more trouble from Selma?"

"No. A body has been found in the lake. It could be Zohar. Do you want in?"

"Of course. What about my release paperwork?"

"This takes precedence."

I smiled. "Happy to accept those terms. Let's go."

"Give me a minute to call this into the forensics team. I'll need them to sweep the scene."

I headed outside with Monty, who was yawning and scratching. I'd only made it a few steps, before an unhappy looking Zohar appeared and swirled around me.

"What's going on? I've been trying to get in and see you, but there's magic around this building.

It stopped me from getting in. Why were you arrested?"

"Hey, Zohar. Long story short, someone at the Magic Council has a grudge against me. It's all been sorted."

"I got worried you wouldn't be able to help me. Brodie is worried, too."

"Tell him not to be. He's okay, isn't he?"

"Sure. We've been talking, and he's doing fine. He said he misses you."

"Odessa, is our ghost here?" Olympus watched me as he locked the office.

"Yes. He's been trying to get in to see me."

"That won't happen. The Magic Council ordered increased security measures after a series of break-ins. No ghosts allowed."

"That's hardly fair. I've done nothing wrong. I'm the victim," Zohar said.

"He's still not happy." I said.

"Ghosts have been distracting the workforce," Olympus said. "An office had to be shut for a week while three poltergeists were removed."

"I wouldn't do that. I just wanted to make sure everything was going to plan with the investigation," Zohar said.

"Everything's good," I said to him. "And you should probably come with us."

"Why? What have you found?"

"Possibly your body. Do you want to take a look?"

He grimaced, and his form flickered. "Not really. But I need to. It could show me how I died."

"I'll translocate us there," Olympus said. "Forensics is on the way, but I want to take the first look."

"Who found the body?" I said.

"A guy doing some fishing. Luke Krauss. He thought he'd snagged the lake's kraken. It turns out, he got more than he bargained for when he pulled up Zohar."

"Poor guy. That's not the kind of shock you ever want. Zohar, follow us to the lake."

"Sure. I'll be right there."

Olympus caught hold of my hand and cast a translocation spell. A second later, we were at the edge of Witch Haven Lake. It was a large, serpentine shaped lake, popular with wild swimmers and people who liked to fish.

Zohar appeared a few seconds later and hovered close by me.

"Hey! Over here." Luke waved his arm over his head as he spotted us. He had lived in Witch Haven all his life. He was normally a cheerful guy, who always had time for a chat, but he didn't look so cheery today.

"Hey, Luke." Olympus strode over. "I hear you didn't get the catch of the day."

He took off his black baseball cap and wiped his brow, before pushing back his gray, receding hair and tucking it underneath. "I'd say, I didn't. When my rod caught something heavy, I was worried I'd snagged the kraken. It took a few minutes of tugging before I realized what I'd gotten. I almost pitched out of my boat, I was so surprised. And I don't know if I did the right thing, but I brought the body onshore. This lake gets awful deep in parts, and I didn't want it getting lost."

"You didn't do any harm by doing that. The water will have washed away most of the evidence. Let's see what we've got." Olympus stepped closer, his gaze on the body. "You know Odessa. She's helping with this investigation."

Luke nodded at me. "Of course."

"That's me." Zohar said. "I recognize those clothes. Did I drown, or was I already dead when I ended up in there?"

I nodded and then shrugged, my gaze flicking over his sodden body, which was already looking a little bloated.

Olympus carefully examined the body then looked up at me. "What do you think?"

"It's Zohar."

"Zohar who?" Luke said.

"Zohar Delarosa."

"You can tell that by his clothing?" Luke said. "Did you know him well?"

"Oh, not really. But I have a knack for these things."

He gave me a puzzled look but didn't ask any more questions.

Olympus turned the body over. It was definitely Zohar.

"I need to sit down. The smell is too much for me," Luke said. "If you don't need me, I'll head downwind and pack up my gear."

"You're good," Olympus said. "Thanks for letting me know what you found so quickly. We'll take it from here."

Luke backed away and sat watching from a distance, occasionally wiping his brow and shaking his head.

"Zohar's got rocks in his pockets," Olympus said. "Whoever did this tried to weigh him down so he sank."

I nodded, not comfortable around the body. I looked at Zohar. His expression was blank. "How are you doing? It must be odd for you to see this."

"It's weird. And it feels so final. There's no coming back from this. Of course, I'm a ghost, so I know that, but seeing this... I have to accept I'm a goner."

"We'll find out who did this," I said. "And now we've got your body, it'll be easier to figure out the cause of death." I'd already spotted red marks on Zohar's face. His sleeves were pushed up almost to his shoulders, and there were marks on his arms, too.

Olympus stepped back and stared out over the lake. "Zohar could have been thrown in from the edge, or someone may have used a boat to take him out to the middle. They hoped if they got out far enough, the kraken would eat the body and destroy the evidence."

"Our kraken doesn't eat people. She's a vegetarian. Her favorite foods are pumpkin and watercress. They were wasting their time trying to use her."

Olympus looked back at the body. "They'd have needed a vehicle to move Zohar here. It's a good thirty-minute walk from the house. Even if the killer was strong, they couldn't have carried Zohar that far. They'd also have been seen."

"Which links to the tire tracks Fire Fang found."

"But who was driving the car?"

"I might be able to help with that. I've been doing some asking around, and I spoke to Finn from the smoothie bar. He's Elsbeth's alibi."

"Sure. He's been checked out."

"He wasn't sure whether Elsbeth arrived by car. But if she did, she could have brought Zohar's body here then ditched the vehicle."

"If it was her, that's cold. Kill your husband, move the body and dump it, and then head out to get something to drink." Olympus shook his head. "I'll ask around, see if anyone saw a boat or a vehicle parked by the lake early that day."

"And have you spoken to Zohar's neighbors? I met Kasper. He reckons he saw Elsbeth driving away from the house not long before Zohar's body vanished."

He nodded. "I'm not sure how reliable he is. The guy has terrible eyesight."

"It's worth looking into. Especially if Zohar was moved here in a car. Elsbeth could have done that on her own. Although there weren't drag marks on the grass back at the house, and she wouldn't have been able to move him easily on her own."

"These marks on my head look serious." Zohar was hovering by his body, his expression bleak.

I edged nearer and took a peek at the matted mess of hair. "Zohar's worried about these head wounds."

"I'll get the experts to look at the injuries. The bruising suggests a fight, but some of these marks could have happened in the water, especially if the kraken rolled him around," Olympus said.

"My pendant's missing," Zohar said. "I always wore a jade pendant and never took it off. It was my favorite. My dad gave it to me before he died."

"Zohar said he's missing a jade pendant," I said. "Maybe the killer stole it."

"I doubt it. It's not valuable," Zohar said. "I kept it for sentimental reasons. You wouldn't get much if you pawned it."

"It could have fallen off the body when he hit the water," Olympus said. "If that happened, I doubt we'll find it."

"Or the killer kept it as a souvenir. You know how some killers keep things from their victims," I said.

Olympus gave me the side-eye. "Maybe. But that gets us heading into serial killer land."

I shuddered. "And we don't want to go there."

"Not unless we're forced to. I'll question Elsbeth and Zohar's friends again. Maybe they found the pendant in the house."

I peered at Zohar's body. "What's this red mark on the top of his bicep?"

Olympus squinted at it. "It could have been made when he was pushed into the water. If he didn't go in the first time, his arm might have been injured on the side of the boat. If a boat was used."

I kneeled beside the body. There was a piece of something red poking out of the shirt pocket. I pointed at it. "Can I look at this?"

"Yes, but be careful not to disturb any evidence," Olympus said.

I tweaked out the red fabric to discover a long red ribbon with a trace of magic on it. I ran it through my fingers. "There's something here, but it's weak.

It feels like it had a spell on it. Zohar, does this mean anything to you?"

He shook his head. "There's no reason I'd have a ribbon in my pocket. I don't know where that's from."

Olympus's phone rang, and he answered it. A frown crossed his face. "I can't come right away. I'm waiting for the forensics team to turn up. We've recovered a body from Witch Haven Lake."

I tugged his sleeve. "Is that them?" I pointed to two people approaching, both carrying black bags.

"Oh, I see them arriving. Okay, I'll be there as soon as I can." He ended the call. "Sorry, that was head office. I need to go. Is there anything else you want to look at before forensics take over?"

"I don't think so. Although I'm no expert with crime scenes."

"The team will look over the body and take it away for an autopsy. That should turn up more useful information."

I tucked the red ribbon back into Zohar's pocket and looked at the sad-faced ghost hovering close by. "I'm so sorry this happened to you."

"Me, too. I want to know why it happened and who did this to me."

"We'll get you justice. I promised I'd help, and I'm not backing out."

"Odessa, a word of warning. Be careful getting too involved in this investigation," Olympus said. "I'm happy to have you here since you have a connection to Zohar, but keep your head down while Selma is still after you. Don't take any risks."

"I know. I don't want to give her a reason to arrest me. Again."

"I'll give you an update on the body as soon as I hear anything, but I've got to go." Olympus cast a translocation spell and vanished.

I looked at Zohar again and frowned. As much as I wanted to keep off Selma's radar, I had no choice but to take risks to make sure I kept Brodie. "Come on, Zohar. Let's go home and see if we can figure out who dumped you in a lake."

Chapter 12

By the time I got back to the farm, I was hungry. No snacks were served while I'd been in the cell, and I was ready for a feast. But before I ate, I headed to the end barn to see if Indigo had dropped by to clear it out.

When I pulled back the door, I was thrilled to see it empty and amazed she'd worked so quickly.

I sent her a quick message. *Thanks for dealing with the barn. What did you do with everything?*

Nothing.

What do you mean?

I mean, I went there, but it was already empty. Did you forget you'd cleared the place?

I stared at the message. *There was loads of stuff in here.*

It was gone when I looked. Is that good news, or have you been burgled?

I wasn't sure if it was good news. I was glad there was nothing incriminating for Selma to find, but where had it all gone?

You coming over for food? I told Olympus to invite you.

No, but thanks. I would have, but we had a breakthrough in Zohar Delarosa's case. His body was found in the lake.

No way! No wonder I haven't heard from Olympus. When he gets involved in a case, I barely see him. Life as the girlfriend of a Magic Council head honcho. It's tragic!!!

The ground rumbled, and I turned to see half a dozen scarecrows racing toward me. I let out a squeak of delight. *Gotta go. Thanks again for coming over.*

No problem.

I laughed as my scarecrows scooped me up and passed me around for huge, straw-scented, bone-crushing hugs. I kissed them all, delighted they were free from Selma's interrogation. "You're all back. Are you okay? I've been worried about you. I hope Selma wasn't too awful."

The scarecrows kept hugging and sniffing me, alternating between growling and snarling, as was their way.

I took my time to check over each one. There were a few holes where there shouldn't have been, and one scarecrow had an arm stuck out at a strange angle, but other than that, they seemed to have survived their time with Selma.

"You deserve a treat for what you've been through. Everyone wait here. I'll be right back." I hurried to the kitchen and looked around, hoping to find Brodie waiting for me, but he was nowhere to be seen. Tuffin was also missing. She could usually be found bathing in a patch of sun on the table at this time of day and keeping an eye on the food situation.

I grabbed a bag of powdered pumpkin and gave myself a healthy dose before heading back outside. I touched each scarecrow, giving them a wallop of my reanimation magic. Each one glowed, and their eyes gleamed a brilliant red as my power pulsed through them. It felt so natural to do this. This was what brought me joy, seeing my scarecrows happy.

As I finished the last one, I stood back and smiled. I didn't want to give them up. They meant so much to me. I'd invested time, love, and magic into my scarecrows. Which meant I needed to work on stabilizing this link with my ancestors' magic. If I got that right, I wouldn't need to sever my connection with the scarecrows. I could keep them and have Brodie, too. I just needed to find a workaround to make it happen, without raising every corpse in Witch Haven.

"Now you're all back to full strength, I have a question. Were you involved in cleaning out the end barn?" I said.

The scarecrows shuffled around and wouldn't look at me.

"Is that a yes?"

There was more shuffling.

I caught hold of Abraham, a strapping seven-foot scarecrow with a straw mullet, and formed a two-way connection with him. "Abraham, you aren't keeping anything from me, are you?"

A buzzing filled my ears, but he didn't say anything other than making a few grunts.

"I'm not angry with any of you if you cleared the barn. You must have sensed I was worried and did it before Indigo got here. Is that what happened?"

Again, all I got were grunts, growls, and whistles.

I broke the connection. "If it wasn't any of you, and it wasn't Indigo, that leaves one person who knows I needed to keep that barn a secret." I sent my scarecrows off to carry out tasks around the farm then returned inside, washed up, and made a huge roasted pumpkin, pesto and avocado salad with hunks of pumpkin and poppy seed bread covered in soft cheese. I added a handful of salty chips and made a drink before settling at the kitchen table and stuffing my face.

Usually, when food was around, so was Tuffin, but she still hadn't stirred. Lazy cat.

Once I'd eaten and was feeling more myself, I grabbed my phone and opened a message to Sol. He must have emptied the barn. He knew what I was doing and how risky it was if the Magic Council caught me. I started the message several times but deleted each one.

I didn't want to make things awkward between us. I hadn't spoken to him since Brodie returned, and Sol must be disappointed in me. But I wanted to make things right between us. Sol was a good friend, and he'd helped me so much more than I'd initially realized. He'd helped turn around the farm, made my life simpler, was fun to be with, and didn't object when I got him messed up in these ghost mysteries. And he was still helping, even though I didn't deserve it.

Zohar swirled through the door.

"How are you doing?" I set down my phone. My awkward conversation with Sol could wait a little longer.

"I'm getting over the shock of seeing my body."

"That must have been grim. But it won't be long until the Magic Council has figured things out. Maybe don't watch the autopsy, though."

"I'm staying away, but I'm not hopeful they'll solve this. I stayed behind and watched the team as they dealt with my body. They were more interested in talking about what they were going to have for dinner than figuring out what happened to me." Zohar spun around me. "Don't give up on me. I need you on this until the end."

"Of course. You've got me. After all, we have a deal. I help you, and you help me with Brodie. Is he around? I hoped to see him."

"No, he wants to spend more time on his own."

My heart lurched, and I gripped the edge of the table. "He's not struggling, is he?"

"A bit. But he keeps telling me he doesn't want to leave. He even told me about some ghost vessel you have planned. That sounds interesting."

"It's a work in progress, but I'm hoping it'll be the way I get Brodie back for good. Which is why it's so important he doesn't cross over."

"He won't. He'll stick around for you." Zohar pursed his lips. "I don't suppose you've got one of those vessels going spare for me, do you?"

"Oh! No, this'll be a one-time deal. What I'm attempting with Brodie has never been done before, and it'll take a huge amount of magic."

"That's a shame. I had things I wanted to experience before giving up on this world. I still can't believe this is it for me."

"You'll have a new adventure to go on soon," I said. "You can have a lot of fun being a ghost."

"I guess. I was thinking about making some changes while I was alive, though. Maybe even moving back to my old town and catching up with people I'd ignored for too long. This fresh start in Witch Haven wasn't so great."

"It's been mentioned you were having trouble settling in. You didn't like Witch Haven?"

He shrugged. "It was okay. The people are nice, but I had a great set of friends where we used to live, and I didn't even mind my job. But Elsbeth insisted we give up everything and have a new start. She wanted us to focus on our relationship. She said now we didn't have money worries, we didn't need jobs to get in the way. We would fix what was broken because we had more time."

"It didn't go to plan?"

"We tried for a bit, but it was hard work. I get you have to compromise in a relationship, but it was too much change, too fast. We were exhausted from trying so hard. We should have accepted we were wrong for each other and moved on. If that had happened, I might still be alive."

His sadness hit my heart, and I struggled to think of anything useful to say. No words seemed enough. "At least you got to see Hester and Ballard one last time. Catch up with your neighbors and remember the good old days."

Zohar squinted at me and shook his head. "Have you got a laptop around here?"

"Sure. What do you need it for?"

"I want to show you some messages from Ballard. They'll show our amazing neighbors in a different light."

I fired up my laptop, and Zohar talked me through how to access his email account. Once it was open, I ran a search to find Ballard's emails. I found some from three years ago and opened the first one.

I can't believe you won't help. You know how difficult the situation is. If it had only been one of us unemployed, we'd have managed. But Hester's been laid off, too. It's been over a month, and she hasn't gotten any work. I know you're good for it. Why won't you help?

"Ballard and Hester were having money troubles?" I said.

Zohar nodded. "That's one of the better emails. Keep reading. Ballard got vicious."

I read through another dozen emails, and each one got more spiteful. The last one had me cringing.

Just because you came into money doesn't make you any different from us. You always were a selfish jerk. We're about to lose our home. I'll even accept a loan if you're too tight to help friends in dire need. You've got so much. You can't need it all. Share!!!!

Help us! Hester is crying every day. I can't believe you're so coldhearted you won't put your hand in your deep pocket and help old friends. What's the matter with you? If you don't help, you'll be sorry.

I sat back in my seat and stared at the screen. "These messages are intense."

"There were phone calls, too. In the end, I blocked his number. It just got too bitter. I felt sorry for the guy, but what did he expect me to do?"

"Give him money?"

Zohar turned away. "I didn't realize things had gotten so bad. I figured one of them would get a job. I kept telling him that, but Ballard didn't listen. Then the spiteful messages and calls started. After that, I didn't want to help."

"How bad did it get for them?"

"We don't talk about it, so I'm not sure. They had to move, but they're working now, so things are looking up. We pretend it never happened. It's easier that way."

"This gives Ballard a great motive for wanting you dead. I need to speak to him again. Give me his number. I'll see if he's free to come over and discuss these messages."

Zohar gave me his details, and I made a quick call. "Ballard, it's Odessa. I could do with your help. Could you come to my farm?"

"I guess so. What do you need help with?"

"It's about Zohar. It's important."

"Oh! Sure. How do I find you?"

"Head into the village and ask the first person you see. Everyone knows where I live, and they'll point you to the pumpkin farm on the edge of the village."

"Okay. Shall I bring Hester and Elsbeth?"

"No, just you."

"Uh... you sure?"

"Positive. This information is sensitive."

There were several seconds of silence. "I'll be there soon."

While I waited for Ballard to arrive, I cleaned the kitchen and then hunted around, hoping to find Brodie. Despite calling his name several times, he didn't show.

Zohar drifted around too, his expression suggesting he was lost in thought.

"Would you mind checking on Brodie again?" I said.

"I'm not keen. The last time I looked in on him, he told me to get lost. He was being grouchy."

"That's not like Brodie. He's usually a friendly guy."

"I guess he's got a lot on his mind. He's about to make a life changing decision."

I picked at my nails. It shouldn't be a difficult decision. After all, we'd agreed to spend the rest of our lives together.

Zohar drifted over and gave my shoulder an icy pat. "He'll come good. Don't worry about Brodie."

A knock at the door distracted me from my worries, and I opened it to find Ballard outside. He hurried in before I invited him.

"Those scarecrows are freaky. Do they belong to you?" Ballard pushed the door shut and peered through the window.

"They're supposed to be freaky. Well, I prefer scary or intimidating. I make them. It's what I do for a living."

He kept staring outside. "One tried to bite me."

"It was just meant to be a friendly nibble, but they're wary of strangers. They won't come in here, though, so you're safe."

"I'm glad to hear it." His gaze flicked to my poor attempt at a suspect board. "My name is on there!"

"Are you surprised? You were staying with Zohar when he died." I glanced at Zohar. He was drifting around the kitchen, his attention on Ballard.

"I guess not. And the Magic Council did interview me, but there's no reason I'd want Zohar dead."

"I've found a reason. Zohar wouldn't help you when you had financial troubles. You asked him for money, and he refused."

Ballard grabbed the back of a chair. "You know about that?"

"Zohar showed me the emails you sent. You sounded angry. You even wrote that he'd be sorry."

He tipped back his head and sighed. "Everything fell apart when I was made redundant and got a lousy payout. I figured I'd find something else, but it seems companies want young, upcoming guys, not middle-aged ones, five years out of date with their knowledge. I kept applying for things but barely got any interviews. We were just getting by when Hester lost her job, too."

"That must have been tough."

"It wouldn't have been so bad, but we had a big mortgage, and with no money coming in and little savings, we were desperate. I figured, since we were such great friends with Zohar and Elsbeth, there'd be no trouble with them giving us money. It wasn't a lot we needed, and it would only have been short-term, just until we got on our feet."

"Zohar didn't help you, though," I said.

"I was so surprised when he wouldn't. They've got more money than they know what to do with. It's why they built that huge house for just the two of them. The place has ten bedrooms!"

"And after the surprise faded?"

"I got angry. And it wouldn't fade. I guess you could tell that from the emails. I couldn't get my head around why Zohar wouldn't help, but he refused point blank. He said it was our mess to deal with. I even begged for a loan and offered to pay interest, but he wasn't having it."

I looked over at Zohar, and he shrugged. "Ballard was always such an independent guy. I knew he didn't really want my money."

Ballard walked to the window and looked out of it. "Hester got depressed. There were days when she didn't get out of bed. We'd find a pile of bills on the doormat, and she'd burst into tears and retreat under the duvet. Nothing I could do would help. I felt I was losing everything. Eventually, we put our place on the market and moved to a studio apartment. One window looks out on a fast food drive-through, and the walls are so thin, I hear my neighbor in the bathroom. I hate it there."

"I'm sorry to hear that. Did you ever tell Zohar how bad things got?"

"Of course. And I told him what I'd do if the roles were reversed, but he said if he started giving out money to friends and family, there'd be a never-ending demand, and he'd give away his fortune." Ballard shook his head. "That would be impossible. You know how much the crystal jackpot is."

"What did you do when you realized Zohar wasn't going to help?"

"There was nothing I could do. He cut off contact and blocked me from calling. He also told me not to bother Elsbeth. I ranted about it to Hester, but it got us nowhere. We sold the house we loved, moved to a different part of the country, and made the best of it. We've both got jobs now but not doing the kind of thing we enjoy."

"Since it ended so badly, how come you're visiting now?"

"Zohar reached out a couple of months ago. He was apologetic and invited us to visit so he could make amends. I figured, why not? I hate holding grudges. So we arranged a trip. And I thought it would do Hester good."

"You're friends again?"

"Kind of. We talked little about the past. And Zohar was too busy showing off all the things he had now."

"Rubbing your nose in it?"

Zohar swirled in front of me. "No! Well, not deliberately. Although maybe it looked like that. Jeez, I've been such a jerk."

I arched an eyebrow at him. He'd gotten that right. "Ballard, you must see how those emails give you a motive for killing Zohar."

He turned and faced me. "Of course. But I have an alibi. I went in half a dozen stores the morning of his death. And Hester was with me. Ask around if you don't believe me, but I was nowhere near the house when he died."

Ballard made some excellent points. He had a great alibi, despite having an amazing motive.

"Odessa, could you give Ballard a message for me?" Zohar said.

I nodded. "Sure. Ballard, Zohar has something to say to you."

"What is it?"

"I'm sorry, my friend. I didn't take it seriously when you asked for help. I was worried about being taken advantage of. I didn't know how to handle having so much money. It was the wrong thing to do."

I passed on the message. "Zohar does seem regretful."

Ballard nodded slowly. "I appreciate that. I mean, it doesn't change our situation, but it's time to move on. For all of us. Is there anything else I can help with?"

"No. But thanks for coming over."

"Are you going to take me off your board?" Ballard glanced at the suspect board. "I'm innocent."

"I reckon I might, since you can't be in two places at once." I walked him to the door.

"I'm surprised the Magic Council didn't question me about those emails. You're a better detective than they are."

"It helps I have Zohar to talk to. He gives me the inside scoop on all the secrets," I said.

Ballard looked past me. "I guess it must. Sorry things had to end this way, Zohar. Take care."

We said our goodbyes, and Ballard dashed away, giving any lingering scarecrows a wide arc.

I turned and looked at the suspect board. "What do you reckon, Zohar? Is he innocent?"

"We can rule out Ballard. He had a good reason for wanting me dead, but it wasn't him. He wasn't in the house."

"I agree. So, who's next?"

Chapter 13

I stood in front of a full-length mirror in my bedroom and smoothed my hands down my black and orange dress. I checked the message on my phone and frowned. I'd had a summons to dinner from Indigo. Luna and Storm were also going.

The last thing I wanted was company, especially not from my well-meaning but nosy best friends. I could pretend I was ill. That would get me out of dinner. I knew what they'd want to talk about, but I wasn't in the mood to be grilled about Brodie. When he was back, they could know everything.

I sat on the edge of my bed and sent a quick message. *Not feeling good. Rain check on dinner?*

Not a chance. The response came from Indigo. *This is a girls' night in. You have to be here.*

What if I'm contagious?

We'll take the risk. You're coming to dinner.

I have a headache, and my stomach's not feeling good. I don't think I can eat.

There was no reply.

I'll catch up with you another time.

That message also didn't get a response. Maybe Indigo was sulking because I wasn't going for food.

I'd just put on my comfiest lounge pants and a big gray sweater with a pumpkin face on the front to chase away the evening chill, when there was a thud on the front door.

I walked over and opened it. Fire Fang bounded in, his red eyes glowing as he growled at me.

"What are you doing here, boy?" I risked a quick pet of his head.

"He's with me. We're taking you to Indigo's house." Storm marched along the driveway. "You don't look ill to me."

Of course, trust my friends to decide for me, despite me making it clear I wasn't in the mood. "You shouldn't be here. You don't want to get sick. You always say how unproductive you are when you get ill."

"There's nothing wrong with you. Let's go." She stomped up the porch steps.

"I'll be terrible company."

Fire Fang nudged me with his nose.

"You're not missing out on girls' night." Storm gestured me out the door.

"If I'm not in the mood, then I'm not going." I crossed my arms over my chest.

Fire Fang head-butted me so hard in the back, I almost fell over.

"Hey, less of that. I don't want to eat dinner. You can't make me go."

"Fire Fang won't stop until you move," Storm said.

"What's he planning on doing, head-butting me all the way to Indigo's house?"

"He'll probably drag you. Get some shoes on and let's move." Storm picked up my keys and purse.

"I can't. I'm not dressed for dinner."

"You look comfortable, and that's all that matters. Although lose the fluffy orange slippers."

There was no way I was getting out of this dinner while there was a powerful weather witch and her fiery sidekick determining my fate. So, with a scowl on my face, I changed my shoes, and we headed outside.

"You can bring Tuffin if you like," Storm said.

I shot her a glare, still not thrilled at being ordered around. "I haven't seen her for a while. She must have found somewhere extra cozy to nap. And there are mice in the barns, so she won't go hungry."

"How are things working out between you two?" Storm kept hold of my purse and keys. She was using them as a ransom to make sure I followed her.

"Some days, I think she hates me, and others, I get the impression she barely tolerates me. And I'm still not used to the smell of fish in the house. I might have to set her up in a barn on her own, so she can stink the place out. I want nothing putting me off my muffins in the morning."

"Spend time with her every day," Storm said. "It'll strengthen the familiar bond."

"Like you do with Fire Fang?"

"He's no one's familiar. He's a free-wheeling hellhound mutt, who I've yet to find the perfect home."

I grinned at Fire Fang as he loped in front of us. "He's found his perfect home. He's not going anywhere."

"Yes, he is. My apartment isn't set up for a huge hellhound."

"You've been doing okay so far."

Storm grunted. "We've had our moments. He keeps trying to sleep on my bed."

I looked at Storm, and my annoyance shifted to concern. Dark circles sat beneath her eyes, suggesting she hadn't slept properly for a while. I'd been so wrapped up in my problems, I'd barely had time to check in with my oldest friend. "How's everything going with the PI business?"

"It's going. Every day, I get some weird case coming through."

"And Eden? Any new leads?" Storm's younger sister had been missing for years, and Storm was on a never-ending quest to find out what happened to her.

"I've hit a wall." Her voice was quieter than usual. "I thought I was onto something with the last lead, but it came to nothing. This guy messed me around and then vanished. If I ever find him, I'll make him pay. I have space in my deep freeze for scum like that."

I nodded along in sympathy. Eden's disappearance had everyone stumped. She vanished in the middle of the night, leaving no clues as to what had happened. The Magic Council had searched for her, but they'd admitted defeat after six months. Storm never did. She'd never give up on her sister. It was one of the many things I loved about her. She could be intimidating, blunt, and sometimes rude, but she was unswervingly loyal to the people she loved.

"I've also got an ongoing problem with an annoying black cat that keeps coming round the apartment. It gets upstairs and paces the corridor, howling. It sometimes sits under the window and wails, too. I asked the neighbor next door to keep her cat in at night, but it isn't hers. I don't know where it's come from, but it needs to get lost."

"You could send Fire Fang out to give the cat a gentle reminder. Nothing violent, of course."

"I've done that. Every time I let him out, the cat vanishes. It's like she's magic. She clicks her fluffy paws, and she's gone. I'm hoping it'll move on soon." Storm yawned loudly. "Thanks to the cat and my late-night searches for Eden, sleep has taken a backseat."

"You should take a few days off. You could catch up on your sleep during the day when the cat isn't around. I always feel like I'm operating with only half a brain if I don't get a good night's sleep."

"I'll sleep when I'm dead," Storm said.

We arrived at Indigo's house to discover the renovation work still ongoing. There was scaffolding at the front, and the external walls were painted in a fresh coat of gray-white paint.

"Watch out for flying brushes," Storm said. "The house is still cranky about the work being done."

The front door was open, so we headed into the kitchen. Indigo stood at the stove, while Luna sat at the table with a drink in front of her.

"Hey! I heard you got arrested again." Luna grinned at me. "What was it for this time?"

"A simple case of raising the dead."

"Oh, so nothing important."

"Nope." I sat at the table with Luna and accepted a drink from Indigo. "It was a test that went wrong.

I was unlucky because Selma Black wandered past the cemetery as the magic was taking effect."

"What test were you doing?" Storm joined us.

"I'm refining my reanimation magic. You know me. I like my scarecrows to be the best."

"You're not supposed to make any scarecrows while Selma's watching you," Indigo said.

"I wasn't. But I'm allowed to test my magic, aren't I?"

"Not if it gets you arrested," Luna said.

"You must have been using a lot of power to raise corpses." Indigo wandered to the table with a serving spoon in her hand. "And I had Silvaria on the phone complaining about you. She even canceled our dance class because she wants to keep an eye on the bodies."

"She doesn't have to worry. I made sure the links to the dead were severed before I left."

"What magic were you using?" Luna said.

"The usual." I grabbed a chip from the bowl in the center of the table and stuffed it in my mouth. "How's everything with everyone else?"

"We're good," Storm said. "And we're much more interested in you."

"My life is the same old, same old." Here was the grilling I wanted to avoid.

"Olympus was telling me about the case you're helping with." Indigo set bowls of meatball pasta in front of us and joined us at the table. "Now you've got the body, it should be easier to figure out what happened."

"I hope so. The autopsy needs to be done, but I should be able to lay the ghost to rest soon."

"Who's looking good for it?" Storm said.

"There are several suspects, but the wife looks guilty to me."

"I've never had much to do with the Delarosa's," Indigo said. "I like Elsbeth, though. She doesn't strike me as a killer."

"They never do," Storm said. "They're the ones you need to look out for."

"The ghost isn't being a problem, is he?" Luna said.

"No. He's been helpful. And I want to get him closure by finding out what happened to him."

"I didn't know you were close to Zohar Delarosa," Storm said.

"I'm not."

"So why are you keen to get him to cross over? Let the Magic Council figure this out."

"All this talk of dead people is making me hungry." Indigo winked at me as she slurped up spaghetti. She could see I was sweating under the interrogation.

No one spoke for a couple of minutes as we tucked into the food.

"What was going on with that barn you wanted me to clear out?" Indigo said.

I sucked up a strand of spaghetti. The grilling wasn't over just yet. "Sorry about that. I didn't mean to waste your time. Olympus got my scarecrows released, and they cleared it for me."

"Did you ask them to do that?"

"No, but sometimes, they just know to do the things I want. Especially the ones that have been around a long time. We've developed a strong connection. It's like a psychic link."

"Where did they put all the stuff?" Indigo said. "It looked neat when I was there. I never figured your scarecrows were all that tidy."

"I didn't ask. I should check. Actually, I should do that now. The... things in there are important."

Storm shoved me back into my seat. "Eat first. They won't have done anything bad to the stuff they moved. What was it, anyway?"

"Oh, you know, scarecrow stuff." My gaze went to the door.

"Which means, you can hang out with us if it's not important." Indigo pierced me with a glare. "Unless there's something you're not telling us."

"Of course there isn't." I stuffed half a meatball in my mouth and chewed.

"Any more sightings of Brodie?" Luna said.

I took a moment to consider what to tell my friends. I'd already admitted to seeing him, so was there any use hiding he was back for good? It would be less of a shock when I got his ghost into the vessel if they knew some details.

"He's back. At least, his ghost is here," I said.

"Whoa! You've seen him again?" Storm said. "You're positive?"

"I am. But Brodie's having trouble adjusting."

"What's he adjusting to?" Luna said. "The guy's been a ghost for over three years. He must be used to that by now."

"That's the problem. He finally found his way back to me, but when he did, he wanted to cross over. He thinks his unfinished business is complete, so it's time to leave. And I don't want him to go."

Luna reached over and caught hold of my hand. "It'll be hard if Brodie goes, but at least you can say a final goodbye."

I swallowed down the tears threatening to turn me into an emotional mess. "I was so certain he wouldn't leave me. He's my one true love, and I was prepared to wait for as long as it took to get him back."

"Get him back how?" Storm said. "Would you be content with his ghost lurking in the shadows of the farmhouse?"

"That's not how it'll be. We're working on a solution."

"What solution? You're going to set him up in a barn and have ghost and witch date nights?" Indigo said.

"No! Nothing like that."

"Tell us what you have planned. We can help," Luna said.

"Not yet. I'm not ready." They'd reject my ghost vessel idea. They'd think I was crazy and tell me it was impossible.

"It won't be enough for you being with a ghost," Storm said. "Maybe you think it'll be like a gothic romance, but Brodie can't give you everything you need."

"He can." I gripped my fork and stabbed a meatball. "You don't understand."

"You bet, I don't." Storm snagged a meatball off my plate and threw it for Fire Fang.

"But we're trying hard to understand. It would help if you didn't shut us out," Luna said.

"This is something I need to do on my own. I promise, once it's done, it'll make sense. But I don't want anyone to talk me out of it. And I definitely don't want to fall out with any of you over this."

"It sounds like you mean business," Indigo said. "You're sure you've thought this through?"

"Don't worry, you won't have to rush over and save me from a stupid Odessa drama."

"Hey, your dramas are never stupid. They're usually adorable," Indigo said.

"And often funny," Luna said.

I didn't find anything funny about this situation, so I focused on my food.

"How's Sol handling this?" Storm said.

I pursed my lips. "I haven't seen him. I've been meaning to get in touch, but Zohar's death has distracted me."

Storm arched an eyebrow. "What a convenient distraction. Did you know, Sol's thinking about leaving Witch Haven for good?"

The meatball on my fork fell onto my plate and splattered me with sauce. "I didn't know that. He hasn't even told me he's quit working at the farm."

"I saw him this morning. He asked how you were doing, so I assumed you weren't talking."

"We are. I mean, there's no reason we shouldn't talk. But I didn't want to make things complicated between us."

"You don't mind if Sol leaves?" Indigo said. "You were getting on well the last time I saw you together."

"I like Sol," Luna said. "He was helping to make you laugh again."

I tried to ignore the little stab of sadness in my heart. "I laugh all the time."

"Yes, but not your real laugh. We hear the laugh you do when you're trying to make everyone think you're having a good time, when secretly, you wish you were in bed with a bag of cookies."

"That's ridiculous." I ate my fallen meatball as I tried to imagine the farm without Sol. I couldn't do it. There were memories of him everywhere, and he was an important part of my life. I did care for him deeply. I maybe even loved him a little.

"Just because you fell hard for one guy doesn't mean you can't fall for another," Indigo said. "Brodie was your first love, but there can be more. It'll be different, and there'll be times when you wonder if it's the right thing, but Sol is your second chance at happiness. Don't have regrets. You need to speak to him before he makes a decision about whether to stay in Witch Haven."

"I've pledged my heart to Brodie," I whispered.

"It's your heart. Take it back and give it to Sol," Storm said. "Or keep it for yourself. Spend more time with Sol and see if it works for you. If it doesn't, go back to your fantasy of loving a ghost."

"Storm," Indigo cautioned.

She shrugged. "I'm just saying, there's always a fallback plan. If one guy doesn't work out, try another."

"I'm not a serial dater. That's not my style. I knew with Brodie as soon as we met. Everything felt right." I didn't miss the exasperated look passing between my friends. Maybe things hadn't been perfect with Brodie, but they'd been good enough. And starting again with someone else seemed exhausting. What if something bad happened to Sol? Then I'd have lost two people I cared about. And I was getting Brodie back, so considering another man, even one as great as Sol, was pointless.

"We're here if you need our help," Luna said. "We just want to see you happy."

"Thanks. I am. Or at least I will be really soon."

I was grateful the grilling about Brodie was over, and we enjoyed the rest of the evening with good food and chat.

I was happy and relaxed by the time I walked back to the farm with Storm and Fire Fang. We'd only made it about halfway when something glinting among the trees caught my eye. I slowed and peered through the foliage.

"What have you seen?" Storm said. "Another ghost that needs your help?"

"No. It's a traveling wagon. What's it doing tucked back here?" As I got closer, I spotted a harness at the front of the wagon for horses. It was dark brown and barrel shaped with several small glass windows on the side. The back had two doors, and one side was painted with a mural of a free running unicorn.

"Let's go take a look." Storm pushed through the trees, Fire Fang cutting a path in front of her.

"This is cute. It must be someone's vacation home." I walked around the wagon, admiring the unicorn on the side.

"Shall we see if anyone's home?"

"There aren't any lights on. You don't think it's been abandoned, do you?"

"There's only one way to find out." Storm rapped on the back door.

There was no answer.

"Hello? Is anyone home?" I said.

There was still no reply.

Storm tried one door, and it opened. "Shall we?"

"Maybe we shouldn't," I said. "If the owner comes back and finds us snooping, they won't be happy."

"We're not snooping. We're looking after their property. And if it's been abandoned, we need to know who it belongs to so we can return it to them or report it to the Magic Council. A nice looking bit of kit like this could get stolen." Storm pulled open both doors.

There was no one inside, but there was a small counter, a single bed at the back, and a couple of bags on the floor.

"Since no one is in, let's take a proper look." Storm pulled out a set of small steps and set them on the ground. She hopped inside. "Fire Fang, stay out here and let us know if anyone shows up."

He growled his reply then settled by the steps.

I hurried up the steps and joined Storm inside the wagon. The place smelled faintly of cedarwood. There were dark blue curtains at the windows, and the bed was neatly made.

"I'll take the bags. You look around," Storm said.

"That won't take long." I headed to the bed and checked it over. The sheets were fresh and looked like they hadn't been slept in. I stepped back and kicked something small under the bed. I kneeled down and peered under it.

I inched my fingers under the small gap, caught the end of whatever I'd kicked on a fingernail, and eased it out. I lifted it up so I could see it in the moonlight.

It was a jade pendant with a broken chain.

Chapter 14

After making a call to Olympus to tell him we'd discovered Zohar's missing pendant, we opened the bags in the wagon and took out the items. Most of it was clothing, but there was also a big bundle of money, along with travel documents.

"I've never heard of Paulo Mitherino," Storm said. "He can't be from here. He could be passing through and stashed his wagon here thinking it wouldn't be noticed."

I looked over the documents. There were travel details for an around-the-world trip with an open-ended ticket. "I don't know him either. But he must have money if he's going to all these places."

"I wonder if he wants someone to carry his bags," Storm said.

"You should hang around and ask. Although..." I pointed at the pendant. "Since this is here, it could mean Paulo is connected to what happened to Zohar."

"Hmmm, I may overlook that if I get to hang out on all these beaches. This guy must be a sun worshipper."

I chuckled. "I never figured you for a beach bunny."

"You should see me in a pair of rabbit ears."

"Is there anything else useful in the bags?" I peered at the contents of the open bags.

"Nothing I can see. The clothing is all designer, though. Whoever this guy is, he blows more on a single shirt than I spend on a month of groceries."

I checked the side pockets of the bag and discovered a passport. I flipped to the picture, and my eyes widened. "This is a photograph of Zohar! But the name doesn't match. This passport is for Paulo Mitherino."

Storm studied the passport for several minutes, using a small light ball to see it clearly. "This is a fake. A great fake. You have to look closely to see it isn't legit."

"Why would Zohar have a passport made out in another name?"

"You'll have to ask your ghost friend that question. But most people get fake passports because they're escaping from something."

"I need to get Zohar here." I closed my eyes and focused on summoning him. He didn't appear. I tried again, but he was either ignoring me or occupied with Brodie, because he didn't show up.

"These clothes and money must belong to him," Storm said. "Zohar was making plans to travel."

"Without Elsbeth? I know things were bad between them, but was he considering doing a moonlit flit? And did Elsbeth know about it?"

"Has she mentioned he was going away?"

"No, but then Elsbeth is good at not telling the whole truth."

A fierce warning growl rumbled outside.

"Storm, call off Fire Fang!" Olympus yelled.

Storm grinned. "He'll only give you a friendly nip if you make any sudden movements."

"Nothing feels friendly about this. He has my arm in his mouth."

Storm whistled. "Fire Fang, drop your new toy."

There was more growling, but then the door creaked open and Olympus appeared, wiping down his arm with a hankie. He looked at the bags we'd rifled through and frowned. "You didn't tell me you were tampering with evidence."

"We're only very carefully tampering. But you need to look at this." I showed him the passport.

Olympus thumbed through it. "This is odd. And illegal."

"All the travel documents are for one person," I said. "Zohar was planning a long vacation under a fake name."

Olympus took a few minutes to look through the bags and take pictures. "Where's the jade pendant?"

"On the floor. I kicked it under the bed, so had to get it out. I haven't touched it since I realized what it was and who it belonged to."

Olympus examined it then placed it in an evidence bag.

"It's a match for the one Zohar lost," I said. "Maybe he fought his killer here."

"Or the killer used this wagon to transport Zohar's body," Olympus said. "Although it's hardly discreet, and it won't be a match for the tire treads found by the house. And something this unusual moving through the village would have been noticed."

"Something bad must have happened here for Zohar's pendant to be left behind," I said. "And he hasn't mentioned anything about a hidden wagon and plans to leave."

"Maybe the killer is using this as a hideout and they dropped the pendant," Olympus said.

"But if this place belongs to someone other than Zohar, why are his things here?" Storm said.

I studied the bags again. "The killer could have stolen them, along with the pendant."

"It doesn't look like it's worth much." Storm examined the pendant through the evidence bag.

"Zohar said he kept it for sentimental reasons. It was a gift from his dad."

"If someone did take it, they could have known how much it meant to Zohar. They wanted it because they knew it would hurt him to lose it," Storm said.

"Which means his killer is someone close to him," I said. "A friend, maybe."

"Or his wife," I said.

Storm's phone buzzed in her pocket. She took it out and checked the message before stashing it away. "I need to leave. Duty calls. Good luck with the rest of the search."

After a quick round of goodbyes, she left the wagon with Fire Fang.

"Is Zohar here?" Olympus said. "We need to find out what he knows about this wagon."

"He's not. I tried to summon him so he could explain himself, but I had no luck."

"Which suggests he's hiding something."

"Or he's busy."

"Doing what? He's a ghost who wants his murder solved. That has to be his top priority."

I tilted my head from side to side. "Sure. You're right."

Olympus narrowed his eyes at me. "Is there something I'm missing?"

"Nope."

"Uh-huh. How did you find the wagon?"

"Luck. I was walking home after having dinner with the girls and noticed the moon glinting off a window. I had no idea this wagon was linked to Zohar."

"Let's hope your luck holds so we can solve this. I'll take it from here," Olympus said. "I've got a team not far behind me, but I wanted to get here first to make sure you weren't snooping around too much."

"Hey! I'm allowed to snoop. I'm practically a full-time employee of the Magic Council."

Olympus grimaced. "Trust me, you don't ever want that. Get back to the farm and speak to Zohar. This is a piece of the puzzle he decided not to tell us about, and we need to know why."

"Sure. I'll see what I can find out." Although I wasn't hopeful he'd be forthcoming. Zohar had concealed this for a reason, and he'd be unlikely to share that reason with me.

I headed off and left Olympus to do his thing. Putting the clues together, it looked like Zohar was escaping from Elsbeth, Witch Haven, or his old life. But why? To start anew somewhere else, where no one knew him? He may not have decided where that new home would be, since there were thirty stops on his ticket. Other than the money in the bag, I had no clue if Zohar had access to other assets. Was he willing to give up the crystal jackpot? Had things gotten so bad, he was washing his hands of everything?

I was walking through the center of Witch Haven when someone called my name. I turned to see Hester waving as she hurried toward me.

"I'm glad I've seen you. How are things going with the investigation?"

"We're making progress. We've just made an important discovery," I said.

"Oh, what's that?"

"Um... It's still being looked into, so I can't share much." Hester fell into step with me. "Do you know if Zohar had plans to travel soon?"

"Travel? No, not that I know of. Although he often talked about it. Elsbeth told me they'd had a couple of luxury vacations and even been on a cruise. She didn't like it because it made her sick."

"This will sound like an odd question, but has Zohar ever gone by another name?"

Her eyebrows flashed up. "No! Why would he do that?"

"It's just something we found, and we can't figure it out."

"I'm sorry I can't help. I haven't known Zohar and Elsbeth all my life, so it's possible he changed his name. Can you find that out?"

"I imagine so. The Magic Council will know how to search for name changes." I glanced at Hester.

"I don't know if you've been told, but Zohar's body has been found. He was left in Witch Haven Lake."

Hester's hand went to her mouth. "That's awful. What a terrible thing to do. Oh! But it makes sense now."

"What does?"

"Two people from the Magic Council visited Elsbeth. She went to her room after they'd gone and won't come out. She said she didn't want to talk. I hope she's okay. I wouldn't want to be alone after learning such horrible news. Maybe I should get back to the house."

"I expect Elsbeth won't want to be on her own for too long," I said. "She'll appreciate having a friend around."

"Of course. But before I go, there was something I needed to tell you. I'm not sure if it's relevant, but I don't think it's been mentioned by anyone, and it was a big reason why Elsbeth and Zohar were so unhappy."

"What's the reason?"

"They were fighting partly over the money and their move to Witch Haven, but Elsbeth always wanted a large family. She's great with children and joked she wanted at least a dozen babies. I was surprised when they didn't start making babies as soon as they married. But a couple of years went by, and no children came along."

"Not all couples have children straight away," I said. "Or maybe they changed their minds."

"I know. So I didn't ask about it, but Elsbeth used to take me to baby stores and look at the tiny outfits and toys. Suddenly, that stopped. It seemed weird, and I wanted to make sure she was okay, so I checked in with her."

"And did they change their mind about having a family?"

"No. Elsbeth still wants kids. The problem was, Zohar concealed the fact he was basically infertile." She leaned closer. "Slow swimmers. It would have been a miracle if he'd fathered a child."

"That's a big thing to hide from your wife. Zohar should have told her, especially since he must have known how badly Elsbeth wanted children."

"Elsbeth said she'd come to terms with never having children. They were talking about fostering, but she always wanted a baby, and most children in the care system are older. They were still looking into it, though."

"A secret like that could blow a marriage apart."

"I think that's the way it was going. As well as admitting to Zohar having slow swimmers, Elsbeth confided that he'd become even more uptight and angry since they got all that money. Elsbeth was pressing him to go for more tests and use the money to improve their chances of getting pregnant. Apparently, every time she brought up the subject, he started yelling, so she'd back down."

"That's sad. Some things you can't buy with money, no matter how much you want it."

"Maybe not. Elsbeth also told me she'd looked into surrogacy. She even paid a young woman a deposit to rent her womb in the hopes Zohar would agree to it."

"Well, that's one option. What did Zohar think?"

"He was so angry and insisted Elsbeth get back the money. He said he didn't want another woman carrying their baby."

"I imagine Elsbeth didn't take that too well."

"She was devastated. She wanted to give a child the best life possible and thought she could now they had no money worries. But Zohar didn't want to know." Hester shrugged. "I wonder if he saw it as an assault on his manhood. You know, guys get funny about things below the waist. They never want to admit to having problems. We all have problems down there. It's nothing to be ashamed about."

"Err... sure. It was wrong of him to conceal that from Elsbeth until they were married."

"I agree. He trapped her in the marriage. I tried to talk to Elsbeth about it when we got here, but she brushed it off and said there was nothing to worry about. She said she was glad she had all this free time, and children tied you down. Although... her free time was spent fighting with Zohar."

"You don't believe she's given up her dream of becoming a mom?"

"Not for a second. Elsbeth was unhappy because Zohar couldn't give her what she desperately needed."

We stopped at the end of the road that split in two directions, one path leading to my farm.

I turned to Hester. "This will sound odd, but does Elsbeth have any special skills?"

"What kind of skills are you asking about? She's great with make-up. She always makes me look good when we have a pamper session."

"Not that. Zohar was a big guy, and Elsbeth is tiny. I was wondering if they'd fought and things got rough, whether she'd know how to protect herself."

Hester blinked rapidly. "You don't think she killed him, do you?"

"With the troubles they had in their marriage, it's got me wondering. Maybe they were arguing about Zohar's fertility issues. He could have lost control, and Elsbeth killed him in self-defense. But she'd have needed to know how to handle a guy as big as Zohar and not get hurt. Does she know any kind of martial art?"

Hester chuckled. "Elsbeth's not a secret assassin. Her passions are fitness and fashion."

"What about strong spells? Elsbeth was the better magic user out of the two of them, wasn't she?"

"That's right, but her family are healers. She uses plant-based magic. That only helps people. She couldn't use it to hurt anyone."

I nodded as I recalled the marks on Zohar's body. I hadn't examined him properly, but I hadn't noticed any magic burns.

"I know they were having problems, but I'm certain Elsbeth's not behind this," Hester said.

"Really? You don't think it was an accident and Elsbeth panicked and hid Zohar's body while she figured out what to do next?"

Hester's mouth twisted to the side before she shook her head. "I can't see her doing that. And she has an alibi."

I didn't comment. She had a sort of alibi, but she'd taken a long time to get to the smoothie bar and hadn't mentioned using a car to get there. Something didn't add up with Elsbeth's alibi.

"Odessa, you can't think it was Elsbeth." Hester touched my elbow.

"You admitted she vanished for a while. What was she doing?"

"Elsbeth is known for getting easily distracted," Hester said. "I bet it happened that day. She fought with Zohar, needed to clear her head, and lost track of time. While she was out, the place was burgled, and Zohar died."

"Yet the burglar moved the body. That's an odd thing to do."

"Yes, I suppose it is." Hester looked around as if seeking inspiration. "I hope you have an answer soon. Zohar deserves justice, and Elsbeth needs to get on with her life. I'll stick by her. I'm sure she's innocent."

I nodded. Elsbeth wouldn't have much of a life to get on with if she was found guilty. And the clues were pointing to her. The fight before Zohar died, her dodgy alibi, the troubles they were having trying to start a family. And, with Zohar dead, Elsbeth wouldn't need to share the crystal jackpot.

Maybe I should accept the direction the clues pointed and only focus on Elsbeth as the killer.

"You don't mind me telling you this information, do you?" Hester said. "I don't normally gossip, but I want this solved. I liked Zohar, although I've always been closer to Elsbeth. It's unfair what happened to him, though. If it was Elsbeth... well, I'll have to accept that. But I won't believe it until she confesses."

Whether she meant to, Hester was definitely stirring with this gossip, but her intentions seemed genuine. She wanted to stick by her friend but could see how bad things were looking for Elsbeth and wanted the truth to come out.

"This could be useful," I said. "Thanks for passing it on."

"No problem. I should get back. I was picking up a takeaway for me and Ballard. Elsbeth wanted nothing. She said she wasn't hungry. Now, I know the reason. I'll see if I can coax her out. Maybe she'll want to get things off her chest." Hester bit her lip. "I really hope she didn't do it."

We said our goodbyes, and I headed to my farm.

I walked up the porch steps and in through the front door. I set down my purse and stood in front of my poorly put together suspect board. Every new piece of information only led to another twist in this mystery.

I wrote down jade pendant on a sticky note and stuck it on the board. The discovery of that pendant was an oddity. Zohar said he never took it off, but it was in the wagon. That meant he could have been there at some point. Had there been a fight, and it got torn from his neck? Or maybe the killer took it out of spite because they knew how important it was to Zohar.

The words red ribbon went on a sticky note, and I stuck it on the board. That was another strange thing. That ribbon in Zohar's pocket had a trace of magic on it. Why did Zohar have that, and what was the ribbon used for?

I stood back and examined the board. All these clues were connected, but I just didn't know how they joined together.

Chapter 15

"Hey, wake up."

I rolled over and shot upright in bed as I came face-to-face with Brodie. "You're here!"

He grinned. "I am. Sorry I haven't been around much."

"That's okay. Zohar said you've been doing a lot of thinking. You haven't changed your mind about staying with me, have you?"

"No, babe. I'm staying right here. It's where I belong. But I've been thinking about the future and what we should do. We have to make this work."

My stomach fluttered with excitement. "So have I. I've got so many ideas. I've been thinking about our future for over three years, so I've probably got too many ideas. We can start with the best ones, though."

He chuckled and pressed his icy lips against my cheek. "I figured you might have. So I planned a day for us."

"A day?" I climbed out of bed and stuffed my feet into my orange slippers.

"Yes. I want to take you out, so it's just the two of us with no distractions. We can talk over everything and make our plans."

"Aww, that's sweet. But in case you've forgotten, I'm in the middle of solving Zohar's murder. And this farm doesn't run itself."

"You can take a day off. I used to twist your arm to do it all the time."

I grabbed my robe. "Sure, but it was different back then. The business has grown, and I've got a backlog of orders. Although, technically, I shouldn't be making any new scarecrows, I hate to keep my clients waiting any longer than they should."

"You should definitely take the day off if you've been told not to work. Come out with me, and we'll have fun. It'll be just like old times."

"What about Zohar? He said he's been helping you, so I need to return the favor. And I found a clue yesterday. A hidden wagon. Zohar is linked to that, so I need to speak to him about it. He wasn't around last night, so I figured you were keeping him busy." I headed into the bathroom and closed the door. Brodie and I had been together a long time, but there were some things we never shared.

"Zohar is fine." Brodie kept talking to me through the closed door. "And if it takes another day to figure out what happened to him, he won't mind. He's an easy-going guy."

"He wants his killer found. He may not like it if I take a day off to have fun with you."

"I've checked with him. He's cool."

"Are you two getting along okay?" I quickly freshened up in the bathroom.

"Sure. And Zohar realizes we need time alone. It's been over three years, and I've missed you like crazy. Forget the farm and Zohar's murder. Focus on us."

I grinned at myself in the mirror. "I've missed you, too. And I want to spend the day talking all about the two of us."

"Sooooo, does that mean you're coming out with me?"

I opened the door and grabbed clean clothing. I gestured for Brodie to turn around.

"Come on. I've seen you naked loads of times."

"This is different. We were both alive the last time you saw me."

"I'm almost alive. And I always feel alive when I look at you getting your clothes off." His eyes gleamed as he chuckled.

My cheeks flushed, but I got changed in front of him. I needed to get used to having Brodie back in all ways.

"You're still as beautiful as ever," Brodie said. "I'm the luckiest guy alive. Well, dead, but you know what I mean."

I ran a brush through my hair and applied the tiniest bit of make-up. I wanted to spend the day with Brodie, but there was so much to do on the farm. And I couldn't abandon Zohar. Even if he said he understood about me taking time out, I wanted his murder solved. And I needed someone around to keep an eye on the scarecrows if I vanished for the day. That someone used to be Sol, but I could hardly ask him to drop by and scarecrow-sit while I went on a date with my dead boyfriend.

"What's on your mind? You don't want to hang out with me?" Brodie settled his cold arms around my waist and tugged me against him.

I snuggled into his chilly embrace. He felt much stronger than the last time I'd been around him. "I want to spend time with you, but I was thinking about Sol. We could easily go out if he was here."

"Sol is your assistant?"

"Kind of. He was doing well here, and I was considering making him a partner in the farm."

Brodie moved back, his cold arms sliding away from me. "This is our place. We don't need anyone else involved."

I turned to face him. There was a glimmer of jealousy in his eyes. "Brodie, you've been gone a long time, and I was struggling even when you were here. Sol has been great. He revolutionized the farm. Even the scarecrows like him."

"The only person your scarecrows like is you. I learned to give them a wide berth a long time ago."

"They're not so bad. And Sol has a knack with them. He was great for this place and knew what I was thinking, even before I did."

"You like this guy. Should I be worried?"

"No!" I didn't like lying to Brodie about my feelings for Sol, but I hadn't done anything bad. There'd been some mild flirtation and a moment or two of weakness, but that was it. I hadn't crossed any boundaries.

"You don't need this guy. We can handle the place between us. But not if you burn yourself out. You need a day off. You don't want to run yourself ragged trying to solve this murder and not have enough time for us."

With guilt rolling around inside me about my near miss with Sol, I nodded. "You're right. Let me fix the scarecrows up with work for the day, and then we can have the morning off."

"How about the whole day? We could be busy."

"Why? What have you got planned?"

His grin was wicked. "Something that'll benefit both of us. And I've arranged for food to be delivered, so you won't need to stop for breakfast. I want to take your mind off murder and the scarecrows, so we can enjoy ourselves."

"Give me half an hour, and I'll be ready to go." I raced around, gathering my scarecrows and setting them to work.

As I dashed back into the kitchen, I looked around for Tuffin.

Brodie drifted into the room. "All set?"

"Just a minute. I can't find Tuffin. Have you seen her?"

"Can't say I have, but I haven't been here all the time. You know what cats are like. They're so independent. She's probably out mouse hunting. She'll be back when she's ready."

"I guess so. But she loves her fish. I'm surprised she hasn't been complaining that there's been none left for her. I'll put some down, just in case she comes in. If it's gone when we get back, at least I know Tuffin's dropping by when she gets hungry."

"Sure, but hurry up. We don't want to miss the best part of the day."

I had nothing cooked, so opened a tin of tuna and put it in a bowl. Tuffin wouldn't be happy about the tinned goods, but it was the best I could offer at short notice.

Brodie ushered me out the door a minute later. "I've missed hanging out with you."

I linked my hand with his and instantly felt my magic drain.

He shot me a sorrowful look. "Sorry, babe. I can't stop tasting your magic. I've missed that pumpkin flavor."

"It's not a problem. And it won't be forever."

"I put some powdered pumpkin in your purse. I figured you might need it if we were spending time together. I don't want you getting too tired."

"Thanks." I grabbed the bag and munched down some sweet powder, giving me and Brodie an instant boost.

"You don't mind me using your magic, do you? It helps keep my thoughts together when I'm fully juiced."

"Of course not. What's mine is yours, and you need it to stay in a solid shape. I've missed this, too. I've missed everything about you." I chuckled. "Well, maybe not your habit of leaving socks on the floor in the bathroom."

"That habit was adorable." He kissed my cheek, leaving an icy tingle behind.

"So, where are we going? Is it far from here?"

"It's a short walk away. And it'll be quiet, so no one will disturb us."

"It sounds perfect." I was so happy, walking with my ghost boyfriend and chatting about old times and future plans. All my dreams were coming true, and I was so close to getting everything I wanted that I was almost bursting with excitement.

"Here we are." Brodie stopped outside the cemetery gates.

I looked through them and then back at him. "I don't understand."

"I needed a quiet place where we wouldn't be disturbed. The dead are hardly going to get in our way."

"Brodie! This isn't funny. We can't have a date in a cemetery."

"Sure we can. The residents won't mind."

I frowned as I looked into the cemetery. "Silvaria will hate us for being here." And I didn't love the idea, either. When I'd pictured spending a romantic day together, I'd imagined woodland walks and stops at cute cafes, not bones, headstones, and crypts.

"The place I found for us is tucked away in the back. Silvaria won't even know we're here."

"She will. You don't know Silvaria like I do."

"I do. I remember her. She's a mean old witch, but so long as we're respectful of the graves, there's nothing to worry about."

"Brodie, I'm not sure about this." I resisted his tug on my arm. "There's something I haven't told you about the last time I visited the cemetery."

"Did you do something bad?" He grinned at me.

I gripped the cemetery gate. "Not intentionally. But I made Silvaria angry."

"That's not difficult. Although I'm intrigued. You're such a good witch. Let's get inside. Breakfast will be here soon, and I got your favorites. You can tell me everything while you eat."

Reluctantly, I let Brodie lead me into the cemetery. I wasn't sure about being here, not after raising the dead.

I crept along, checking out each grave, but they were as silent as they should be. Maybe I was reading too much into this. And if I was going to get this link with my ancestors to work, I had to try again. And it would be easier with Brodie here. I could channel power into him and see what happened.

"This is us." Brodie gestured behind an ancient, broad oak tree, and I spotted a picnic blanket laid out.

"Excuse me. I've got a food order for Brodie. Can... can you take it?"

I turned to see a young guy of about eighteen racing toward me, clutching two large bags. His gaze kept darting to the graves.

"Sure. That's for me."

He practically threw the bags then turned tail and raced away.

Brodie chuckled. "Someone doesn't like spending time with the dead. Or maybe he's scared of Silvaria."

"Poor kid. I hope you tipped him well."

"Sure. I used your account to pay. After all, I've got no money."

I rolled my eyes at him. "So I bought myself breakfast?"

"I promise, it'll be worth your while. You set up, and then we'll talk."

I grinned as I pulled out takeout cartons. Brodie always used to do this when we were together. It sometimes meant I got behind with my work, but I enjoyed myself when he sprang a surprise day out. And today was important. We needed to focus on our future.

I opened the first carton and frowned. It was smoked salmon and scrambled eggs. Not my favorite breakfast. "Is this for you?"

"Babe, the dead don't eat. I got you one of everything off the menu. I didn't know if your tastes had changed since I've been away."

"Nope. Still a sweet girl through and through. I hope there are muffins or croissants in here. Or even better, warm, sweet waffles."

"I'm sure there will be. Nothing but the best for my girl."

I found plenty more savory breakfasts but finally discovered a sugar encrusted blueberry muffin. I pulled it out, opened a takeout coffee, and took a sip. The whole time I'd been sorting the food, Brodie had been drifting around.

"Is everything okay?" I asked.

"This will sound creepy, but this place feels like home. I'm mixing with my own kind." Brodie's gaze moved over the cemetery.

I grimaced, the piece of muffin I'd swallowed lodging in my throat. I had to cough several times before I could speak. "This isn't your home. Your home is the farm, with me and the scarecrows."

He turned and drifted closer. "About that. I've been thinking about our future home." He settled next to me and ran a chilled finger down my arm. "I want to move."

"Get a new place in Witch Haven?"

"No, leave the village."

I set down the coffee. "You've mentioned it before, but I didn't think you were serious."

"I am. There's no point in us hanging onto the past. And you only stayed here because of me. Now I'm back, and things can change."

"That's partly true, but everything I care about is here. My best friends, my business, my scarecrows. I don't want to leave those behind."

"You've got me now, and we can start somewhere new. Wipe the slate clean and forget every bad thing that happened and the sadness you felt after I was gone. All I've got here is bad memories."

"They can't all be bad. We had amazing times while we were together and you were alive. We can make plenty more happy memories when you're in your scarecrow vessel."

"I don't remember many of those old memories," Brodie said. "Since I've been a ghost, I've changed. I sometimes don't feel myself."

I caught hold of his hand. "You're not having dark thoughts, are you? You said you weren't experiencing those."

"Since I found my way back to you, things have been shifting. I don't know whether it's because the clock is ticking and I need to make a decision about our future, but I know something is changing inside me. It doesn't feel like a good something."

I refused to panic. Everything was under control, and Brodie wouldn't change into a ghost ghoul.

"You're just excited now you're back, and we have so many possibilities to consider."

"It could be that. But I'm worried about what will happen when I come back for good. What if people don't accept me? Or they think it's unnatural and don't want me here? If we go somewhere no one knows us, we won't have awkward questions to answer."

"They'll accept you! Everyone loved you, and they'll be thrilled when you're back. Even if you will be a little different."

"I just want to get out of here. This is the place where I lost you. It's the place where I lost myself for a long time."

I kneeled in front of him. "You've been through tough times, but getting rid of everything and starting again is extreme." I hated the thought of leaving, but part of me understood Brodie's trauma. I may have felt the same if I'd died and gotten lost for so long.

"I'm right about this," Brodie said. "Ever since I found my way back to you, all I've wanted to do is take you away from all of this. It's why I took time for myself. I needed to find a way to make you understand."

"I'm trying to. And I want you to be happy. But what would we do if we left Witch Haven?"

A smile crossed his face, while I struggled to muster one. "We could try anything. You could sell the farm, and we could set up something together. Something we'd both enjoy."

"No pumpkins? No scarecrows?"

"Babe, they were always your thing."

"And working at the mines was your thing. If you want to go back to doing that, I won't stop you."

"I don't want to do that. I didn't mind it, but now, we can be free. You'll get plenty of money from your business, and the land must be worth a fortune. Sell up, release your assets, and we can enjoy them together. How about setting up a hotel? Something classy."

My nose wrinkled. "That sounds like hard work."

"Harder than dealing with a bunch of out-of-control scarecrows?"

"They're not out-of-control. Well, rarely." I leaned closer to Brodie, worried at how serious he was being about this move. "I don't want to give up my life here."

"Then we have a problem. Because I don't want to stay."

I chewed on more muffin, even though I was no longer hungry. It felt like I was giving up too much if I moved. But then there was Brodie. I didn't want him to leave me, but if he wouldn't stay here, we had to find a compromise that worked for both of us.

"Sorry, I'm pressing you to make a huge decision, and I've only just sprung this on you. We don't have to decide straightaway," Brodie said. "But how about we take a break from Witch Haven? Once you get me in that vessel, we could rent out the farm for a year. Someone could take over, and we could go have fun."

"Rent it out?"

"Sure. What about that Sam guy you hired? Would he be up to the job?"

"Sol. And I doubt he'd want to rent the farm. He's thinking about leaving Witch Haven."

"No matter. Someone else will be interested."

"No one can manage the scarecrows without me around."

"Sure they can. Give them the right orders, and they'll behave. Or shut them down for a bit."

"Brodie! They aren't toys. You can't just turn off their power supply."

"Babe, they kind of are. You're their source of power."

"No! It's not that simple."

"If you want me back for good, you might have to shut them down, anyway. Unless you've changed your mind about us being together."

"Of course not." I raked a hand through my hair. "I've been thinking about how to get you stable in the vessel."

"Great. And..."

"That's one of the things I wanted to talk to you about. I stopped by the crypt the other day and tested the link."

"Babe, that's amazing. Why didn't you tell me?"

"Because it didn't go to plan. The magic is powerful, but it came with a side effect."

"What's that?"

"I raised the dead."

Brodie whistled low. "No way. Did you mean to do that?"

"No! I was just testing my ancestors' power."

"So what happened to the corpses?" Brodie tugged me to my feet.

"They settled down once I told them to. That's why Silvaria was so unhappy with me."

"This means your ancestors' power will work on me. You link to them, and we'll use that power to get me in the vessel. I'll stay stable, and we can have all the adventures we want." He drifted closer. "And I can hold you like I used to. I've missed that most of all."

I wanted that too, but I also didn't want to reanimate every body this side of Witch Haven. "I'm not sure about trying again."

"Try for me," Brodie said. "I want to know you can do it, so I don't give up hope. And I want to get a sense of that power. I bet it's incredible."

"Sure, it's strong. But until I can control it, I shouldn't use it."

"Let's give it a go. What's the worst that can happen?"

"An army of undead takes over the village and eats everyone."

He laughed. "You can handle a few corpses. And we'll be careful. And I'm here, now. I can help."

With Brodie by my side, I felt like I could achieve anything. "If I'm careful, I'll try again. You watch over the cemetery. If any graves move, I'll have to stop."

"Whatever you need. But this will work. I know it." Brodie grabbed hold of me and spun me around. "I'm finally getting you back. After all this time." He planted a freezing kiss on my lips.

I giggled, so happy to finally get what I wanted.

"Let's do it now."

"What about the food? And we've barely talked about our future."

"We'll have all the time in the world to do that soon. Please, I'm too excited to wait."

I indulged him with a smile, even though my stomach was twisted up with worry. I had to make sure the dead didn't rise again.

"Babe, for me." He flashed me a smile.

"Okay. Let's see what I can do."

Brodie led me to my family crypt, and I opened the door. He stood by it and watched the graveyard.

"I just need to borrow a little something from an ancestor to get the magic going," I said.

"I can sense the power without you evoking it. I'm sure your ancestors will be happy to lend it to us. After all, they want to see you content. And you will be with me," Brodie said. "You're my forever girl."

"And you're my forever guy. Just give me a minute to get my focus." I placed a hand on the wall of the crypt and connected with my ancestors. Their energy vibrated around me, welcoming me in.

"Are they happy you're here?" Brodie said.

"I think so." I leaned against the wall, drinking in the energy.

"How's it going?"

"A little quiet would help."

"Sorry," he whispered. "I'm excited."

"This is just a small test," I murmured to my ancestors. "I want to see what's possible. I hope you'll help."

A gust of wind rushed through the crypt, and a coffin lid slid open.

"That's a good sign?" Brodie said.

"They're on board. Let's see what happens next." I selected the smallest finger bone I could find and held it between my hands. "How's everything going outside?"

"It's as silent as the grave." Brodie laughed. "You're doing great."

I walked over to him as magic pulsed through me in powerful waves. Everything seemed fine. The magic held and felt stable. But it was strong, and I needed all my focus to channel it.

"Whoa! Your eyes are glowing." Brodie peered at me.

"I feel so alive. There's so much power in the dead. It almost feels like too much."

"Let me help with that." Brodie grabbed hold of my hands.

"No, wait! I'm not—" There was an ear blasting explosion and a flash of light, and darkness took me.

Chapter 16

A warm, wet rasping feel across my cheek made me stir. I groaned and tried to push it away, but after a second, the sensation resumed.

I inched open an eye to discover Fire Fang looming over me. Drool slid off his fangs as he licked my face. I shuffled away then moaned again. Every muscle hurt, and the back of my head ached. I was flat on the floor inside the family crypt.

Fire Fang whined and settled next to me, resting his giant head on my stomach.

"I'm okay, boy. At least, I think I am." The place was freezing, and it was dark. How long had I been unconscious? "Brodie? Are you in here?"

He didn't reply.

Fire Fang growled softly.

"Can you sense his ghost?" My ears were ringing, and I kept seeing double every time I looked around.

Fire Fang whined again.

"Is Storm with you?"

He looked over his shoulder and then back at me.

I tried to get up, but the effort had my stomach flipping and black dots dancing in my vision, so I lay back on the cold floor and closed my eyes.

Fire Fang licked my face again, forcing me to stay awake.

I gently pushed him away. "I'm good. I just don't feel ready to move." I reached into my pocket then remembered my phone was in my purse, and my purse was on the picnic blanket in the cemetery. "Fire Fang, will you fetch my purse? Go sniff it out."

He didn't move.

"Please. I have to call for help. Or maybe you can go get Storm."

He stayed where he was, looking like he was intent on guarding me.

I pressed my hands into the cold stone, trying to connect to my ancestors' energy. The link felt dead. There was nothing there. I couldn't have used it all when Brodie connected with me, could I?

And where was Brodie? He must have seen what happened. Why hadn't he gone for help? By the lack of daylight and ache in my back, I'd been unconscious all day.

A deep worry bit into me. What if the connection had gone wrong? The magic was too powerful and blasted Brodie apart rather than making him stable. Or what if I'd forced him to cross over? I could have lost him.

Tears pricked my eyes as I stared at the ceiling. This should have worked, but it felt like a giant failure.

"Odessa, where are you?"

I turned my head. Was that Sol? "Hey! Help. I'm in the family crypt."

Footsteps pounded closer, and Sol appeared in the doorway a few seconds later. His eyes widened as he raced over to me. "What happened to you?"

"I made a little mistake."

"Are you injured? Do you need me to take you to the hospital?" Sol kneeled beside me, not paying attention to Fire Fang's menacing growl, warning him not to touch me.

I petted Fire Fang to reassure him Sol was a safe person to be around. "Nothing's broken. Although I think I whacked my head when I hit the floor. And I feel dizzy."

"You could have a concussion."

"I just need to rest. Stay with me for a few minutes until I feel better."

Sol took off his jacket and covered me with it. His warmth seeped into me, and I instantly felt perkier.

I snuggled into the jacket. "How did you know I was here?"

"I didn't. But I stopped by the farm to say goodbye, and your scarecrows were acting weird. They were running around looking for something. I know how connected you are to them, so I figured something must have happened to you." Sol clasped my hand between his and rubbed briskly to get the circulation going. "I looked all over the farmhouse and in the barns and fields and couldn't find you. I was walking past the cemetery when I heard growling. That's when I saw your family crypt open."

"My scarecrows must be frantic with worry." I tried to sit up again but flopped back on the floor, Sol's hand cushioning the blow. "I need to get back to them."

"You need to look after yourself. The scarecrows will be okay. We'll get them calm." He stroked my hair off my forehead. "I'm worried about you. I should take you to the hospital."

"No, I don't want to go there. I have to get back to the farm." I needed to find Brodie and figure out what happened to him. It must be something bad if he'd abandoned me.

"Have you got healing magic at home?" Sol said.

"Sure. You know what I've got. I always have things on hand in case either of us get injured."

"Then I'm taking you there. I'll carry you."

"Once I'm on my feet, I'll be fine to walk. And if not, Fire Fang will let me ride him."

Fire Fang grumbled as if not sure he would let me do that.

"No arguing. You're injured, frozen, and your lips are blue. And where is Brodie? Why isn't he helping you?"

"Um... he was helping. He was here. Something happened."

Sol's expression hardened. "Put your arms around my neck. I'll take us home."

I was too weary to protest and looped my arms around Sol's neck. He scooped an arm under my legs and lifted me effortlessly.

Fire Fang growled but stepped back and allowed Sol to help.

"Sorry," I whispered to my ancestors. "I hope you can forgive me."

The stones faintly rumbled.

"Oh, wait! I need my purse. It's at the back of the cemetery," I said.

"Fire Fang, go get it," Sol said. "I don't want any delays in getting Odessa safely home."

Without a second of hesitation, Fire Fang loped away and met us at the gate a moment later with my purse. He also had several sausages sticking out one corner of his huge mouth.

Sol took the purse and tucked it under my arm. "Go home to Storm. And thanks for looking after Odessa."

"Yes, thanks, Fire Fang. I'll get you a big treat for this."

He turned and headed back into the cemetery, no doubt planning to finish off the rest of the long abandoned picnic food.

Sol strode away, his pace brisk as we headed to my farm. "Are you going to tell me what's going on?"

"I'm not sure what happened. Or where to start." The movement made me queasy, so I clung on tight.

"This has to do with Brodie, though?"

"It does. He had an idea about how to stay stable so he can use his new vessel."

"The human-like scarecrow, you mean?"

"Yes."

Sol was quiet for a moment. "You'll need powerful magic to make that work."

"I will. I'm planning on taking it from my ancestors. The magic was stable when I tried it. At least, it was stable until Brodie made contact before

I was ready to pass it on. There was an explosion and then... nothing. I must have passed out."

"Odessa, that was dangerous."

"I can handle it."

"Even a witch as powerful as you has limits. If all your ancestors channeled their magic at the same time, it must have overloaded your system."

"I felt in control. Well, most of the time." I adjusted my grip around Sol's neck, getting a whiff of his apple wood scent. "I'm worried I hurt Brodie, though. When I woke, he was nowhere to be seen. What if he's gone?" I didn't hide the tears trickling down my cheeks.

"He won't have left you. Not if he has any sense."

"That's no comfort. Something terrible could have happened to him. What if my magic destroyed him?"

"You wouldn't do that."

"Not deliberately. But..."

"You lost control?"

I sniffed. "Yes."

"This guy has your heart, and you want him back so badly, you'd never destroy everything you worked so hard for. You're willing to sacrifice everything to keep Brodie."

"It's not a sacrifice. Not when you love someone."

He sighed. "Odessa, you deserve so much more than what's lurking in the past."

"It's not my past. Not anymore. Brodie's back, and he's my present. It's where I knew he'd end up. We can build the rest of our lives together." I swallowed back more tears. "That's if I haven't ruined everything."

"This isn't your fault. Brodie was wrong to take the magic before you were ready. Did he even ask if he could make the connection to your ancestors' magic?"

"No, but he was excited. He just wanted to get back to me."

"Brodie should know better than to mess with such powerful magic."

"He didn't mean any harm. He got carried away."

"And look what happened to you." Sol shook his head. "You need to hold off from using your ancestors' magic to bring Brodie back until you've properly tested it without him interfering."

"I don't have time."

"If you keep taking these risks, it'll kill you. I can feel how fast your heart is racing. You're under too much strain."

I chewed on my bottom lip. "Brodie is talking about crossing over. I need to give him an excellent reason to stay."

"You're the excellent reason. And if he's telling you you're not a good enough reason to hold on to until you make things perfect, then he's the wrong guy for you."

"It's not that." It kind of was exactly that. Brodie had pushed me to test the link. Had he set up the picnic in the cemetery just so he could try the magic?

"He shouldn't be pushing you. He's kept you waiting for over three years, so a few weeks of testing while you make everything right shouldn't be a struggle for him."

I leaned my head against Sol's shoulder. "I just want my happily ever after. It's all I've ever dreamed about."

"I know. You want your fairy tale ending with Brodie. No one else will do."

"I... That's what I always thought I wanted."

"Sometimes, what you think you want is not what you need. How about changing your dream? You never know, you might find an even better ending."

"An ending with you?" I whispered.

"Would that be so terrible?"

I closed my eyes. "I'm sure it wouldn't. You're a great man, Sol. You've always been good to me."

"And I'll keep being good to you, even when you end up passed out in a cemetery after helping your dead boyfriend. Who, in my opinion, is a jerk and doesn't deserve you."

I kept my eyes closed, not wanting to fight with Sol. Where was Brodie? He had to be here.

We reached the driveway to the farm, and Sol walked along it.

"You said you'd dropped by to say goodbye," I said. "Are you leaving Witch Haven?"

"I figured it was best if I went. You'll soon have Brodie back. That's if you don't destroy yourself trying to help him. He can work on the farm with you."

"Maybe. Although he's not keen on staying, so you might not need to leave. We were talking about renting the farm for a year and trying somewhere new."

Sol looked down at me, surprise in his eyes. "You love this place, and all your friends are here.

The scarecrows would follow you anywhere, but if you're not running the farm, what would you do with them?"

"We were figuring it out. Brodie even suggested you might like to take on the farm."

Sol grunted. "I'll pass. There are too many memories here for me. It would be like living with my own ghosts, working here every day and not having you around."

"I told him it was a bad idea. But I don't know anyone else who can handle the farm like you. You're really leaving?"

"That was the plan. I was going tomorrow."

I wanted to tell Sol I'd miss him and didn't want him to go, but that was selfish. I'd made my decision, and I was sticking with Brodie.

The ground rumbled, and a few seconds later, we were surrounded by scarecrows.

Shamrock tried to grab me out of Sol's arms.

"Relax, everyone. Sol is looking after me. I had an accident, so he brought me home."

"And I need to get Odessa inside and get her full of healing magic," Sol said. "Everyone back off."

All the scarecrows took a step back but matched Sol's movements like they were stalking prey as we headed onto the porch.

I fished my keys out of my purse and handed them to Sol. He unlocked the door, and we headed inside. All the scarecrows bundled in, too.

Sol walked into the living room and settled me on the couch. "Don't move. I'll go get the healing magic."

The scarecrows crowded into the room, and each took a turn touching my head. When it was Shamrock's go, he tried to form a connection with me, but I could barely hear him, I was so weak.

"Something wrong?" he said.

"Just a problem with my magic. It's getting fixed."

"Someone do this to you?"

"No. It was an accident. Have any of you seen or sensed Brodie around here today?"

They all shook their heads.

I jumped as something thudded against the wall. "Brodie?"

There was no answer.

"I need you all to help me. Go search the farm and look for Brodie. You know what he feels like. I'm worried about him. I could have hurt him with my magic," I said.

"Don't want to leave you," Shamrock said. "You're vulnerable."

"I have Sol looking after me. I'm safe with him."

"And I'm right here. We have all the healing spells I could find." Sol brushed past the scarecrows and sat beside me. He uncorked a vial of healing magic and passed it to me. "Drink this, and then you need to rest."

I looked at my scarecrows. "You know what you need to do."

With reluctance, they left the room, leaving me with Sol.

His hand gently stroked across my forehead. "I was so scared when I saw you on the floor of the crypt. I thought you were dying."

"I'm made of strong stuff," I whispered. "Hey, have you seen Tuffin anywhere?"

"You're worrying about your cat at a time like this?"

"A bit. If I'd had her with me, I wouldn't have been so badly affected by that magic. We have a solid witch familiar bond. I could have made use of that."

"I haven't seen her. But then I've not been around much."

"Could you check her bowl in the kitchen? I left food in it this morning. If it's gone, I'll know she's been home."

"Sure. I'll get you something to drink, too. Could you handle anything to eat?"

I pressed my hand against my stomach and shook my head. "No, but a cup of strong, sweet tea would be amazing."

Sol stood and left the room. A second later, the air chilled, and Zohar appeared. His eyes were wide and his face set in a frown. "What's going on? Where have you been?"

"Hey, Zohar. Getting myself in trouble," I said. "How about you?"

"Worrying about you. And where's Brodie?"

I forced myself to focus on him, despite my eyes trying to close against my will. "He didn't come back here after this morning?"

"No! When I couldn't find either of you, I panicked. I thought you were going back on our deal."

"I'm still helping you. I thought Brodie explained that we'd planned a day off so we could figure things out." I wriggled around, trying to get comfortable and keep myself awake. "But there's lots I want to talk to you about."

"Oh, sure. I remember him saying something about that. I didn't expect you to be away for this long, though." Zohar flickered in and out of focus, although maybe that was my eyes misbehaving.

"I don't think that was the plan. Brodie definitely told you what we were doing?"

"Yeah, I just forgot. My memory is lousy." Zohar floated around the room. "You don't look so good. And your energy feels weird. Kind of drained but also wired."

"You can thank my ancestors for that. I'll be fine in the morning. I just need to rest." I closed my eyes. There was something I needed to speak to Zohar about, but my thoughts were a scramble.

"It might take more than a good night's sleep to fix you. And what's that guy doing in the kitchen?"

"That's Sol."

"Are you seeing him? Brodie won't like that. I get the impression he has a jealous streak."

"Not my Brodie. He can trust me." I yawned. "Sol works on the farm. He found me injured and helped me home. He's a good guy."

"I guess that's okay if he just works for you. But you don't want to make Brodie jealous. It might destabilize him. When we were talking, all he could focus on was getting back to you."

"He will get back to me. We're almost there."

Sol came in with a tray in his hands. He also had the suspect board. "You've been busy."

"Oh, yes. I tried to make a suspect board, but it's not half as good as yours. Any sign of Tuffin?"

"No. And the food is still there." Sol set down the tray. He handed me a mug of tea and then another healing spell. He settled on the edge of the couch and sipped his own coffee. "I can give you a hand with the board, if you like."

"If you don't mind. But you must have packing to do if you're getting ready to leave."

"Everything is done. And I'm not leaving until I know you're okay." Sol nodded over his mug. "Talk me through the suspects. I'll set everything up and make it easy to read. Unless you want to sleep."

"Don't sleep. Get my murder solved. If this guy can help, tell him everything," Zohar said.

I brushed him away. "Sure. I do need to solve this. And the ghost I'm helping is here. Zohar, meet Sol."

Zohar gestured at the board. "Hi. Now, get a move on."

I swiftly brought Sol up to speed on Zohar's death and all the suspects still in the frame.

After about half an hour, I was close to falling asleep again, and Sol was standing by the suspect board, looking over the details he'd added. "If I had to guess, I'd say Elsbeth did it. The fights, the money worries, the problem with having kids. It could have been too much for her, so she killed Zohar."

Zohar had hovered around as Sol worked on the board. "I'm beginning to think that, too. Although I hate the idea of my wife killing me."

"The problem with that is Elsbeth has an alibi. It's not perfect, but she'd have struggled to kill Zohar. He was a big guy."

"Her alibi is the smoothie bar, isn't it?" Sol said.

I stifled a yawn. "Yep."

Zohar shook his head. "That place. She was always going there, three or four times a week. I once teased her she'd get fat if she had too many smoothies. It didn't go down well."

"No kidding." I couldn't stop yawning. "And I like smoothies, but four a week might be too much."

"Why else would Elsbeth go there if not for the drinks?" Sol said.

I closed my eyes. "The serving guy was friendly and cute. Maybe he was the reason Elsbeth went to the smoothie bar so much."

"What are you suggesting?" Zohar said.

I forced my eyes open as an idea hit. "Elsbeth's alibi. What if it was faked? The guy working at the smoothie bar, Finn, said he liked her. He also mentioned Elsbeth wasn't happy at home. Could she have asked him to cover for her? Her alibi has holes in it, suggesting it was decided upon quickly. Maybe the reason the alibi is suspect is because it's not real."

"Why would Finn give Elsbeth an alibi?" Sol said. "He'd get in trouble if he got caught lying to the Magic Council."

"If they're more than just friends, he might do it," I said.

"No, Elsbeth wouldn't cheat. She was loyal, even though we were having trouble," Zohar said.

"I need to check out Finn again. He sounded genuine, but I should have dug deeper."

Zohar zoomed around the room. "Elsbeth wouldn't be unfaithful. But... I'm beginning to doubt every aspect of my life. What if she did cheat? We must find out."

I tried to sit, but Sol shook his head. "You have to rest. We've done enough for one day."

"No, Odessa should look into this. She could be onto something important." Zohar frowned as Sol almost walked through him and grabbed a throw off the back of a chair before tucking it around me.

"You need sleep." Sol sat next to me. "And use at least two more healing spells before you go anywhere."

"I'll be okay. Thanks, Sol. It's been helpful talking things over. With everything on the suspect board, it made me realize there could be more to Elsbeth's alibi than I'd first thought. Oh, and the wagon. Zohar, I have to ask you about that."

His gaze shot my way and then flicked to the wall. "Wagon?"

"Yes. The hidden wagon with the money and travel documents in a different name. What's going on?"

"Um... I need to go. I'll see you later." He vanished.

"Zohar! Wait. I have to find out why you're keeping secrets."

"Hey, Odessa." Sol brought my attention back to him. "I'm glad the suspect board helped, but you need time to heal. You've been through a trauma."

"But Zohar's not telling me everything. How can I solve his murder, if he's not being truthful?"

"We can figure that out tomorrow."

A sneaky yawn came out. "Before I rest, could you check on the scarecrows? See if they've found anything."

Sol sighed. "You sent them to look for Brodie, didn't you?"

"I did. I'm worried about him. And Zohar hasn't seen him, either. I have to know what went on at the cemetery."

"Fine. So long as you don't move from the couch. Or would you rather go up to bed?"

"The couch is great."

"You rest, I'll deal with the scarecrows, and then you can tackle the murder tomorrow."

"With you?"

Sol leaned down and kissed my forehead. "With me."

Within seconds, my eyes were closed, and I was lost to a deep, drugging sleep.

Chapter 17

Once my eyes had closed last night, they hadn't opened again until late the next morning.

I yawned and stretched, feeling much better after all those healing spells and a good night's sleep.

Shamrock and Marmaduke were standing guard in the living room doorway, but Shamrock bounded over the second I made a noise and loomed over me.

I waved him back a few steps. "I'm good. I survived the night. Where's Sol?"

Shamrock placed a hand over mine to form a connection. "Had to go. Said goodbye."

"Oh. Did Sol say he was going for good or that he'd be back?"

"Don't know. Told him to stay. Tried to force him."

"Shamrock, I hope you didn't hurt him. And I need to have a word with all of you. Sol hid the fact you've been mean to him. You've injured him."

"Not on purpose. He's weak."

"You're too strong. No more hurting Sol. He's a friend. A great friend. Tell everyone else not to injure him."

"Doesn't matter now. He's gone."

My heart gave an unhappy thump. I wasn't ready for Sol to be gone. We had so much we needed to say to each other, and I still hadn't figured out how to apologize for not keeping him in my life the way he wanted. Maybe there was no apology that would be good enough. I couldn't give Sol what he wanted, so the kindest thing to do was let him go.

"Did you find Brodie?" I said to Shamrock.

"Not here. Glad."

"Shamrock, that's not nice. He's staying for good. Well, hopefully. So long as I can find him and figure out what went wrong at the cemetery."

"Hope not. Sol better."

"Get used to the change. Sol has gone, and Brodie's back. And I need to get up and work on a murder. I have an alibi to double check." I looked at the perfect suspect board and smiled, but it was tinged with sadness. I could always rely on Sol when I needed something done right.

After shooing out the scarecrows, I took a long shower and dressed. I still felt tired but was much better than yesterday. But there was a faint whisper of sound in my head. It reminded me of my ancestors. I felt terrible about what happened. They were strong, independent women, and I'd potentially messed things up.

I ate a much needed late breakfast and drank a strong mug of coffee while listening to the whisper. Could it be their power inside me? Had I made our connection permanent?

As I headed into the living room, I found Zohar lurking by the suspect board. "Morning. Are you ready to grill Finn with me?"

He nodded. "Sure."

"Is everything good? You don't look like you're having a fun day."

"I'm dead. How am I supposed to look? I'm not waving the flags because I'm no longer breathing."

"Zohar, don't give up. We're making progress."

"Slow progress. You're supposed to be helping me."

I crossed my arms over my chest. "I needed a time out. Almost dying will do that to a girl."

"Try actually dying." He winced. "Sorry, I'm frustrated. You're doing a great job. Better than the lazy Magic Council."

I walked over to him. "I get it. We all have off days. Yesterday was one of mine. Let's get out of here and rough up a suspect."

His eyebrows flashed up. "We're really going to do that?"

"Nope, but I thought it might sound more interesting to you."

We left the farmhouse and headed to the smoothie bar.

"You still think Elsbeth cheated on me?" Zohar said.

"Let's keep all the options open. It would be a solid motive for your murder if they were seeing each other behind your back."

Zohar didn't speak for the rest of the walk. I felt sorry for the guy, but we couldn't look away from this possibility because it was uncomfortable.

There was hardly anyone in the smoothie bar when we arrived, and Finn was reading a book. He put in a page marker and placed the book down as I approached the counter with Zohar.

"Hey, you're back again. Did you get hooked on my smoothies, or was it my adorable smile?" He winked at me.

"Sadly, I'm not here for a smoothie or a smile." My gaze shifted to the heap of dark chocolate brownies behind the counter. I could smell the warm chocolate and sugar.

Finn chuckled. "Are you sure I can't tempt you?"

I dragged my gaze from the chocolate temptations. "I wanted to talk to you about Elsbeth again."

"Sure. There's not much else going on. It's the slump before the lunchtime rush. What do you need to know?"

"Would you consider Elsbeth a good friend?" I leaned against the counter and studied his expression.

"I wouldn't say we were friends. She's a great customer, though. And as I said, always generous with the tips. I like to give good tippers my extra special attention. You know, a free upgrade on a smoothie or a taster sample of brownies. It makes sense to keep the best customers on side and give them incentives to come back and fill the tips jar."

"Is that the only reason Elsbeth comes by several times a week?"

"Sure. What other reason would there be?"

A group of half a dozen women came through the door and settled at a table.

"Give me a minute," Finn said. "I'll be right back." He gathered up menus and hurried to the table.

Zohar drifted to my side. "This isn't getting us anywhere. That guy's too young for Elsbeth. She likes older guys."

"I have to make sure Elsbeth's alibi is legit. It's patchy. What if she lied to us?" I kept my voice low, since I didn't want to look like I was talking to myself.

I turned over the book Finn was reading. The title was: *How to manifest your best life with positive thinking*. I flipped open a few pages and the page marker fell out. I grabbed it and stared at it. It was an ultrasound of a baby.

Finn rushed over and grabbed the picture. His sunny disposition had vanished, and perspiration blossomed on his forehead. "You shouldn't have seen that."

"Why not?"

"You just shouldn't." He tucked the picture away.

"Who's the lucky lady?"

"It's... it's a friend's scan. She thought I'd like to see the baby."

"Are you broody?"

"No! I mean, maybe. I... it's not important. Forget you saw it."

Now I was interested. No one sweated and stammered that much unless they had something to hide. "Which friend?"

"You don't know her. She's not from around here." Finn placed a glass on the counter. "Let me get you a smoothie on the house. Then we can talk about Elsbeth."

I pointed at the ultrasound picture in Finn's pocket. "I think we already are."

He clattered ice into a blender. "The triple mocha chai ginger blend is amazing with oat vanilla ice cream."

"No, thanks." I tapped the counter to get his attention. "I can find out who the scan belongs to. I'll give it to someone at the Magic Council, and they'll contact the hospital. They'll tell them whose baby it is."

Finn tossed a banana and some strawberries into the blender then stopped. He rested his hands flat on the counter and dropped his head. "Don't do that."

"Then tell me who the mother of this baby is."

He kept his head lowered. "It's Elsbeth's baby."

Zohar made a choking sound. "That's not possible. We can't... I mean, I can't. No!"

"Does that mean you and Elsbeth are more than friends? Since you have this picture, it suggests you have a connection to the baby, too," I said.

Finn pulled out the picture and looked at it, a smile on his face. "It's mine. I'm going to be a dad."

"I don't believe I'm hearing this," Zohar said. "Elsbeth was unfaithful to me."

I gestured him to be quiet. "How long has the affair been going on?"

"Almost a year. I met Elsbeth after she moved to Witch Haven, and we clicked. She's funny and pretty, and I wasn't lying about the tips. To begin with, we were friends who flirted. I knew she was married, so I never took it seriously. I don't make a habit of stealing other men's wives."

"I'd like to see him try." Zohar swirled away but soon whizzed back, his angry glare focused on Finn.

"What changed between you?" I said.

"Elsbeth came in one day, and it was obvious she'd been crying. Her eyes were red, and she ordered three giant sharing brownies and ate them all herself. We got talking, and she stayed after the place closed. I realized then that I really liked her. Like, a lot. Things progressed quickly after that."

"I'm going to kill this guy." Zohar lunged at Finn, but I grabbed him, twirled him in a restraining spell, and yanked him close to my side so he couldn't touch Finn.

"Err... is everything okay? What did you just do?" Finn said.

"Kept you safe." I shot a warning look at Zohar. "Does the Magic Council know about your relationship with Elsbeth?"

Finn's gaze flicked around. "No way. And we had no plans to tell them. We both realize how bad this looks. I'm having an affair with the woman whose husband is dead. Of course, if the Magic Council found out, I'd be the prime suspect."

"Or Elsbeth. She's my prime suspect. Be honest with me, are you covering for her? Did she ask you to give her an alibi for the morning of Zohar's death?"

Zohar growled and twisted in my restraining spell. "Let me at him. He seduced my wife. He's the reason we were unhappy."

"I shouldn't say anything," Finn said.

Zohar almost broke free of my spell. I yanked him close and held on tight to stop him from getting away. "Give me a minute. I have a problem to deal with. While I'm gone, you think about what you want to keep a secret and how honest you need to be. It could get you off the suspect list for murder."

Finn backed away. "Err... sure."

I pulled Zohar outside and slammed him against the wall. "Calm down. I need to talk to Finn without you messing things up. This is a crucial piece of the puzzle."

"I don't care. It's all his fault. I'd have been happy with Elsbeth if it weren't for him."

"Is that true? It sounds like you and Elsbeth were struggling before you came to Witch Haven. I don't agree with Elsbeth cheating on you, but that's not the only reason things went wrong in your marriage."

"It is! What else could it be?"

"I'll get to that. But first, I need to find out if Elsbeth lied about her alibi. Will you behave if you come back inside, or do I have to bind you in a spell and leave you out here?"

He grunted several unintelligible words then nodded. "I'll behave."

I headed back into the smoothie bar, with Zohar behind me. Finn was serving the table of women, but as soon as he saw me, he hurried back.

"So, Elsbeth's alibi?" I said.

Finn clutched a menu. "She didn't do it."

"I'm sure you want to believe that, since you're involved with her."

"It does make me biased, but Elsbeth is sweet and kind, and she's pregnant with my baby. She wouldn't do anything to put the baby at risk. She's wanted kids for a long time."

"Finn, did she ask you to lie for her?"

He rearranged empty glasses in front of him and folded several paper napkins. "She called me in a panic and begged me to cover for her. She said she'd gone to the house after an argument with Zohar and found him dead. Elsbeth freaked. Everyone knew they were having troubles."

"She found Zohar's body?" I said.

"That's what she told me, and she sounded terrified. I told her to get out of there. Leave the house and come here. I knew how bad things would look if she had no one to confirm where she was."

"Elsbeth specifically asked you to cover for her, or did you say you'd help?"

He lifted his chin. "She asked. And I'd do it again, because she's no killer. And she so desperately wants this baby that she wouldn't have done anything to risk it. If things had gotten physical between them, she'd have run, more to save the baby than herself. This child means the world to her. Me, too."

"Elsbeth could have used her magic to kill Zohar and move his body," I said. "Have you considered that?"

"She's got magic, sure, but ever since Elsbeth got pregnant, it hasn't worked. It's what alerted her she might be pregnant. Apparently, the same thing happened to her auntie when she was pregnant. She barely uses any spells because they backfire. Elsbeth even went to the doctor about it, but he told her not to worry. He said it was because hormones were changing, and things would settle as the pregnancy progresses."

That was convenient. But if it was true, it ruled out Elsbeth.

"Did Elsbeth ever talk about getting rid of Zohar for good?" I said.

"No, but she told me she wanted a divorce. She'd even spoken to Zohar about it, but he said he'd only divorce her if she gave him the money from the crystal jackpot."

"Really?" I glared at Zohar, but he refused to look at me.

"Elsbeth was even considering it, because she was so done with the relationship."

"Lies!" Zohar smashed into a row of chairs, sending them clattering to the floor. He swooped around the table of ladies enjoying their smoothies, making them shriek and spill their drinks.

"What's going on? There's something else here, isn't there? I could sense the vibe was off." Finn backed away.

I ducked as a chair almost hit me. "I should have mentioned Zohar's ghost is here. He heard everything you just said."

A row of glasses smashed to the floor as Zohar whirled around in a rage, making the place freezing.

"Zohar's here?" Finn ducked behind the counter.

"He can't cross over because he was murdered. And he's not happy about Elsbeth keeping secrets." Although they'd both been keeping things from me. Zohar hadn't mentioned a conversation about a divorce with Elsbeth, or his infertility, or the wagon. This couple was full of secrets and lies.

"Get him out of here," Finn said. "He's ruining the place."

"I'll ruin you," Zohar growled as he swooped over the counter. "You destroyed my marriage."

"That's enough!" I grabbed Zohar in another restraining spell and hauled him out of the smoothie bar.

He shoved into me and sent me sprawling to the ground. I rolled over and threw out a stronger restraining spell, trapping Zohar so he could barely move. I reeled him in like a line caught mermaid and grabbed hold of his arms.

"Congratulations. You just demonstrated why your wife wanted you dead. Control your temper."

Zohar bared his teeth. Then the fight drained out of him, and he slumped forward. "I'm sorry. But I got so angry when I heard Elsbeth cheated. All this time, I was trying to save our marriage, and she couldn't be bothered. She went with another guy."

I kept the spell in place. "You've been fighting for something that ended a while ago. Neither of you have been happy in the marriage, have you?"

"No. But I didn't want to give up."

"Maybe you should have accepted it and moved on."

"Why didn't she divorce me? Why cheat?"

"You know the reason for that. Is it true you wanted the money from the crystal jackpot win in exchange for a divorce?"

Zohar looked away and shrugged. "That was between me and Elsbeth. She wanted out, and I wanted proper compensation. I didn't want to be a divorcee. It gives a guy a stigma, you know, like he doesn't know how to keep a woman happy."

"Better that than stay in a miserable marriage. And if you'd taken the money, Elsbeth would have been left with nothing. That wasn't fair. She must have been feeling trapped and desperate."

"Desperate enough to kill me."

I nodded slowly. "Maybe. And Elsbeth has no alibi. She got Finn to cover for her. Although it's strange she claims to have seen your body."

"She's lying. That's all she does. She killed me then made out someone else did it."

"Maybe she said that so Finn wouldn't think she was guilty. He might feel differently about her if he knew he was covering for a murderer."

Zohar groaned. "She really did it. I don't remember seeing her just before I died."

"Do you remember fighting with Elsbeth that morning?"

"Vaguely. My memories are muddled. We fought a lot."

"You do remember her asking for a divorce, though?"

He nodded. "She did. But I wasn't willing to let Elsbeth go. I didn't want the relationship to end. I only ever wanted to marry once. I loved Elsbeth. I still do. If I could have fixed things, then I would. But it seems Elsbeth checked out a long time ago."

"Hold on to those thoughts, and there's more we need to discuss. But first, I have to call this in to the Magic Council. Don't go anywhere near that door." I jabbed a finger at the entrance to the smoothie bar.

"Sure. I'll stay here."

I put in a quick call to Olympus and told him what I'd discovered then returned to Zohar. "Someone from the Magic Council is coming. They'll get a statement from Finn and then arrest Elsbeth."

Zohar's form flickered in and out of focus. "We had our problems, but I didn't realize she'd become so unhappy. I overlooked Elsbeth's flaws, but she couldn't do the same with me. Was I so bad that I deserved to die?"

"No, but you were both unhappy. And from everything I've heard, you weren't a perfect guy. You had a temper and kept your infertility a secret from Elsbeth. Is it any wonder she was miserable?"

"I thought I'd fix that problem. There were still doctors I planned to visit. I knew, eventually, I'd give Elsbeth what she wanted."

"Really? Or were you holding onto a lie? A baby won't fix a failing marriage."

"I was willing to try anything."

"It's the worst idea to have a child when your marriage is struggling."

He heaved out a sigh. "You're right. I even talked to Elsbeth about adoption, but everything was so unstable between us that it felt wrong to bring a child into a troubled home. It was a stupid thing to try."

"Not stupid. You were worried about your marriage and wanted to make things right."

"You see. I am a good guy."

The air around us heated, and a second later, Olympus materialized.

He nodded at me. "I sent a team to the house. They're bringing Elsbeth into custody. I'll get Finn's new statement and then join them. Is everything okay with you and Zohar?"

"It will be. Zohar will be ready to move on soon."

Zohar's shoulders slumped. "I don't feel ready. I just feel sad."

Olympus headed into the smoothie bar to speak to Finn.

"Let's get out of here," I said. "I've solved your murder, but we still have unfinished business to deal with."

"What's that?"

"Help me with Brodie."

Chapter 18

I'd given Zohar space all morning, so he could come to terms with the discovery Elsbeth had killed him. But I'd clock watched the whole time. I needed Zohar's head in the game to help with Brodie. I hadn't seen him since the incident in the cemetery and was almost tearing my hair out with worry.

I had so many concerning possibilities running through my head about what happened to him. I needed Brodie back. He wasn't gone for good. There'd be an explanation for his absence.

I headed outside and over to the barn where I'd last seen Zohar. He was still drifting around it, looking sad. "How's it going?"

"I've been better."

"Shall we focus on Brodie? It'll take your mind off Elsbeth. And I'm getting worried about him."

He waved a hand at me. "You should be."

"Why? What do you know?"

"I saw him an hour ago. He's angry with you."

"With me?"

Zohar nodded. "What did you do to him?"

"Nothing! You should have told me he was back. Is he okay? I've been terrified I did something bad to him."

"It looks like you did."

"What did he say?"

"He's disappointed in you."

"What? That makes no sense. He's okay, though?"

"Just annoyed. Brodie said you failed him."

My jaw dropped. "I don't understand. Failed him how?"

"He didn't say much, and he was only here for a few minutes, but he said something about a magic link going wrong. You took back the magic too soon, something like that. I wasn't really listening because I was thinking about Elsbeth. What will happen to her?"

"She'll be questioned and charged." I shook my head to try to make sense of everything Zohar had told me. "I didn't take anything back. Brodie connected with me before I was ready to give him the magic. It wasn't my fault it went wrong. What else did he say?"

"Not much. Oh, Brodie did say he wondered if he'd made a mistake coming back. You're not the witch for him."

My stomach dropped to the ground, and I rested a hand on the barn as a wave of dizziness hit. "That doesn't sound like Brodie. Are you sure you heard him right?"

"Not for definite. Like I said, I've had a lot to process. My afterlife has imploded, thanks to my cheating wife."

"You must have misheard." Brodie was never moody or difficult when he'd been alive. Maybe he'd changed since becoming a ghost. Change happened to us all, and ghosts who'd been around a long time could become despondent and lose hope.

Guilt punched into me. This was my fault. Had Brodie become jaded because he'd been a ghost for too long? I should have worked harder to find him. I needed to get him back with me as soon as possible, so I could show him how incredible the world was and how much fun we'd have once he was back.

"Is Brodie around now?" I said. "Can you go get him? I need to make this right."

"I haven't seen him for a while. Maybe he won't come back."

"Please, I need him here."

"You should leave Brodie alone."

"I can't. Leaving him on his own is making things worse."

"He wanted you to know..."

"What? Is it important? What do I need to know?"

Zohar's mouth twisted to the side. "He said he's seeing the tunnel of light again."

"No! Tell him not to go. Go get him. Stop him!" I reached for Zohar to give him a shake, but his form wasn't solid, and my fingers slid through his arm. He looked like he'd been drained.

"I can try to stop him." Zohar hesitated, not seeming keen to move.

"Are you okay?" I forced down my panic and focused on him. "Are you seeing the light, too?"

"I'm seeing nothing but a gray, bleak future. My wife's a cheater and a killer. It's shameful."

"That's all?"

Zohar looked away. "What else would it be? Hey, what do you need to do to get Brodie back for good?"

"Strong, stable magic. I'll use it to keep his vessel animated and ensure his ghost can safely live in it. Why?" I walked slowly back to the farmhouse.

"Just curious. Brodie talks about it a lot."

"We're excited to get it right. But to do that, he needs to come back."

"What magic are you using?"

"My ancestors' reanimation magic." I stepped in front of Zohar, so I had his full attention. "Brodie is still excited about this, isn't he?"

"I wouldn't say excited. The guy was complaining when I saw him." Zohar shrugged and looked around before whizzing close. "Are you sure he's the right one for you?"

I moved back. "Yes, I'm certain. Brodie's just having a bad day. Maybe he got spooked because we tried the connection and it didn't work. And I got injured, too. He must not want to risk me trying again."

"Brodie mentioned that." Zohar held my gaze and ducked his head by my ear. "You're certain he's the one for you?"

"I... yes. Why do you keep asking?"

"No reason." He drifted away. "I wondered if you were having relationship problems, just like me."

"Has Brodie changed his mind about coming back to me?" I said, more to myself than Zohar.

"I mean, maybe. The guy's always saying he loves you, though. At least, he tells me he does. But being a ghost isn't simple. I struggle, and I've only been doing this a short time. I can't imagine what it must be like being stuck as a ghost for years and not knowing what's going on."

"Brodie is struggling, isn't he?" Guilt burrowed deeper into me.

"He's struggling with something. I don't know what I'd have done if I hadn't found you to help me." Zohar smiled at me. "You're a sweet witch, Odessa, and you deserve the best. Even though I'm not happy to learn Elsbeth killed me, at least I know the truth. It gives me a kind of bittersweet closure."

"Thanks, Zohar. I'm being too hard on Brodie, aren't I? I can't imagine what he must have gone through. His sudden death then not being able to cling to the memories that kept me going while I looked for him. He's been through so much pain and worry. I keep expecting him to be the same guy I knew. But, of course, that's impossible."

"It's amazing Brodie stayed together all these years. He's a strong ghost. Like, really strong. Weirdly strong."

"I'll try harder to get him back, and we can rebuild everything and adjust to what's changed." I looked around the yard before heading up the porch steps. "I really need to talk to him. I have to make sure he's doing okay."

"I wish I could help, but Brodie's not around. I could go look for him, if you like. I don't want to annoy him, though."

"Please, check in on him. I need Brodie here so I can test the magic link." My phone rang, and I answered it when I saw the caller was Olympus. "Hey, how's everything going?"

"Not great. We've run into a few problems with Elsbeth's arrest."

I gestured Zohar over so he could listen in. "What's the problem?"

"We took Elsbeth into custody and questioned her about her fake alibi. She admitted she got Finn to lie for her."

"That's good news."

"Yes, but she said she panicked after finding Zohar's body at the house. She was too scared to go inside in case the killer was there, so she phoned Finn, got herself an alibi, and fled."

"Do you believe her?"

"I'm wavering. And Elsbeth won't admit to killing Zohar and moving the body. She keeps saying she didn't do it. She admits to panicking and getting a fake alibi but not the actual murder. And there's another problem."

"Which is?"

"That wagon you found hidden in the trees."

"What about it?"

"There's no evidence Elsbeth has ever been inside. There are no fibers or prints that link to her. Nothing to connect her to it."

"Maybe she wiped it clean."

"No. It's not been wiped down. My team did a thorough search and found plenty of other prints and evidence of use but not by Elsbeth."

"How did Zohar's pendant get in there, then? I wondered if they'd fought and it fell off."

"If it did, Elsbeth miraculously concealed the fact she'd ever been there."

"Okay, but that doesn't mean she's innocent. I can't explain what you found in the wagon, but she faked an alibi. She was at the house right around the time Zohar was killed."

"That's true. And she also confirmed she lied about how bad things were with Zohar. She desperately wanted children, and when she had a happy accident with Finn, Elsbeth decided things needed to change. She refused to stay in a marriage that couldn't give her what she wanted."

"So Elsbeth killed Zohar to get free of him and keep the money so she could raise her child with Finn?"

"It's a theory. And Finn is sticking by her."

Zohar scowled and shook his head. "It's so unfair. I would have eventually given her a baby. She didn't have to shack up with someone half her age. Maybe Finn helped her kill me."

"Have you checked Finn's alibi?" I said to Olympus.

"He was at the smoothie bar at the time of the murder. His boss confirms it, and we checked his phone records. He got a call from Elsbeth that morning. It was when he was at work. He couldn't have been involved with killing Zohar or moving his body."

"Neither could Elsbeth. Finn told me she has been having trouble with her magic, so she couldn't have used it to move Zohar after she killed him."

"If she killed him," Olympus said. "And we tested her magic. It's not stable."

I blew out a breath. "Those are some serious problems. And if Elsbeth didn't use magic, she'd have been seen by her neighbors. There's that nosy one who knows everything about Zohar and Elsbeth's movements, so she wouldn't have been able to sneak past him. He even saw her driving away that morning."

Neither of us spoke for several seconds.

I tipped back my head. "This isn't adding up. Some of it fits, but not all. Has the autopsy been done? Is that any help?"

"Yes, and we got nothing from Zohar's body. It was a dead end."

I chewed on my lip. "Do you think Elsbeth is innocent?"

"We're going over the evidence again. You should do the same, too. Elsbeth seems guilty, but there are too many factors making me doubt her guilt."

"Sure, I'll do that. Anything that can help." We said our goodbyes, and I shut off the phone.

"Elsbeth didn't do it?" There was a hopeful note in Zohar's voice.

"Maybe she is innocent." I headed back inside, stood in front of the suspect board, and looked everything over. "There's something we're missing. You were killed at the house, but your body was found in the lake. Somewhere along the way, you were also in the wagon you decided not to tell me about. Something you still haven't explained."

Zohar looked over his shoulder. "Um—"

"No! Don't you dare vanish on me again. No more secrets."

He sighed. "I didn't tell you because it's not important."

"Were you planning on leaving?"

Zohar didn't say anything for a long time. "I was desperate. I wasn't planning on going forever, but I thought if I left for a while, Elsbeth would realize what she was missing out on. She'd see how important the marriage was and give it another go. I'd never have bothered if I'd known she was cheating. I'd have filed for divorce and gotten everything."

"Or you could have let Elsbeth go so she could be happy with another man. She was finally having the family she's always dreamt of. She didn't go about getting it the right way, but neither did you. Threatening to take everything would have made her fearful for her baby's future."

"I never said I was perfect," Zohar said. "But I didn't deserve to be killed."

I studied the suspect board again. "You were leaving Elsbeth, though?"

"Yes, for a while."

"Under a fake name?"

"Only because everyone knows my name. I'm part of the crystal jackpot winning couple. I needed space to breathe, where no one would bother me. It seemed the easiest way to go about it."

I kept inspecting the board. We needed help with this puzzle. I scrolled through the contacts on my phone and stopped at Sol's name. Here was another puzzle I needed to figure out.

I called his number, using the pretense of the murder to speak to him. When it went to voicemail,

I hung up, not sure what I wanted to say. Instead, I sent a message. *Need my murder solving buddy back. Are you still around? And thanks for looking after me. Again.*

That felt inadequate, and I was about to redial, when the room grew cold, and Brodie appeared.

My heart skipped a beat. "You're back."

He grinned at me. "I am. Are you ready to have me back for good, babe?"

Chapter 19

I raced over and embraced him, not minding the freezing chill. "Of course. I was so scared when you vanished from the cemetery. Where did you go? What happened to you? Was it my fault?"

He stroked a hand down my hair and chuckled. "All these questions."

"And you need to answer them. I've been so worried. I didn't mean for you to connect to the magic so quickly. I wasn't ready to pass it on to you."

"Yeah, I figured that out when it went wrong." His smile slipped.

"I didn't mean to fail, but you could have given me some warning." I stepped out of his chilly embrace. "That was supposed to be a test. Not an attempt to get you back."

He sighed and drifted away from me. "I know. I'm so sorry. I got overwhelmed. I've been so frustrated being stuck as a ghost and not knowing where you were or what to do. I'm scared as well."

"Scared of what?"

"This will fail, and I'll be drawn into the light. I can't bear the thought of being without you." Brodie floated closer and pressed an icy kiss against my lips. "I want to do that properly, without making your teeth chatter."

"And we will, really soon. But I need to recharge my magic before we try again."

"You don't. You're my all-powerful super witch. And I've been working on the vessel. I think it's ready."

"You have?" I tilted my head. "Wait! You were here all this time?"

"Yeah, in and out. I wanted to get things right, so the next time we tried, it worked."

"You weren't injured? You came here to work on your vessel right away?"

"Pretty much."

"But... you should have come to see me. And you left me in the cemetery after the magic went wrong. I was there for hours. I woke in the dark, and it was freezing cold. I got scared."

"Oh, well, I didn't come back here right away," Brodie said.

I narrowed my eyes. "So what happened? You touched me, the magic flipped out, and that's the last thing I remember. What did you do after that?"

"I don't remember much." He drifted away, nodding at Zohar, who hovered by the door, looking like he wanted to flee. "I was excited about testing the link, so I grabbed your hand, and then there was an explosion."

"Yes, and I collapsed. Didn't you think about going to get help for me?"

"I didn't know you were hurt. And I lost track of time. The magic blasted me away. I scattered."

"Where? Why couldn't you come back when you got whole? You should have checked the cemetery, not hid here tinkering with your vessel."

"Sorry, I should have tried harder. I'll do better. But you're never alone for long. You have all those scarecrows looking out for you."

My hands clenched. "We're supposed to be in this together. Why do I suddenly feel more alone than ever?"

"Because you're stressed. Babe, I had to get my vessel right. Time's running out for me, and I can't lose you. If the vessel doesn't work, we could have the most powerful magic in the world, and it won't matter."

I wasn't buying this. "Brodie, what's going on? You do want to be back with me, don't you?"

"Absolutely. It's all I've ever wanted. Why do you think I've stuck around all this time?"

I nodded but still wasn't happy. If the roles had been reversed, and he'd been injured, I'd have moved heaven and earth to get back to him. It sounded like Brodie hadn't been that bothered to find out if I'd survived or not.

"Babe, I really am sorry. I'm struggling to keep my thoughts in order. The more time I spend with you, the more I feel myself shifting. And I'm so done with being a ghost. I want back with you full time. I want the magic link to work and my vessel to be stable so we can be together. I know you want that, too." He reached forward and caught hold of my hand.

"I do." I let some of my frustration go as I breathed out slowly. "Sorry, it's been a rough couple of days.

I thought we'd solved Zohar's murder, but now I'm not so sure." I glanced at the suspect board.

"Zohar doesn't mind waiting a bit longer, do you, buddy?" Brodie said.

Zohar didn't meet Brodie's gaze. "I guess not. In a way, I'll be glad if it wasn't Elsbeth who killed me."

"Most of the clues still point to Elsbeth being your killer." Although I was also having doubts about her guilt. "Brodie, give me a day to recharge. I can work on Zohar's mystery, and then we can try the link again. But slower this time. And no grabbing the magic until I say so."

Brodie shook his head. "There's no need to wait. Come see what I've done to the vessel. You'll love it."

I didn't move. "Where are you getting all the energy to manipulate this vessel?"

"I've been taking it from you. And Zohar," Brodie said. "I didn't think you'd mind. And I got a huge jolt of power when I connected with your ancestors. Those ladies were awesomely strong. I wish I'd known them when they were alive."

"So do I. And I don't mind you using my energy. Although it makes sense now why I've been feeling so tired."

"The sooner I get in that vessel, the better. I'll be tapped into all the Grimsbane magic, so you won't get drained so easily." He tugged me to the door. "How about we get the rest of our lives together started?"

Although I was still angry with Brodie, my heart melted a little. It was everything I wanted to hear. "Sure. Let's go take a look."

We walked out onto the porch, and I was surprised not to see a single scarecrow. They must be keeping themselves busy and, hopefully, out of trouble. We reached the end barn, and the doors were wide open.

"Brodie, we still need to keep this a secret. The Magic Council won't be understanding if they discover what we're attempting to do."

"They'll be impressed. Why hide your power?"

"To stop the farm from being shut for good. They think the scarecrows are dangerous. Until we get this magic absolutely right, we need to keep this between the two of us."

"Where's the fun in that? I've been a ghost for over three years. When I'm in the vessel, we're going out to celebrate."

"And we will but not right away. We have to take our time and get this right. And we need to figure out how to tell everyone about what's been going on."

"Babe, you used to be so much fun." Brodie jiggled my arms and tried to charm me with a smile.

"This isn't about fun. This is about making sure I keep the farm, you, and my scarecrows. That'll take careful negotiation, and I need to make sure the Magic Council is on our side."

"I won't let them stand in our way of being happy. We deserve this. You deserve this. Come inside. And prepare to be impressed."

Brodie didn't seem to realize how risky this was. But all thoughts of cautioning him left my head as I saw the enormous scarecrow in front of me.

"He's impressive, isn't he?" Pride traced through Brodie's tone.

I slowly circled the scarecrow. Although it had elements of my original design, it was bigger, taller, and magic pulsed out of it in uneven waves. "How long have you been working on him?"

"Just now and again, when I had free time. I tweaked your original design."

"Tweaked! I wanted your vessel to look human, so you'd blend in." I had to crane my neck back to see the scarecrow's eyes. This design was the opposite of blending in.

"Why blend in when I'll be so powerful? We can become the power couple of Witch Haven. We'll be unstoppable."

"Why would we need to be that? We won't have anyone after us. Well, maybe the Magic Council. Everyone will simply be happy to see you back in whatever form you take. But this..." I waved at the scarecrow.

"He makes a statement."

Looking at the scarecrow, I wasn't sure what statement Brodie wanted to achieve. "This'll need a lot more magic to keep it stable. Something smaller—"

"This will work. I got a taste of the power coming from your ancestors, and you're connected to it now. You can feel it inside you."

"I... I can. How do you know that?"

"Because we're connected. When I touched you, our magic joined. This is the way it's supposed to be. It's the only way you can get me back." Brodie's expression darkened. "And why shouldn't I get a say in how I look? I want something strong that'll support me forever."

I studied the scarecrow carefully, testing the magic and stabilizing it as I pulsed power into it. "I mean, if this is what you really want. But it'll take some getting used to."

"It'll still be me. And sure, I made improvements, but nothing else has changed."

I inspected the scarecrow's arms. They were bulky, and there was something flat and hard on the underside. I pressed it and a blade shot out. I leaped back and tripped over a bundle of hay.

Brodie chuckled as he helped me to my feet. "I thought you'd like that."

"Not really. Why would you add weapons to your scarecrow? You don't need the blades. You'll have magic."

"It pays to be prepared."

My mouth twisted as I stepped away. "Brodie, I'm not sure this is a good idea."

He drifted closer and wrapped his arms around me. "I know this is scary. It's terrifying me, too. I want to make sure we get this right, though. I don't want my vessel to break down in a few years or be vulnerable to attack."

"Why would anyone attack you?"

"Remember what happened at the mine? If I'd been stronger and faster and able to fight better, I'd still be with you. Instead, I was killed because of the trolls' greed. That's never happening again. When I'm back, I'll be strong, so I can protect us both."

My heart went out to him. "You make it sound like we're going into battle."

"And you sound like you don't understand me." Brodie moved away. "I'm different. I've been through a traumatic experience."

I hurried after him. "Of course, you have. And I'm trying to understand. It must have been terrifying when you were in the mine and there was nothing you could do."

He looked over his shoulder at me, and there was bitterness in his eyes. "I didn't die straightaway. I lingered for hours. Both my legs were broken. I tried to get out, but..."

"Oh, Brodie. I never knew about your injuries. I always hoped it was quick, so you didn't suffer."

The bitter look remained on his face. "There were times when I wondered if you even bothered to find me."

I caught hold of his hands. "Brodie, I never stopped. And I know, we've changed over these past few years, but I still love you."

"It's no use telling me. You need to show me. Bring this vessel to life. Fill it with your ancestors' power. I want to be back."

I looked at the scarecrow again. It would take time to get used to being around such an intimidating vessel. His eyes glowed, and he was over eight-foot tall. But I could handle it. And Brodie was right. Inside, it would be him, so I had nothing to be afraid of.

"Let's do this," I said. "I've stabilized the magic. We'll run some checks and then give it a test. But just a short one."

"Whatever you say. I just can't wait to be back in a proper body."

I tried not to be distracted as Brodie hovered around and asked questions, while I tested the magic and checked the boundaries of the power radiating from the scarecrow. It was so strong, I could barely contain the energy. But when I tried to turn down its resonance, Brodie caught hold of my hand and shook his head.

"No changes to the magic. I've tested dozens of variations, and that's the only one that'll hold. That was where you were going wrong. You didn't have the energy jacked up. This will keep me going."

"Sure, but it'll also take all my focus. I can't handle this and my scarecrows."

"Then give the scarecrows a long vacation. Once you've gotten used to this energy, you can slowly bring them back a few at a time."

"I can't sever all the links at once. It'll be dangerous. Not just to them, but for the customers they work for."

"Contact your customers and let them know they need to put their scarecrows in storage for a few weeks. You could say you're making essential repairs to the magic links. That way, you'll know they're no risk to anyone. You get me stable, we spend some time together with zero distractions, and then we move forward."

That sounded nice, but I hated letting down my customers. "We move forward with my scarecrows alongside us?"

"If you must. But I reckon a few weeks without monitoring them all the time will make you realize how much you've been missing out on."

"I don't miss out. The scarecrows bring me joy."

"You say that now, but I remember how stressed they make you. And you'd often work till gone midnight on those things. It put a strain on our relationship."

"We were happy. I don't remember any strain."

"Because I never said anything. I know how much you love them, but there's another way to live. We can have a better life with no scarecrows."

I wasn't giving up my scarecrows. Even if I had to put them on ice for a short time, once I figured out Brodie's vessel, they were all coming back. I wasn't letting a single one go.

"I love it when you get that stubborn look in your eyes." Brodie kissed my forehead. "If you can work out a way to keep those scarecrows, then they're all yours. Just as long as I get to keep you forever, too."

His warm smile took the edge off my frustration. "That's what we always planned. You and me, together forever."

"But only if you hurry up and get my vessel stable."

My hands were shaking with excitement as I moved over to the scarecrow and poured more magic into him.

"That's it. You're almost there. I can feel it getting stronger," Brodie said.

I kept testing and tweaking, making tiny adjustments to ensure the connection was as stable as possible. I wiped a hand across my forehead, and it came away damp. I rolled my shoulders and blinked my eyes. "I need a break. Doing all this intense magic so quickly is draining."

"Take five minutes. But then we carry on. You're close."

I took out my phone to see if there were any messages from Sol. There was no reply to my message about needing my ghost buddy back. I was too late to keep Sol in my life.

"Are you expecting a call?" Brodie said.

"Oh, no. It's just... Sol. I'm worried about him."

"Why? He just works for you."

I stared at my phone. "I know. But it's complicated."

"Odessa, what aren't you telling me? Were you seeing that guy?"

I set down my phone and looked at Brodie. "No, we never went on a date or anything like that. But Sol was always good to me. He looked out for me when I was on my own."

"If I ever see the guy again, I should thank him. Otherwise, you'd have been out here alone."

"Sol made sure I never felt alone. He'd get here early and stay late, and he took amazing care of the scarecrows. And... There was a time, when I wondered if there could be something more between us."

Brodie's eyes narrowed. "You want to be with him, instead of me?"

"No! You're my first love. My forever love. But I was on my own for a long time. My resolve got weak."

"You must have known I'd never give up on us."

"Of course. But late at night, when I was on my own and had no one to talk to, I got lonely. It felt like you were never coming back. I had a few moments of weakness. And... I care for Sol. I don't want him unhappy. He was always honest with me about how he felt."

"How did he feel? Was he hitting on you when I wasn't around?"

"No, at least not in a creepy way. But he saw a future for us, and I feel like I've let him down. I hinted that maybe there could be something between us, but then you came back..."

"And spoiled your fun?"

"Don't be like that. I just don't want to think of Sol hurting." I lifted my chin to meet Brodie's hard gaze. "I still want him in my life."

"You don't need him. You have me. And you can't have a guy working here if he's got a crush on you. It would be awkward. I don't want him around."

Stubbornness flickered through me. Brodie had been back five minutes, and he was trying to call the shots. "I want Sol to stay. He's been amazing for the farm."

"Forget him. You only need me. Besides, we're leaving the farm and starting anew. You'll have forgotten this place in a couple of months."

"I never agreed to leave for good," I said.

"Witch Haven will soon be in our past. No more pumpkins, or scarecrows, or guys working for you and making inappropriate suggestions."

"Sol never did that. He was always respectful."

"I don't care about this guy. You're happy with me." Anger lit Brodie's eyes. "Is he the reason you're making excuses about my vessel?"

"I'm not making excuses. This is the toughest magic I've ever done. You can't rush it."

He didn't look convinced. "When you said you hadn't been able to get the vessel right, I figured it was because you were having problems with the magic. But it sounds more like you were having problems convincing yourself you wanted me back. Are you disappointed I found you?"

"That's not fair. I've worked so hard looking for you and trying to get you back. I've tested dozens of models to find one that's the perfect fit."

"And yet it took me only a few days to make it work. Something doesn't add up."

I crossed my arms over my chest. My gaze flickered over Brodie several times. His expression was sharp, his eyes full of anger, and irritation radiated off him. I'd never seen him like this. Even when the scarecrows had tested his last nerve, he'd still been patient with them.

"Something's not adding up for me, either," I said.

"Is it because you have a crush on the guy you hired after I died?"

"I didn't... okay, I had a small crush. But I still love you."

"It feels as if you couldn't wait to replace me." Brodie raked his hands through his hair. "Babe, let's not fight. You're confused and tired. Don't fail now. We're so close to success."

A success I wasn't certain Brodie wanted me to share in. "Before I finish this vessel, I have questions."

"No questions. Babe, we need this."

"And I need answers. Did you ever do anything you shouldn't with my scarecrows?"

"What? No! Focus on what's important." Brodie nudged me toward the scarecrow.

"This is important to me. And you know me well enough to realize how much each scarecrow means to me. I put my heart and soul into them, and they remain a part of my family forever."

"Got it. The scarecrows are awesome. Now, can we..." He gestured at the scarecrow.

"Not yet. A ghost I helped once told me to be careful of your dodgy dealings, because they were drawing the wrong attention. What did she mean by that?"

"I have no clue. Why would I do anything to your scarecrows?"

"That's what I'm trying to find out. Not all of them make it, and you were always keen to clear up after I was done with my failures. I figured you recycled them in keeping with the farm's ethos, but I never asked what happened to them."

"How am I supposed to remember what I did with a few broken scarecrows? Forget about that."

"Did you ever have any dealings with Arietta Frost?" I said.

He blinked several times. "No. Why would I?"

"Because she was the ghost who told me about your dodgy deals. And although she wasn't a warm and fuzzy ghost, she had no reason to lie to me about you."

"She must have. She was confused. All ghosts get confused."

"Arietta also said you were a serial dater. Of course, I didn't believe her. You've always been true to me, haven't you?"

"Angel, don't do this. Not now. As soon as I met you, I knew I wanted to settle down. You were the right one for me."

"Did you ever date other women when we were together?"

He put his hand over his heart. "Don't listen to Arietta. She was a bitter, twisted woman."

"How would you know that, if you had nothing to do with her?"

"I knew of her! You're making something out of nothing."

Brodie was lying to me. "If I went to Arietta's old business and asked for records of you selling my scarecrows to them, I wouldn't find anything, would I?"

He shrugged. "Do what you like. But your hesitation suggests you don't want me back. You don't want the happily ever after you've dreamed of. Maybe you think you'll get it with this Sol guy."

His words hit me like a slap in the face. I'd always wanted this, but now it was in front of me, it felt wrong.

"Is it because I'm not a real man? You don't see me like you used to?"

My heart felt lodged in my throat as it beat out an unhappy rhythm. There was something wrong, and I'd been hiding my concerns ever since Brodie came back. It wasn't just the hint from Arietta that Brodie hadn't been honest with me, but it was other things I'd brushed away. The fact he didn't know what I liked for breakfast, and the way he'd dismissed my scarecrows and the farm, when he should have known they were important.

Brodie scowled at me. "You're not denying it. You don't want to be with me, anymore."

"I do. But answer this question for me first."

"Okay, if it'll set your mind at rest."

"When did we first meet?"

He groaned. "No more tests. What's wrong with you?"

"Nothing. And this isn't a test. I just want to know if you remember it the same as me. It was unusual. A real memorable meet."

"You know my memories aren't great. Why test me on something so unfair?"

"If you can't remember that, tell me when I have my birthday."

"You're being so difficult."

"I'm not. It's hard to forget, even if you have been a ghost for a few years."

"You probably wish it was on October thirty-first, the way you're so obsessed with scarecrows and pumpkins."

My heart thundered out my panic as I took a few seconds to stare at the floor. This couldn't be happening, but I had to face facts that something was horribly wrong here.

An icy chill revealed Brodie had moved closer. "Sorry, babe, but I'm so frustrated with this situation. Give me a minute to think, and I'll remember everything. You wanted to know how we first met and when your birthday is, right?"

I looked up at him. "You guessed correctly. It's October thirty-first."

He grinned. "It wasn't a guess. You see, I remember. Now, stop messing around and let's get on with our life together."

I licked my lips. I couldn't believe I was about to say this. "There won't be any new life together. Because I don't think you're Brodie."

Chapter 20

Brodie's mouth dropped open, and then he laughed. "Of course I am. Who else could I be? You know me."

"I do. And my Brodie would never be so pushy about getting this vessel right. He wouldn't grab magic off me and drain me whenever he likes. He also wouldn't forget my birthday or that my favorite breakfast food is sweet pumpkin muffins with a dark chocolate frosting. Never mind the smoked salmon and scrambled eggs. Talk about yuck. And he would never disappear when I was hurt, alone, and scared. So, who are you really?"

He stared at me without blinking, and I stared right back. My insides were shaking, but my resolve was firm. I didn't know who had taken the form of my dead love and was pretending to be him, but I was determined to find out.

Brodie blinked first and looked away, his gaze settling on the scarecrow. "You're clever. I thought I had you fooled." The voice that came out was deep and guttural. It sounded like a demon.

"Maybe you did for a short time. I wanted Brodie back for so long that I refused to see the flaws.

But you messed up one too many times." I raised my chin, not wanting to say the next words, but knowing they had to come out. "My Brodie is dead. He died over three years ago in a mining explosion. He crossed over, and he's moved on. He's never coming back to me."

"Babe, I'm right here if you want me to be." The ghostly looking Brodie chuckled. "But I have a feeling you're not going to want me around for much longer. I can play the good guy loser if that's what'll make you happy. Or would you rather I turn into the other guy? The one who was a replacement for your dead boyfriend."

Rage replaced my sadness in a flash. "Whoever you are, you deceived me. You're a liar."

"You didn't seem to mind all those kisses I gave you. They felt like the truth, didn't they? And I have no objection to keeping a witch around for my entertainment. I love the taste of your power." He smacked his lips together.

"You're disgusting. You preyed on my desire to be happy."

"It's hardly my fault your obsession for something you could never have blinded you to the truth. Although I'm proud of myself. I never realized I was this good of an actor. I should go into show business. Although my new vessel may cause alarm, but then everyone will be too afraid of me to say anything." He chuckled that deep growling laugh again. "So, shall we get on with it?"

I stood in front of the enormous scarecrow. "You're not having this vessel. And you're not using my ancestors' power to get what you want. Leave this place. You don't belong here."

"Oh, little witch, it's not going to be that simple." He rushed me in a blur of movement, and I just dodged out of his way with a split second to spare. Hot energy blasted past me, filling my nose with a foul, sulfurous stench.

The second I inhaled, I knew I was dealing with a demon. I backed away, my hands held up, warning magic sparking. "You're a shape shifter."

"You've got me. And don't you love this form, babe?" He laughed again. "If you behave and finish what you started, I may even visit you late at night and give you a reminder of the good old days with Brodie."

My stomach clenched with disgust. "Never touch me. And stop using Brodie's form."

"How about I make you a deal? You give me that vessel and the power I need to live in it, and I won't burn this place to the ground."

"That's a hard pass."

"You love this weird farm and the strange magic that comes out of those pumpkins. And I feel the sickeningly sweet love you have for those scarecrow monstrosities that strut around like they own the place. You won't let that go. This farm means everything to you."

"It does. Which is why I'll fight until my last breath to make sure you don't get what you want." I raised my hands. "Stop looking like my boyfriend and leave." I slammed out a reveal spell, intent on seeing what I was dealing with.

He flew to the ceiling then spiraled down around me, the air no longer cold but hot and spicy and flaring with danger as my hair burned.

"Give me what I want, witch. My patience has run out. I played the nice guy, the sad guy, the lonely idiot who just wants to be with his witch girlfriend. Boo, hoo. It's been exhausting and tedious, and I'm done playing games."

"Then go find your own body. Stop living this lie." I dodged out of his way as he grabbed at me.

"If it was that simple, I wouldn't be wasting my time on you."

I shot out a knockback spell. "Did something go wrong with your magic? You can't change to another shape, so you had to borrow a ghost. That's a low stoop, even for a demon."

His eyes glowed red. "Spending time with you has been torture."

This time, I laughed. "You're stuck. What did you do, shape shifted into the wrong form and someone blasted you apart? Or did a powerful witch take your body when you were mid-shift? That must have stung."

"You witches are all the same. You spout goodness, but you're dark and twisted inside."

"So, it was a witch. And I'm not twisted."

"Your magic is pure, is it? You feed off the earth. You suck it dry to support your scarecrows."

"Wrong. I nurture the land. I fill it with my love, and I cherish it. In return, it fuels my magic. It makes me strong."

"All that powered orange gunk you shove down your throat juices you up. You're a witch on steroids. It's wrong. You're unnatural."

"Maybe I enjoy a little too much of Mother Nature's candy, but I always protect the things I love the most. And I'll make sure you pay for what you've done. You almost had me convinced. I almost gave you everything you wanted."

"And you still will."

"No, I won't." I thrust out a powerful knockback spell, but it didn't have its usual sharp edge. It slammed into the demon, and although he wheeled back, within seconds, he was launching himself at me.

Claws skimmed my cheek, and a fiery blast slammed into my back. I staggered forward, my skin on fire as I rolled across the hay to extinguish the magic on me.

I hit the wall and came to a stop. Then I was up and running before this demon attacked again. More of his hot magic sprayed around, dazzling me. I dodged and weaved, avoiding the magic and blasting my own over my shoulder, not sure if I was hitting the target.

The back of the barn was getting near, so I ducked into a stall and skidded to a halt. There was a trail of blood on the floor and a pile of black fur. My stomach flipped, and my eyes filled with tears as I dropped to my knees. "Tuffin?"

A deep laugh rumbled behind me, too close for comfort. "You kept asking where that annoying furball was. I couldn't have her planting doubts in your head. As soon as she saw me, she realized I wasn't quite myself. Well, not quite Brodie."

I stroked a finger over a piece of fur. "So you killed her?"

"I had to ensure her silence. Oh, and if you're wondering where your wonderful Sol is, I got rid of him, too."

Heat bubbled from the tips of my toes and spread through my body like wildfire, heating me from the inside and tinging the world red. My tears were gone as hot, angry, desperate rage boiled inside me. I took the anger and threw out the most powerful spell I knew. The destruction spell slammed into the demon's chest and blasted him through the wall of the barn.

But I wasn't done. I raced after him, hopped through the hole, and kept pounding him with magic. "You killed my familiar, you killed Sol, and you lied to me. You used my dreams against me. I'm going to destroy you."

The demon batted away my spells, but each time they made contact, his form changed. Brodie vanished, and a large, thin, gray-skinned demon with claws and narrowed red eyes appeared. Horns curled around his ears as my next spell slammed into him, wiping away the last of his disguise.

I bared my teeth and thrust out another spell. He caught it and smashed it between his hands, dispersing it into the air. "Enough! I deserve that vessel. I've been too long without a body. No more games, witch." He lunged and wrapped his fingers around my throat, lifting me off my feet and slamming me through the hole in the wall, tearing my skin on the broken wood.

He tossed me to the floor and stood over me, panting out hot, acrid breath that made my stomach churn. "I cannot hold this shape for long. You will give me what I need."

"I'd rather die."

"I can make that happen."

"If you kill me, where does that leave you? You need me to channel the magic."

He snarled at me. "Then I'll keep you alive, but it won't be a life worth living. You'll be my prisoner. I'll keep you chained in the darkness and alive just enough so you power me. I'll drain you of that Grimsbane magic until you're a husk. You'll beg me to end your life every day, but I'll always enjoy tormenting you."

"Never going to happen." I tried to roll away, but the demon stamped on my chest.

"If you're good to me, I may come and see you as the wonderful Brodie. Mr. Perfect never set a foot wrong when he was alive, isn't that right? He didn't get involved in shady deals with your scarecrows or see other women behind your back."

"You're right. He never did any of that." The words rasped out of me, tears running down my cheeks.

"Are you sure? You were asking those questions yourself. And I got to know Brodie when I was living as his ghost. I even have some of his memories. He was unfaithful to you, and he hated your scarecrows. And he took the ones that didn't work and sold them on the black market for use in spells."

I wanted to block my ears to shut out his lies, but I couldn't move my arms. And a tiny part of me knew some of that was true.

"So much for your wonderful guy and the happily ever after you had planned. He deceived you and lied to you. And it's no wonder. You deserve it. You're so naïve, accepting the things people tell you. You should have learned by dealing with these murders and meeting troubled ghosts that everyone lies. The world is bitter and twisted, and you don't fit in. Even your friends don't think you should be here."

"My friends love me just as I am."

"Is that so? What about the tormented Indigo, who almost destroyed this place when she was a teenager? Or the messed up Luna, who hid her secret failings from her family for so long that it almost killed them. And then there's Storm, the most messed up of them all. A witch who can't let go of her past. She revels in it, even though it's a toxic bog of failure and loss."

"We've all had our struggles." I tried to get a hand up to cast a spell, but my muscles were shaky, and nothing wanted to work. "Leave my friends out of this."

"I can't. I know all about them thanks to the time I've endured with you. And don't you see, you're the misfit in the group. Everyone in this world is damaged, wrong, and deceitful. That's what makes them normal. And that's what makes you a mistake."

"I'm not a mistake." I gulped back angry tears. "And maybe Brodie wasn't perfect—"

The demon grated out a laugh. "You've got that right. It was so easy to possess the whispers of memory I found from him and manipulate them. The man was weak and as easy to corrupt in death as he was in life."

I inched back as the pressure from his foot eased. "His ghost was in Witch Haven? You actually found him?"

"You poor, deluded witch. What I found wasn't Brodie but a broken, insane, ghost ghoul. When I realized his connection to you and the power you had, I couldn't resist taking advantage. And here we are. I'm about to win."

"No, you're not." I stuck my fingers in my mouth and whistled for my scarecrows. The floor didn't shake, and there were no approaching footsteps as my boys came to my rescue.

The demon cackled. "You've been so busy with your wonderful Brodie, you didn't notice your scarecrows vanishing. You should check the bonfire around the back."

My breath whooshed out as a lancing pain sliced my heart. "You're a monster."

"Yeah, babe. But I'm your monster, so you'd better get used to it."

I rolled away and slammed into a heap of pumpkins. I fired up what was left of my magic and plunged my fists into two pumpkins. I fed off their energy, charging my magic and feeling the primal pumpkin power race through my veins and chase away the tiredness, shock, and fear. I was going to kill this demon for everything he'd done to me, every lie he'd told, and for every second he'd deceived me.

With the pumpkins still attached to my hands, I turned. I caught a hint of shock in the demon's eyes as my enormous pumpkin fist landed on his nose, followed by the other, and I didn't stop hitting.

"Stop! Wait. It's me." The demon changed back into Brodie. "Babe, I love you."

His lies only made me madder, and I continued to slam into him. He was weakening as the pumpkin magic coursed through my veins like a welcome embrace. Until that second, I'd not realized how weak I'd become. All this time, this demon had been using me.

What I thought was Brodie was gone. That was a heartrending realization. But I couldn't focus on the pain that was to come.

I hesitated for a second as a wave of sadness hit. That was my mistake. The demon threw himself at me. His power wrapped around me, stealing my breath and squeezing my lungs. I saw double as he dragged me to the vessel and slid a sharp claw across my cheek, drawing blood.

"You're mine now, witch. Welcome to a world of pain."

My arms wouldn't move, and I couldn't get air into my lungs as I slumped against the scarecrow. The connection to my ancestors' magic was wide open, and it poured out of me and into the vessel.

"Let me have it all. Don't hold back. I know how powerful you are." The demon skulked around me, rubbing his hands together and clacking his sharp teeth.

My power drained, my eyes closed, and I got flashes of Brodie, Sol, even a glimpse of Zohar, looking sad. There was also Tuffin and all my friends. This was my life flashing before my eyes, and I was losing it all. It was sliding out of me like the trickle of blood down my cheek.

But as I'd promised this magic sucking demon, I wouldn't give up until I had no breath left in my body.

I dug my fingers into the pumpkins, sucking up the last of their power. It was enough to give me the strength to move.

I waited until the demon was on the other side of the scarecrow before dropping and sliding away. The source of my power had always been this farm, the land, and the pumpkins I grew on it. My ancestors' energy pulsed through the rich soil that created such incredible scarecrows and pumpkins. And I needed to get to that source.

"Hey, witch. Where are you going? If you beg for your life, I may let you live." The demon was following me as I crawled along.

"I'm living. Don't worry about that." I reached the edge of a vat of chopped pumpkin stewing in the barn. It was always here, fermenting away, power infusing through it and becoming potent.

The demon's claws clamped around my head. "You lost, and I'm taking what's mine. That vessel, your power, everything. I'm even keeping you."

I aimed a kick at his stomach, but he barely moved as my foot made contact. I clung to the edge of the vat. I needed to go headfirst into this gooey mess of power. Once I was juiced up, I knew the spell to use.

My magic wasn't meant to destroy, but I could pull out the life force from any creature if I had to do so. And this was one of those moments. This demon had to be stopped.

He pulled me to my feet and grabbed the back of my head with one clawed hand. "Submit to my will."

"Go back to the pit you crawled out of."

He spun me around and ducked my head into the pumpkin.

For a second, I resisted then relaxed, opened my mouth, and chewed. *Wrong move, buddy*.

He pulled me back. "This will go much easier for you, if you stop resisting."

I couldn't speak because my mouth was full of tangy, magic infused pumpkin, and it was flooding my system in a delicious, sweet wave.

"Why are you smiling?" the demon snarled in my face.

I had just enough magic to slam him with a knockback spell. Then I turned and dove into the pumpkin. The vat was big enough that my feet only just touched the bottom, and I stayed submerged for as long as I could, eating and swallowing, covering myself in sticky, orange goo.

I'd gotten so used to being surrounded by energy draining ghosts, the demands of my scarecrows, and even Brodie that I'd forgotten how amazing it felt to have my magic to myself. Not anymore. I had my mojo back, and this demon was about to get a demonstration.

I shot out of the vat of pumpkin and landed on the floor with a soggy splat. It wasn't a Wonder Woman arrival, as I stood there with pumpkin dripping off my hair and clothes, but I didn't care what I looked like. It was how I felt. And that was pretty darn amazing.

The demon stared at me, his eyes narrowed to tiny slits. "What are you doing, witch?"

"Destroying you. You have no power over me, no right to be on my farm, and no claim over any vessel I've created. Demon, leave this place." I threw out my arms and cast a powerful destruction spell. Everything that got in its way would be blown to pieces.

A flash of movement caught my eye at the back of the barn. It was small, dark, and looked like Tuffin. That was impossible.

It was too late to pull back the spell as it shot toward the demon in a solid wave, obliterating everything it touched.

I yelled a warning, and my eyes widened as not only did Zohar's ghost appear, but Sol was suddenly there, too. He had Tuffin in his arms and was racing toward me.

I stared at the wall of magic speeding in their direction. I couldn't stop it, and the spell didn't care what it destroyed. "Go! Get out of here." Were they even real, or was my mind playing tricks on me?

As the destruction spell hit home, the demon roared his anger as pumpkins exploded around us, and I collapsed to the floor.

Chapter 21

As I slowly blinked open my eyes, a sweet, tangy scent flooded my nose. It reminded me of home. I ran my tongue across my teeth and discovered small chunks of pumpkin wedged between them.

I tried to keep my eyes open, but the world was blurry and made me dizzy, so I shut them again.

"She's waking up," an oh so familiar and wonderful voice said.

I risked another peek and found Indigo by the side of the bed I was in. Luna and Storm quickly joined her. I cleared my throat and smacked my lips together. I wanted to say something profound, but all I could manage was, "Errargghhh."

"Just relax. You're in the hospital," Indigo said.

I'd figured out that much from the white walls and the faint smell of bleach and antiseptic. "How?"

"Sol brought you in," Storm said.

"Sol?"

"Yep, he ran all the way from your farm with you in his arms. He was also carrying Tuffin," Luna said. "What happened back there?"

"I... um..." I still couldn't form a sentence. Sol and Tuffin were dead, weren't they?

"Give her space." Storm nudged the other two out of the way. "What you need is strong coffee and something to wash all that sticky orange gunk off you. The nurse tried, but it won't budge. It stinks like over ripe pumpkins, but it set like concrete."

I raised a hand and patted my face. There were chunks of pumpkin attached to my cheeks. My magic was still protecting me, and I couldn't love it any more than I already did.

There were high-pitched, angry voices close by, and a few seconds later, the door slammed open. Shamrock stormed into the room, closely followed by half a dozen other scarecrows.

A nurse was right behind them. "You already have too many visitors. We can't have these things in here, too."

"Sorry, they're my friends." I held out a hand to Shamrock, and he caught hold of it in both of his huge, straw-filled hands. The connection instantly formed.

"You died," he growl-whistled at me.

I'd never heard his voice this panicked. "No. I'm right here."

"Yes. Dead. Lost connection. You dead."

I glanced at my friends. "Did I die?"

"Only a couple of times," Storm said. "The doctors brought you back. And of course, you had a little help from your friends."

A tear slid down my cheek. "Shamrock, the demon told me you were dead. He said he burned you all." My gaze went to the rest of the scarecrows.

"He tried. Idiot. We're not easy to kill. And had to save you. Our Queen."

"You're all okay? Really?" A flame of joy ignited inside me as I felt for the connections I had to my scarecrows. They were intact.

Shamrock nodded and gestured at the other scarecrows hovering at the end of the bed, growling at anyone who got too close.

"I'm so glad you're here," I said.

"I'm not. I insist they all leave at once. And visiting hours ended half an hour ago. Everyone else needs to go, too." The nurse stood fearlessly in the door, glaring at my scarecrows as if she didn't realize they could take her head off if she looked at them the wrong way.

"Shamrock, I need you to do me a huge favor." I cleared my throat again. "You're in charge of everyone. Get the other scarecrows out of here."

"Not leaving you."

"Yes, you must. I'm safe in here. You see, I have my other friends, and they won't let anything bad happen to me. But I need time to recover. I have to rest."

"Witches protect you?" Shamrock's red eyes shifted to my friends.

"They always do."

"We'll wait outside. Guard you."

"Good idea. You do that. But no menacing other patients or the nice nurses and doctors. They have important jobs to do."

"That's right. And we can't do them while we're herding scarecrows around the corridors. Out," the nurse said.

After a few more comforting words to Shamrock, I convinced him to take the other scarecrows outside. They all took a few seconds to touch me to check I was okay and then left.

The nurse looked pointedly at my friends.

"Please, can they stay?" I said. "I've got lots of questions."

"So have we. We're not going anywhere," Storm said.

The nurse huffed out a breath. "Keep it quiet. And only an extra half an hour. I'll be back to check." She shot them all a glare before hurrying out of the room.

Storm handed me a huge mug of coffee so strong it made my eyes water. "There are three sugars in that. Drink up. Then you need to talk."

It was only when I was holding the mug and lifted it to my lips that I noticed a silver ring on my wedding ring finger. It looked like Sol's ring.

I lifted my hand and examined it. "What's this?"

"Like I said, you needed help from your friends to stop you from turning into a ghost. Sol brought you here, and while the doctors worked on bringing you back, he slid that ring on your finger. The second he did, you started breathing, so we left it where it was." Storm patted my hand and looked away but not before I saw the shimmer in her eyes.

"I don't deserve him. I... He's still alive? When I was in the barn, the demon said—"

"Whoa there, speedy. Let's go back a few dozen steps," Luna said. "What demon?"

"Oh, it's a long story." I drank plenty of coffee.

"We've got time. And you're going nowhere," Storm said.

I could already feel my eyes closing, despite the injection of caffeine. "Has anyone got any powdered pumpkin?"

Storm shook her head. "You realize you're an addict?"

"It's all natural."

"So are a lot of other drugs." Indigo tossed me a bag of powdered pumpkin.

I dipped my finger in it and tasted the delicious, sweet goodness. Buoyed by the coffee and powdered pumpkin, I lay back on the bed, not sure where to begin.

"Let's fill in some of the missing pieces for you." Indigo settled beside me on the edge of the bed. "Sol brought you in here."

"Where is he?"

"Right over there. Behind the curtain. Before he collapsed, he insisted you stay together." She jabbed a thumb over her shoulder. "The guy is a mess. He was also covered in pumpkin."

"He'll be okay, though?"

"He'll be fine," Storm said. "Your barn, however, is flattened."

"And there was pumpkin everywhere," Luna said. "When we heard you were in the hospital, I went to see what happened at the farm. You said something about a demon."

"The barn is gone?" I said. "Everything inside is destroyed?"

Indigo nodded. "The one at the end you always keep locked. There's nothing left. Just a mess of wood and pumpkin. So much pumpkin."

My breath stuttered out. Brodie's vessel was gone. But of course, he had never been here. My heart hurt at the thought, but I'd accepted he was lost to me. "I... I was tricked. The ghost I saw, it wasn't Brodie. Well, there were a few memories of Brodie, but a shape shifting demon who'd lost his ability to change form found Brodie's ghost ghoul. He used Brodie to get something I'd created."

"What did you create?" Luna said.

"A vessel for Brodie's ghost to live in." I looked at my friends, expecting to see disappointment or shock, but they simply shrugged and nodded.

"We figured as much," Indigo said.

"You knew what I was doing and didn't stop me?"

"We tried several roundabout ways to get you to see sense, but you dug in your heels. There was nothing we could do."

"We should have blown up the barn," Storm said. "I suggested it several times."

"I was so sure I'd get Brodie back, and when he appeared at the farm, it felt right." I couldn't believe what an idiot I'd been. "I ignored the clues that it wasn't Brodie because I wanted him back so badly."

"What clues?" Indigo said.

"It was little things at first, but I should have known. The demon was only interested in the vessel. He gave himself away several times, but I was so desperate to get my happiness back, I ignored the red flags. I'm a fool."

"You are a huge fool," Storm said, "but we'd have most likely done the same thing."

"No, you wouldn't. You're smarter than me. And it was only when Brodie, or what I thought was

Brodie, was almost forcing me to bring the vessel to life, that I questioned him. That's when the demon revealed its true form. We fought, and I almost lost, but I used my pumpkin magic to send out a destruction spell. But... I saw Sol and Tuffin just before the spell hit. How did they survive? Oh, and Zohar. He was there, too."

"Slow down! This is a lot to take in." Indigo picked a piece of pumpkin off my arm. "Hey, this is coming off."

"It's protecting me. I'm safe now, so I don't need it anymore. It'll flake off over the next day or so."

"That demon didn't stand a chance against you and your pumpkin armor magic," Storm said. "There were bits of demon everywhere. It's gross over at the farm."

"I'll get that cleaned up once I'm out of here."

"Which won't be for a few days," Indigo said. "Don't worry about the mess. We'll fix it."

"Thanks, but it's something I want to do." I was considering protesting having to stay in the hospital, but I was exhausted and aching all over. Killing with magic would never be my specialty, and I was glad of it.

"I'm really sorry about Brodie," Luna said. "We know how much you loved him."

"I did. I do, but maybe he wasn't such a perfect guy. I'll never be sure if what the demon told me is true, but he claimed Brodie hadn't been faithful, and he'd sold my scarecrows on the black market. And he wasn't the only one to tell me about Brodie being less than honest, recently."

"We can always ask around, see if there's any proof," Indigo said.

"I have contacts. They'll find out any dirt. If you're sure that's what you want," Storm said.

"No, I don't want to know. When we were together, we had a good life. I chose to forget the bad times. I don't need to know anything else. Brodie's in my past." I took in a deep breath. "You all nudged me about the problems with Brodie. Sol most of all."

"Sure, but Sol has a serious ulterior motive. After all, he put his ring on your finger," Storm said.

My cheeks flushed, and I looked at the curtain concealing Sol. "Maybe, but even you can't deny he's a good man. The most solid and reliable man I've ever met. And all this time, I've pushed him away because of my flawed memories."

Indigo glanced at Sol's bed. "It's not too late. Any guy who carries you all the way from the farm to here must still have feelings for you."

"Most likely, he's feeling his sore back muscles," Storm said.

The nurse walked back in and over to Sol's bed. She drew back the curtain, put a blood pressure monitor around his upper arm, and pumped it up. She then used a tourniquet and extracted blood from a vein.

I watched her closely, my gaze shifting back to Sol. He looked so pale and still, but his chest was moving up and down.

"Don't worry about Sol. They're just running tests because he hasn't woken up," Luna said. "All the signs are good, though. And we kept an eye on him while you were out of it."

"No, it's not that. I mean, I am worried about him, but I've seen something important. It has to do with Zohar's murder."

"Is that ghost still around?" Indigo said. "Olympus said someone got arrested for his murder. He should have crossed over by now."

"I'm right here." Zohar emerged from under my bed.

Luna leaped back. "Don't be sneaking up on people like that. No wonder my toes have been so cold. I hope you weren't peeking up our skirts."

Zohar's eyebrows rose. "You're all wearing pants."

"Oh! Well, you still shouldn't hide under a bed. That kind of behavior gives ghosts bad reputations." Luna glared at Zohar. "Is this the guy you've been helping?"

I nodded, my attention on Zohar. "I have questions for you. You haven't moved on?"

He looked shamefaced. "I didn't leave because I was worried about you. You must hate me."

He looked so sorrowful and bedraggled that I didn't have it in me to hate him. "You're not top of my best friends list. Did you know about the demon pretending to be Brodie?"

Zohar lifted a shoulder. "I knew he wasn't the guy he claimed to be. He was too powerful."

"Shall we kick the ghost out?" Storm said. "Was he in on the deception, too?"

I tilted my head as I studied Zohar. "I'm not sure. Give me a minute with him."

"Is that a good idea?" Indigo said.

"Yes. And I need to remember what I've just seen. I don't want to fall asleep and forget." My heart was racing as I shuffled up in the bed, bits of congealed pumpkin dropping off me. "Zohar, I know what happened to you."

"You do? What about Elsbeth?"

"Indigo, is Olympus around?" I said. "I need all the suspects in Zohar's murder here. I'd go to them, but..."

"You shouldn't worry about this ghost. Focus on getting better."

"We know that won't happen," Storm said. "What do you need us to do?"

"I need to see Elsbeth, Hester, Ballard, and Finn." I looked at Sol again. "And there's one more person involved in your death. Someone I never considered until I saw Sol get blood taken."

"Who? No one else is being questioned," Zohar said.

"You'll find out soon enough. Indigo, can you..."

"I'm on it. I've just sent Olympus a message." She looked up from her phone. "But after you solve this murder, you're having a vacation."

I sank back against the pillow. "Agreed. A long one."

❧ ❧

I dozed off several times while I waited for Olympus to get everyone together. But an hour later, my hospital room was full, and the nurses were still unhappy with all my visitors.

"Are you sure you're up to this?" Olympus said as he stood beside my bed. "You're a strange color. Kind of yellow."

"It's just pumpkin. I'll be fine. And you don't want to charge the wrong person with murder."

Elsbeth, Ballard, Hester, and Finn stood at the end of my bed, looking nervous, while Zohar hovered by my side. Indigo, Luna, and Storm were a few paces back, standing by Sol's bed. The curtain was pulled back so I could see him, but he was still asleep.

"I won't take up much of your time, mainly because I'm exhausted," I said.

"Killing a demon will do that to you," Storm muttered.

"It wasn't until I was in this hospital that I saw something. It was the missing piece of the puzzle as to what happened to Zohar the day he died."

"What was that?" Olympus said.

"Sol having his blood taken. Do you remember we found a red ribbon on Zohar's body after he'd been pulled from the lake?"

"Of course. It's in the evidence store. It had a faint trace of a spell on it."

"It did. And that spell was used to fake Zohar's death." I looked at Olympus. "If you test the ribbon for a life suspension spell or draining magic, there should be enough left to show the spell used."

Olympus's eyebrows flashed up. "I'll get someone on that right away."

"Zohar didn't fake his death." Ballard shook his head. "I checked him. He was dead when I got to the house."

"It only appeared that way. Zohar used a magically laced piece of red ribbon and tied it around his upper arm. It suspended all signs of life. So, when you checked on him, he appeared dead. When the spell faded, Zohar got up and left the house."

"Why would he do that?" Hester said.

"I saw him, too," Elsbeth said. "When I went back after our fight. He was there. I was so shocked. There was no way he was alive."

"Zohar started that fight, didn't he?" I said.

Elsbeth nodded. "He was in a bad mood that morning. Nothing I could say would make him smile. And he was picking on me about everything. In the end, I snapped. I yelled back, and he yelled louder. He even threw things. I didn't feel safe, so I left. I wouldn't have gone back for hours, but I left my phone behind."

I looked at Zohar, and surprise, surprise, he didn't meet my gaze. "Zohar lied to all of us. He set this up because he wanted to frame you, Elsbeth, and ruin your life. Isn't that right, Zohar?"

He said nothing for several seconds and simply stared at Elsbeth. "I found out about the affair. I picked up Elsbeth's phone one day when a call came in. It was from the doctor. He congratulated me on the good news and said how pleased I must be after so many years of trying. I was stunned. It was then that I realized Elsbeth had cheated on me."

Elsbeth raised a trembling hand to her mouth. "Why didn't you speak to me about it?"

"Because I'd have said and done things I'd have regretted. So, I waited."

"Go on, Odessa, if you're up to it. How did you work this out?" Olympus said.

"Once I'd figured out Zohar didn't die at the house, everything made sense. The travel documents in the wagon with a different name on them, the missing jade pendant, the hidden money and clothing. The clues revealed Zohar was planning a new life."

"He was leaving me?" Elsbeth said.

"You deserved a lot worse," Zohar said.

"He was leaving but wanted to make sure his old life was in tatters. Olympus, can you access the Delarosa's bank accounts?" I said.

"Of course."

"Check for any large withdrawals over the last few weeks. Zohar must have wanted as much money as he could get without Elsbeth becoming suspicious, so he could set up his new life. There might even be a hidden account or something in a different name."

"We'll take a look at that."

"He stole from me, too?" Elsbeth said.

"I should have taken more," Zohar muttered. "But I just wanted out."

"He did a lot worse than that. Zohar tried to frame you for his murder. He wanted you left with nothing," I said.

Elsbeth swayed on her feet, and Hester caught hold of her.

"Zohar staged the scene, so when Ballard came back for their day of golf, he'd find his body. Ballard arrived, saw Zohar dead, the mess suggesting a fight, and while he was making a call to get help, Zohar snuck in and attacked him."

"I must have missed that happening by seconds," Elsbeth whispered.

I nodded. "Most likely. If the timing had been out at all, this deceit would have been discovered. Zohar then fled in a car, which he'd parked at the back of the house on the dirt lane. An entrance only a few people know about."

"The tire tracks had nothing to do with the killer moving Zohar's body?" Olympus said.

"No. Zohar's getaway vehicle left those marks," I said.

Zohar scowled at me. "When Elsbeth came back, she could have ruined everything, but it played into my hands. I heard her coming just as the spell was wearing off, so I took a risk and stayed still. Elsbeth screamed. Then she was on the phone, calling her boyfriend. She sounded terrified, and although I could only hear one side of the conversation, she was setting up a fake alibi. I knew that would get found out and reveal Elsbeth as a liar. She deserved everything she got."

I relayed what Zohar said to everyone who couldn't hear him.

Elsbeth dabbed at her eyes. "He hated me that much?"

"You did cheat on him," Storm said.

"What Zohar did was wrong, but he was hurting and wanted to make you pay," I said. "He knew the Magic Council would find evidence of an unhappy marriage, a recent fight, and a fake alibi, plus his body missing. They'd have blamed you, Elsbeth."

"But Zohar's body would never have been found," Elsbeth said. "They'd have never known what really happened to him."

"True, but there were enough clues pointing directly at you as the killer," Olympus said.

"And when your relationship with Finn was discovered, everyone would have assumed the worst," I said. "Even if you weren't charged with murder, you'd have remained under suspicion and the subject of gossip. You may have had to move and start again somewhere else. Your life would never have been the same."

"I'm confused," Hester said. "Zohar is actually dead, isn't he? I mean, his ghost is here. You have been talking to Zohar?"

"Oh, yes. He's dead. But he never planned to die." I looked at Olympus. "Have you checked for fingerprints on the travel documents in the wagon?"

"Sure. There was only one set of prints on the documents other than Zohar's."

"Have you found a match for those prints?"

"No. There's no one on the system who matches them."

"If you take a set of Ballard's fingerprints, they'll be a match," I said.

Ballard made a strangled sound in the back of his throat. "I had nothing to do with this. I was injured, too. I couldn't have killed Zohar."

"Zohar only wanted you here because he needed an alibi. He used you as part of his plan to fake his death, frame Elsbeth, and leave Witch Haven, while the rest of you picked up the pieces and wondered what happened to his body," I said.

Ballard shook his head, and his anxious gaze shot to Hester. "I didn't love the guy after he let us down, but that's no reason for killing him. We got back on our feet."

"Barely. And we're still struggling." Hester licked her lips. "You didn't have anything to do with what happened to Zohar, did you? You were so angry over the money."

"No! I don't even know how Zohar died. I thought he was dead when I found him." Sweat bloomed on Ballard's forehead, and he dabbed it away.

"That's true. You thought Zohar died at home," I said. "So you must have been shocked when you saw him alive. When was that?"

"I... I didn't see him."

"Zohar, I'm assuming that, when you left the house after faking your death, you went to the wagon," I said.

"I did. The plan was to lie low until it got dark and then leave. Start my new life, knowing Elsbeth's was over."

"Ballard must have seen you. Did you ever leave the wagon?"

"No. I didn't want to risk anyone spotting me."

"You didn't even open the door to get some air?"

"Oh, sure. I mean, I got out a few times and stretched my legs."

I grabbed his arm and yanked him close. "It would have been helpful if you hadn't hidden this. We could have solved your murder in a day if you hadn't lied to me."

He hung his head. "It's not my fault. And I only remember parts of it. I definitely don't remember who killed me. I just remember the pain, shock, and then the darkness."

Ghosts. They were such complicated creatures. "When did you see Zohar?" I asked Ballard.

"At the house! And after the shock of finding his body, we spent most of the day with Elsbeth and then had an early night."

"Ballard." Hester's voice was quivering. "You went for a walk. You couldn't sleep as usual and said the moon was beautiful. You... you didn't do anything, did you?"

"You're remembering wrong. I didn't go out."

Hester stepped away, her hands pressed against her stomach. "You did. And when you came back, you didn't come to bed straightaway. And you always said one day you'd get revenge on Zohar."

"Only to comfort you. You were so unhappy when we moved. I felt like I'd let you down. It made me sick to think I was failing as a husband."

"What happened when you spotted Zohar?" I said. "Did you lose your temper? It must have been a shock to realize you were part of his deception. He didn't want to rekindle the friendship and help you; he wanted to get something out of you and then was abandoning you again. Did you see the wagon?"

Ballard kept his head lowered, but I could see tears on his cheeks. "I thought I was seeing a ghost. I was stunned after discovering Zohar's body and then it going missing. I went for a walk to get my thoughts in order. I saw a light among the trees and took a look. The wagon door opened, and there was Zohar. I almost called out his name, not able to believe what I was seeing. But I saw him smiling, and he was laughing to himself."

"Laughing at you?" I said.

"Probably. He always saw me as a joke. When he went back inside, I marched over and confronted him. I demanded answers."

"Did he give them to you?"

"Of course not. He pretended he was sorry, but only said that so I'd keep quiet. He was using all of us. I couldn't let that happen."

"What did you do?"

Zohar hovered closer to Ballard, but I didn't sense any malice, just a deep regret and sadness.

"Zohar kept telling me to forget what I'd seen and move on. He even had the cheek to offer me money. All those years ago, when he rejected my pleas for help when I needed it, and now, because it fulfilled his needs, he was throwing it at me. I saw red and hit him. I didn't mean to kill him, but we struggled, he hit his head and then didn't get up. I panicked. I was terrified people would think the worst."

"Oh, Ballard. You should have told me. Or gone to the Magic Council," Hester said.

"I couldn't. I had to make things right. I had to make our life together perfect."

"What did you do after Zohar died?" I said.

"Nothing for about half an hour. I sat with his body and cried. Then I found the bag full of money and fake travel documents and realized the full extent of his manipulation. I thought, if I got rid of his body, hid the evidence, I might get away with it, and we could all be free. I didn't mean for Elsbeth to get in trouble." Zohar grasped Elsbeth's hand. "I'm sorry."

She stepped away and shook her head. Finn tucked an arm around her shoulders.

Olympus stepped forward. "Thanks, Odessa, I'll take it from here. Ballard Quinn, you're under arrest for the murder of Zohar Delarosa."

Ballard's body sagged, and he wiped his eyes.

I glanced at Zohar, who stared at me for a second, then blinked out of sight. I was so tired, I could barely keep my eyes open. People were talking, but I couldn't make sense of their words. So I slid down the pillows and went back to sleep.

The mystery was solved. But as for everything else, well, that would wait until the morning.

Chapter 22

I shivered and pulled the covers tight around me. I wasn't ready to wake. Although I'd been in the hospital for over forty-eight hours, I could easily do with another few weeks of not getting out of bed for anything other than essential business.

The cold grew intense, and I forced one eye open. Zohar stood beside my bed. "Hey! You're still here. I figured you'd crossed over."

"I couldn't go. I had unfinished business."

I kept my voice low as I sat up in bed. I checked on Sol, but he was sleeping. "I hope you didn't go after Ballard."

"No! Definitely not. That's not the unfinished business. I need to apologize to you." He caught hold of my hand in a chilly squeeze. "I should have warned you about the demon."

I arched an eyebrow. "That would have been helpful."

"I know, but I was scared. He said he'd rip my ghost apart and suspend me in limbo for eternity if I didn't pretend he was Brodie."

"You knew the demon was deceiving me the whole time?"

"Not at first, but as I spent time with him, I realized something was wrong. I confronted him, and he warned me off."

"Why didn't you drop a few hints?"

"I did! I asked if he might not be the right guy for you. But if I'd said anything else, he'd have realized I was tipping you off. He never left you alone for long."

I sank back against my pillows. "I'm not happy about you keeping the truth from me, but I understand. The demon was clever. He had me fooled until the end. You were only trying to keep yourself safe."

"I put you at risk, when all you've done is help me. I should have been a better man. Well, a better ghost. What can I do to make it up to you?"

As tempted as I was to ask for a huge bucket of triple chocolate and pumpkin brownies, I shook my head. "Nothing. Just move on. Get on with your afterlife and be happy. And stop deceiving people and yourself. You wouldn't be in this position if you were truthful with Elsbeth and kinder to your friends."

"I should never have tried to ruin Elsbeth. Not now she's got a baby on the way. And I regret what I did to Ballard and Hester. They were my friends, and I let them down."

"That's what you can do. Be a better ghost and don't go haunting places and scaring people. Go have fun adventures and make friends."

"Are you sure that's all you want? Nothing else?"

"That'll make me happy."

"What will you do once you get out of here?" Zohar looked at Sol.

I kept my gaze forward. "Get on with my life. Make sure the farm is running again as soon as the Magic Council gives me the okay and then... figure out the rest."

He kissed my cheek. "You're a wonderful witch, and you deserve every happiness. And I'm sorry your barn got destroyed and your friends injured."

"Me, too. But I'll put things back together again. I always do."

"Thanks again, Odessa." Zohar looked over his shoulder. "It's time to leave. I finally see the light."

"Take care, Zohar."

He blinked out of sight.

I looked at Sol's ring. It was a perfect fit for my finger, but I didn't deserve it. I'd treated him so badly as I'd tried to get back something I'd lost a long time ago.

I eased out of bed, quickly used the bathroom, and returned to our room. I walked to Sol's bed and settled beside it. "Zohar's not the only one who needs to make apologies."

Sol didn't stir.

"One day, when you're well again, I hope you'll forgive me. I've been awful to you, rejecting your kindness and leading you on. You deserve someone much better."

Sol's leg shifted under the covers. I checked his face, but his eyes were still shut.

I twisted the ring once more and slid it off my finger. It was too late for us and all because I'd never given Sol a chance. I went to place the ring on his finger, but his hand covered mine, and I jerked back.

"That's yours to keep." His voice was rough and croaky.

"You're awake!"

"Just about. Keep the ring."

"No, it's yours. The magic in it will speed up your healing. How are you feeling?" I tried to get the ring on his finger, but he wouldn't let go of my hand.

"I'm getting there. It helps you're here."

I gripped his hand. "You were always there for me when I most needed you. You've always been around to stop me from spiraling and making a mess. And when you weren't there, I let a demon almost destroy the farm. I let go of my rock and look what happened."

"You saved yourself." Sol opened his eyes and blinked at me. "You always do. And you don't need anyone else to save you, but I've always hoped you might want me to step in now and again to take some of the stress away."

My heart stuttered. "I don't know if I saved myself. We're messed up and in the hospital. And I didn't save you or Tuffin. I didn't even know the demon had you because I was so caught up in my own problems. It was selfish."

"Don't be so hard on yourself. I saw you fighting the demon, and there was no way that creature would have beaten you. You're powerful, magnificent, and unstoppable. When you finally believe that, everything else will fall into place. And maybe you'll find a place for me in the amazing, messy world of Odessa Grimsbane. It's my favorite place to hang out."

I smiled, despite tears clogging my throat. "I want to believe everything you say about me is true. I often do when you're around."

"So keep me around. I'm happy to be your cheerleader."

"You really want to stay, after everything I put you through? I almost got you killed. And I don't know how you escaped from the barn as I cast that destruction spell."

"I'm not sure either, but it had something to do with Tuffin."

"Tuffin is dead." I swallowed around the lump in my throat. "I found her blood in the barn. The demon told me he'd killed you both."

"And demons always tell the truth, do they?"

My cheeks flushed. "Yeah, I learned that one the hard way."

"I'm sorry you didn't get Brodie back," Sol said after a few seconds of silence. "I know how much you love the guy."

"I loved him so much, I was prepared to be deceived by a demon. Everyone else warned me. You did, Tuffin, my friends, but I wasn't ready to believe any of you. It wasn't my smartest move."

"You had to go through it to find things out for yourself. You held onto your love for Brodie for such a long time, and I expect you always will."

"Maybe. But I'm also aware now he wasn't perfect."

"No one is."

"You are. I can't believe you want to stay." Hope lit me up from the inside. I was learning that true happiness came from within me, but it would be enhanced by having Sol in my life.

"Well, if I do, you may have to make it up to me. Starting with a vacation once we set the farm back to rights."

Happy tears sprang into my eyes. "I'd love that. I want you on the farm for good."

"As an employee?"

I sucked in a deep breath. My ghosts were laid to rest. Brodie was gone, and I was ready to face a future without him. I was ready for something new and exciting. An adventure that made my stomach flip, my toes curl, and gave me hope.

"I want to be with you. Not as your boss. I want to work on the farm with you as equal partners."

"You'll always be the boss of the farm. The scarecrows wouldn't have it any other way. But I would love to be your partner."

A choked cry of happiness shot from my lips. "Yes, please."

"Then that's what we'll do." Sol's smile was genuine, but I could see tiredness in his eyes. He still had some healing to do. "But there's no need to rush. We take things at your pace."

"My pace. Right. No more going backward, though."

"Odessa, you were never retreating. You were just facing a different way to me. Now, we're on the same path."

"I know where I want that path to take us." I leaned down to kiss him.

"There's something I need to tell you before those pretty kisses get me distracted. Tuffin is alive."

My mouth dropped open, and I pulled back. "But the blood... and I saw you carrying her."

"She'd been injured but still created a powerful protection spell around us just before your magic hit. Tuffin saved us."

"If she's alive, where is she?"

He pointed to a lump under the covers that I thought was his leg. "She snuck in. Not even the nurses noticed her."

I inched back the covers, and there was Tuffin, sound asleep, snuggled next to Sol's leg. One ear had a chunk missing, and her fur was singed, but she was alive. I wanted to kiss her but placed the covers down so as not to disturb her and swiped happy tears off my cheeks.

Sol gently patted her. "She's got some injuries, but she's getting stronger. I reckon Tuffin will be as good as new soon."

"Tuffin is an amazing familiar. I'm so glad I have both of you."

"I can't wait to get home with you," Sol said.

"Same here. We've got so much to do. And I have so many ideas about how I'm going to make this up to you."

He grinned. "I'll look forward to exploring those."

I lifted the ring, never feeling surer of anything in my whole life. "Sol Vossen. Will you marry me?"

His eyebrows shot up. "You did hear me when I said we could take things at your pace. No pressure."

"This is my pace. I've avoided my feelings for too long. Now, they're all coming out. And this is what

I want. I want you in my life full time. I want to see you every day, laugh with you, cry with you, and make an amazing future together. We have to fill the farm with scarecrows, babies, and happy memories."

"Odessa, I'd marry you in a heartbeat. But are you sure about this?"

I slid the ring onto Sol's finger. "Yes. So, what do you say, will you marry me?"

❧ ❦

I danced around my kitchen, my long pale orange dress skimming the floor as my bare feet tapped across the tiles.

"Oh! Look at you. Like a Halloween goddess. You're so beautiful." Indigo appeared in the doorway, and beside her was Luna. They were dressed in cream and orange silk bridesmaids' dresses, orange flowers woven through their hair.

"So do you. I knew you'd make the perfect bridesmaids." We all hugged and were soon laughing and trying not to cry tears of happiness and smudge our make-up.

Tuffin strutted into the kitchen. She had on a sparkly collar, and her black fur was gleaming. There was no sign of the singed fur, although the missing part of her ear had yet to grow back.

"Tuffin, you look adorable," I said.

"I always do." She glanced at me. "You look passable."

I tickled the top of her head then looked at my two friends. "Where's Storm?"

"Making sure the guests behave. She's taking her role as celebrant seriously," Luna said. "What with your scarecrows being page boys and Storm barking orders, the guests are too terrified to move from their seats."

"Eek! We need to get out there. I don't want any casualties on my wedding day. People are here to have fun, not be too scared to move."

"I can't believe you're getting married before me," Luna said. "I've been non-stop planning for weeks, and you pull it together in less than two."

"Well, I had to move fast. I didn't want to risk losing Sol."

"It would be impossible to lose him," Indigo said. "The man is besotted with you. Even though you almost got him killed, you've got him in your life for good."

I laughed, giving an outlet to my joy. "And I couldn't be happier."

Footsteps marched up the porch steps, and Storm appeared. She was dressed in a demure black dress and wore striking dark eye make-up. "The guests are getting shifty. Get your butt out there if you want to get married today. Nice dress, by the way."

I laughed again. "You, too."

"Are you ready to go?" Indigo said.

"I just need five minutes. Wait right here. I'll be back." I hurried out of the farm, to a quiet copse of trees I'd let run wild for the bees and insects to enjoy.

I stepped along a well-worn path and stopped in front of a small, roughhewn stone. I placed a single orange rose on top of it. There was a word carved into the stone. *Brodie*.

"Hi. We've never said goodbye properly, but today is that day. It's time for me to try something new."

The wind whispered through the trees as my eyes glazed with tears. I'd been hoping that, one day, he'd come back. Now I knew, Brodie was gone for good. And although he hadn't been the perfect guy for me, I'd still wanted a way to remember him.

Sol had been in full support of placing a memorial on the farm, so if I was ever feeling melancholy or thinking about my old life, I could come here. Have I ever mentioned what an amazing guy I have?

I placed a hand on the stone. "I hope you have peace. And I hope that demon didn't cause you pain. I'm sorry we weren't able to spend the rest of our lives together, but I've found happiness. And I hope you're happy, too. I wish you the best."

A warm wind swirled around me, and what felt like a light kiss pressed against my cheek before it was gone.

I touched the spot and blinked away tears. "Thanks. I'll never forget you." I walked back to the farm and smiled to myself. I'd been naïve with first love. I'd thought it would be always and forever, but I'd learned that wasn't the case. Once I opened my heart to Sol, I discovered how blindingly amazing real love was. And I was embracing every second.

I rejoined my friends, picked up my bouquet, orange flowers, of course, and slipped on my shoes.

"Everything good?" Luna asked.

"Yep, perfect."

"No last-minute nerves?" Indigo said as we walked out behind Storm.

"No, I'm not nervous. I'm excited, and I can't wait to marry Sol."

"When you know, you know," Luna said. "Even though I've been inspected by dozens of werewolves, attended terrifying pack meetings, and am still dealing with my parents' demands about the wedding, I'm happy. I just want to be married."

"It'll be your turn soon enough," Indigo said. "But today is Odessa and Sol's day."

Luna grinned. "I promise, I won't steal any wedding ideas. Well, maybe a few."

"You're welcome to them."

Shamrock met us at the end of an outdoor aisle set up next to the farmhouse. We'd decided on an intimate wedding since we'd put it together so quickly and had twenty of our closest friends and family there. Of course, all my scarecrows were also in attendance. And Sol had picked Shamrock to be his best man.

"You look handsome." I tweaked the bowtie around Shamrock's neck.

He extended his arm to me, his elbow crooked for me to take. Not only was he best man to Sol, but he was also walking me up the aisle.

"Just a moment."

I tensed at the unwelcome sound of Selma Black's voice behind me.

The crowd went quiet before they started murmuring.

Storm hurried down the aisle. "Say the word, and I'll dust her."

I lifted a hand. "Let's see what she wants before you do that."

Selma stopped beside me, and her gaze drifted over the watching crowd. "You're getting married?"

"In about ten seconds, so this had better be a life or death situation."

"Or your death will be on the cards," Storm snarled.

Selma pursed her lips. "I didn't know. I have this for you." She held out a letter.

"You shouldn't take that," Storm said.

"What's in it?" I said.

"I was ordered to hand deliver it by my superior. You'll be happy with the contents." Selma kept the letter held out, pinched between two fingers.

"Read it to me," I said.

Her sigh made her annoyance clear. "I'll give you a summary. Your scarecrows, magic, and the farm have been cleared of any wrongdoing. You can begin operations with immediate effect."

My mouth fell open. "How? You were determined to shut this place."

"Ever since your operations were suspended, the Magic Council has dealt with daily calls and complaints. It seems, people love your scarecrows."

"I know they do! I kept telling you that. But what about the complaints you received?"

"They were looked into. They didn't hold up. Congratulations." The word almost choked out of Selma. Her gaze shifted to the waiting wedding party. "And on your marriage."

"Um... thanks." I took the letter and read the contents, Storm leaning in to take a look, and Indigo and Luna joining us.

"Best day ever," Luna said.

"It seems like it." I handed the letter to Shamrock. "Keep this safe."

He tucked it inside his pants.

"Come on. It's time you got married," Storm said.

"Just a sec." I caught hold of Selma's arm and walked her a short distance away. "I never meant any harm. I know some of what I do is unorthodox, but my heart was in the right place."

"Be careful. You're almost admitting to a crime. I can open a new investigation."

I arched an eyebrow. "But you won't. Because although you act like you aren't, you're a decent witch. You're doing your job. And I haven't forgotten you lost an aunt because of magic that went wrong. That'll make anyone jumpy around my power."

She sniffed. "I uphold the values of the Magic Council."

"And so you should."

Selma looked away. "Perhaps I was hard on you. But my work is all I have. My boss told me I may be demoted because of all the complaints."

My heart went out to this prickly witch. "We can't have that. I'll have a word and send over a basket of my special pumpkins and cookies. Would that work?"

Her nostrils flared. "A bribe?"

"Selma! An offer of compromise and friendship. You should try it sometime."

A muscle tensed in her jaw. "I'm not sure I know how."

"Drop by the farm anytime you like, and we can work on that."

"With your scarecrows?" Her horrified gaze went to Shamrock.

"I was thinking with me and Sol, but if you want to go wild and buddy up with Shamrock, I won't stop you."

She hesitated before a tentative smile crossed her face. "Thanks. I'll think about it. Enjoy your wedding."

"I plan to. I'll send you some cake."

Selma nodded before hurrying away.

I rejoined my friends. "Now, where were we?"

"Running out of patience." Storm marched back up the aisle and took her place.

Indigo and Luna followed her slowly, Shamrock behind them, taking his time so I had a chance to greet everyone. I was thrilled to see Hettie Crane had gotten back in time, and she gave me a thumbs-up and a nod of approval.

Sweet birdsong welcomed me as we walked, but my handsome husband-to-be took my attention. Sol stood there in a black suit, his hair neat and face freshly shaven. Just like me, he didn't look nervous, but there was excitement in his eyes.

Shamrock passed me over to Sol, but before he let go, he pointed a finger at him and then slid it across his throat.

Sol chuckled as he held up a hand. "I've got her, buddy. We can look out for Odessa together. Not that she can't look after herself."

"I can. But it's always great to have backup."

Shamrock gave me a hug and then let me go.

I looked at Storm, riots of excited butterflies inside me, and nodded at her.

She glanced around the small group, a rare smile on her face. "We're here to celebrate the joining of my best friend, Odessa Grimsbane, and a guy who isn't too terrible, in a binding ceremony. Personally, I think marriage is for idiots, but I like these idiots, so I agreed to this pairing."

There were a few nervous laughs. Shamrock growled, and everyone fell silent.

I giggled and shook my head. "Relax, everyone. Storm is only kidding. So is Shamrock."

"I'm half-kidding," Storm said.

As she led us through the formalities and joined our hands with an orange ribbon, my heart settled, content to be surrounded by Sol's unyielding, constant love, and my closest friends.

As I leaned forward to seal our vows with a kiss, Tuffin butted my leg with her head.

"Not now, Tuffin." I inched closer to Sol, my new husband.

"This is important. You haven't forgotten the fish cakes, have you? I checked the food, and I didn't smell any salmon. I thought we were having an all fish buffet."

Sol gently nudged Tuffin to one side with his toe. "You'll be so full of fish by the end of the night, we'll have to roll you home. Now, if you don't mind..." He caught me around the waist, tilted me back, and sealed our love with the sweetest, warmest, most heart melting kiss I'd ever experienced.

Everyone applauded, and even Tuffin seemed content as she stamped her paws on the ground, matching the drumbeat footsteps of my scarecrows.

Life in Witch Haven would always be weird, sometimes dangerous, and full of mystery, but with Sol, my familiar, my best friends, and my scarecrows by my side, I'd face any challenge with a smile.

Now, though, it was time to party.

About Author

K.E. O'Connor (Karen) is a mystery author living in the beautiful British countryside. She loves all things mystery, animals, and cake.

If you want to be part of the Witch Haven crew, practice spells, solve a few murders, spend time with amazing witches and their talking familiars, and get a free book, join her weekly newsletter.

Sign up today.

Newsletter:
https://BookHip.com/QKGDWJW
Website:
www.keoconnor.com/writing
Facebook:
www.facebook.com/keoconnorauthor

Also By

Spells and Spooks
Hexes and Haunts
Curses and Corpses
Muffins and Moonlight
Cupcakes and Cauldrons
Pancakes and Potions
Hauntings and High Jinx
Hauntings and Havoc
Hauntings and Hoaxes
The Case of the Screaming Skull
The Case of the Poisoned Pumpkin
The Case of the Cursed Candy
Fire Fang
Silvaria

You know what's coming? More books!

This time, you'll meet Storm Winter, a troubled weather witch with a broken heart, a hellhound hybrid with a secret, and a stray cat that just doesn't get the hint!

The Case of the Screaming Skull is waiting for you.

Would you go head to head with a cursed skull to save your life?

That's the option dumped into my lap when I luck out and get screamed at by an evil skull. So what you may ask? I get screamed at every day by my toddler wanting his candy. But I ask you this: does his scream curse you to a painful death in seven days' time?

Thought not. I win.

I'm Storm Winter, private investigator, with a reputation for taking no prisoners and demanding answers to questions others won't ask. My clients may be terrified of me, but I get them results. So long as they pay me.

Do I love my work? No. Does it give me access to well-connected, underground contacts who help me search for my missing sister? Yes. That's why I do it. The side cases pay the bills, so I can keep looking for Eden.

Back to the case in hand. I have seven days to figure out who used a cursed skull to murder millionaire jinn, Delano Discord, or I'm dead, too.

Was it the suppressed wife, the mistress who isn't what she seems, the sneaky lawyer, the bitter sister, or the too happy to be true son?

They're all suspects, none of them have alibis, and I have a pile of motivation to solve this case.

Care to join me? Great. Just stay out of my way, and watch out that my hulking hellhound, Fire Fang, doesn't tread on your toes. They may break.

9 781915 378361